THE BOOK AND THE BLADE

A.B. FINLAYSON

Parliament House Press

ISBN: 978-1-956136-53-1

Edited by Mary Westveer and Malorie Nilson

Cover by Shayne Leighton

Map illustration by Danielle at CraftyFoxArtsCrafts

For my beautiful wife, Kel.
Who was absolutely no help whatsoever in the writing of this novel.
In fact, none of the best ideas were hers. Honest.

AUTHOR'S NOTE

This novel takes place in God's own country of Yorkshire, and indeed, in God's own City of York. The places mentioned are all very much real (you can have a pint in most of them) but it should go without saying that the people are not. However, it isn't really that simple, and so I've written the following disclaimer to try and clear things up.

This is a work of fiction. Names, characters, ~~places~~, and incidents are either products of the author's imagination or are used fictitiously...except for the names of my friends which I sprinkled in with their permission because I thought it would be funny. Any resemblance to actual events (would be deeply concerning) or persons, living or dead, is entirely coincidental... except for the ghosts. They're real. That is, all the ghosts are based on the 'real' legends and myths contained within the walls of my favourite city.

Well, not Steve. I made him up. Have you met Steve, perchance?

Kings Manor

York Council

Museum St.

The Judges Lodgings

Mansion Hous

Leeman Rd.

Station Rd

Station Rd.

Rougier St.

North Street

Tanner Row

Bridge Street

Si's Pub

Micklegate

Holy Trinity Church

Bishophill Se

Micklegate Bar

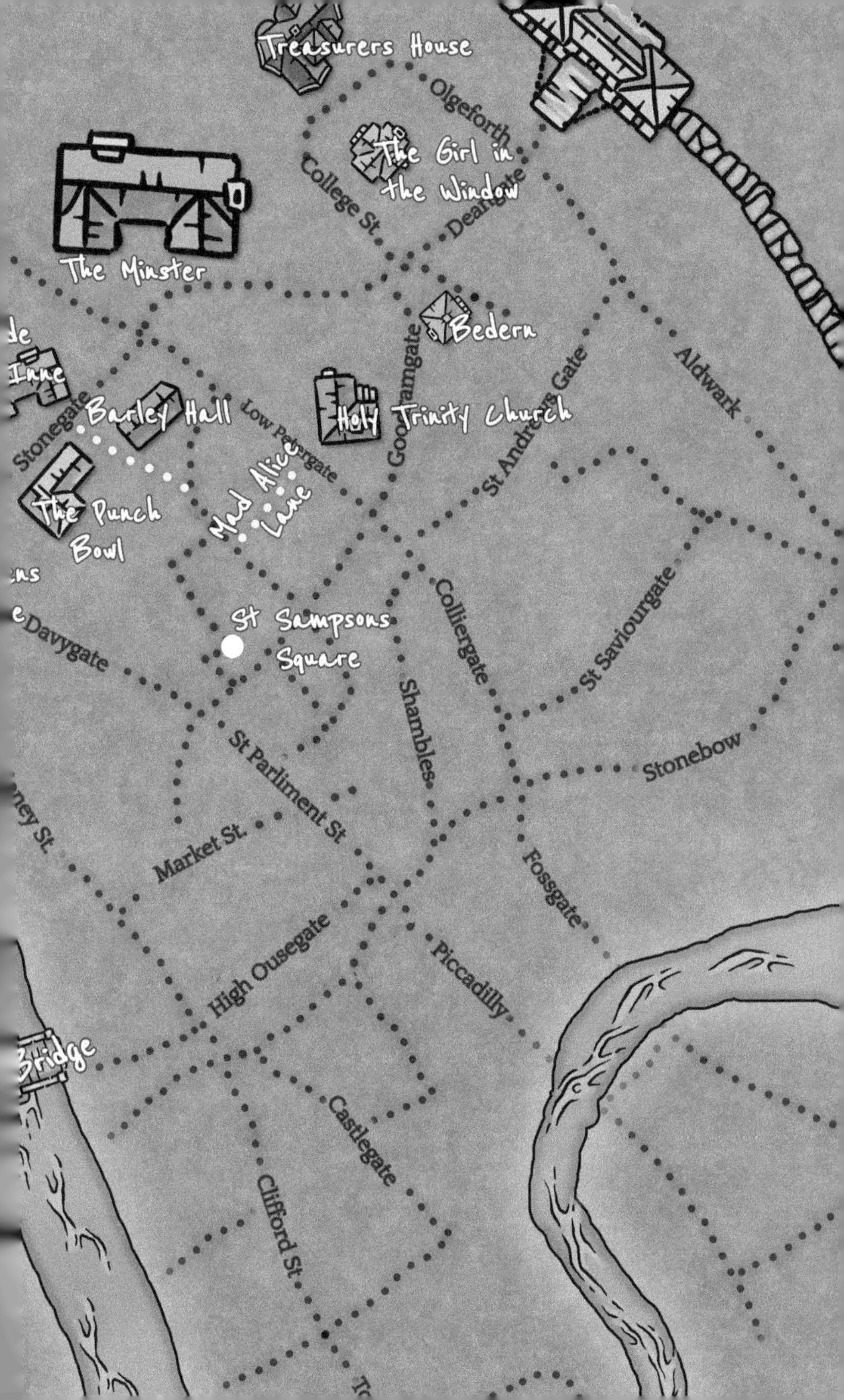

Treasurers House
Olgeforth
The Girl in the Window
College St
Deangate
The Minster
Bedern
Goodramgate
Holy Trinity Church
St Andrews Gate
Aldwark
Inne
Barley Hall
Stonegate
Low Petergate
Mad Alice Lane
The Punch Bowl
St Sampsons Square
Davygate
Colliergate
St Saviourgate
Shambles
St Parliment St
Stonebow
Market St.
Fossgate
High Ousegate
Piccadilly
Bridge
Castlegate
Clifford St

PROLOGUE

We think we know fear, but we don't. Not really. Not the true essence of fear. Sure, fear is part of an instinct to avoid harm; how else would we protect ourselves without the occasional threat of bollock-shrinking terror to keep us in check? But we use the word so loosely—a throwaway catchphrase to describe lonely walks home through dark car parks, bumping into childhood bullies in our nightmares, and penalty shootouts. Thankfully, very few people experience real fear. One of the great mercies of humanity's vast intellect is our own wilful ignorance. We're quite happy to float blissfully along without a paddle, adrift on an invisible sea of terror, so long as we have free Wi-Fi and fried chicken.

This is a story about fear.

And ghosts.

But it's not a ghost story.

Not *a* ghost story, no.

It is many.

It begins with a man in a pub.

PART I

THE NIGHT BEFORE

CHAPTER 1

Arthur settled down on the well-worn leather seat and shifted his arse back. It sank comfortably into the groove he had been cultivating for the last three hours. The half-empty pint glass stood guard over his seat, marking the spot at the far end of the bar for the few minutes he'd nipped out for a smoke. It needn't have bothered. He was the only person on the stools. In fact—he turned his head back and forth—he was the only person in the pub. It was late, and he was drunk, but it was the middle of summer, and the sun was only just beginning to dip over the slate roof tiles on the other side of the street. He had a good view of the bar and the world outside. Just how he liked it. People-watching, Wendy used to call it, back when Wendy was, well...part of his life. He used to enjoy people-watching with Wendy, but that all ended on a freezing train platform just after New Year.

She never looked back.

And now there weren't even any people to watch.

"Where is everyone?" Arthur asked the barman. The man shrugged in reply and pulled another tray of glasses from the washer, momentarily releasing a cloud of steam. It washed up to the dark wooden beams of the low ceiling and curled there for a moment in the cooler air, diluting the naked yellow bulbs that suffused the bar in an atmospheric low glow. As the steam dissipated, Arthur caught sight of himself in the long mirror behind the bar. He raised his glass and said cheers to his reflection, hiding, as it was, behind the usual collection of assorted multi-coloured bottles.

Christ.

He looked down, embarrassed.

I should probably go home.

But not yet. It might pick up.

The City of York wasn't quite the same as its gigantic little brother in the States; this old girl definitely did sleep, but it was a nice evening and nearly the summer holidays. *At the very least, there should be some drunk students hanging around*, he thought.

Arthur gazed at the reflection of the empty pub, then turned in his seat to make sure. Not a soul. He peered out the window at the curved street of Micklegate as a black car trundled along the road outside. A grey-haired old lady struggled up the hill with her head bowed and both hands clasped behind her back, pulling a rickety tartan bag on wheels. A man in a lycra suit ran past her, heading the other way, lifting his knees to tap against outstretched palms as he went.

Twat.

Arthur turned back to the empty pub and raised his empty glass to the barman with a little shake.

Might as well have one more. It might pick up.

The barman looked up, his ginger beard lit with a blue glow from the mobile phone he was scrolling through.

"Another?" he asked as he secreted the phone behind an industrial-sized jar of pickled eggs, which to Arthur's knowledge, had never been opened.

"Cheers, Si."

"Are you sure?"

Course I'm fucking sure, he thought with all the venom he reserved for Netflix when it asked if he was still there. He knew just how many hours of TV he wanted to watch, and he knew just how many beers he wanted to drink, thanks.

One more.

Always one more.

Si swapped out Arthur's empty pint glass with a fresh one, full to the brim. He didn't need to ask what Arthur was drinking; he'd drunk the same beer for years: Deuchars IPA, hand-pulled, made in Scotland. It was the pub's best-selling real ale. Arthur took a sip, and Si placed the card machine on the bar beside him, knowing full well that Arthur wouldn't hand over the card. He never did. And when he tapped the machine, he always did so with the card facing down to hide his name. Of course, there was no need for the charade; as a regular, Si had learned Arthur's full name long ago. But traditions were traditions.

Arthur grinned as the machine beeped. It still made him smile that he no longer had to check his accounts before every purchase. It used to be that Si would take payment before he even poured the drink, but that was years ago, back when Arthur was a student. That handsome, dark-haired young man was a success now—a city planner with a pre-approved credit card. *Here's to my success*, he thought as he raised the pint to an empty pub on a lonely Monday night while the barman returned to his phone.

And all the joy it brings.

An hour later and Arthur was quietly singing along to the music filling the pub, his head nodding away as he tapped out a drumbeat on the bar top:

...and I'm doing just fine, gotta, gotta be down because I want it all.

The pub had filled significantly as the restaurant staff from various Micklegate establishments congregated for a few well-deserved post-shift drinks. The room hummed with life, but Arthur was oblivious to it all and jumped in surprise when Si appeared beside him.

"Drink this," the barman said, not unkindly, as he placed a pint of water in front of Arthur.

Arthur looked at him for a moment, then sang loudly, "It was only a kiss; it was only a kiss!"

Si laughed despite himself and walked off to collect some empty glasses. Arthur wouldn't call him a friend, not exactly; they didn't hang out outside of the pub or go to the football together, but when two men spend so much time together with little more between them than the width of a bar top, it builds a rapport of sorts. The truth was, Arthur knew that Si probably felt sorry for him. He'd seen him here with a large group of friends, the centre of a whirlwind of laughter, jokes, celebrations, and commiserations. Different girls came and went over the years, but the core group of blokes remained the same. Until slowly, one by one, they drifted away, relationships and careers scattering them far and wide across the country.

Arthur was the last man standing.

Or sitting.

Well, swaying.

...my stomach is sick
And it's all in his head now, but she's touching his...

Arthur suddenly went quiet and stared into space, lost in some distant time and place only he could see.

He grinned slightly, then fumbled absentmindedly with the small tower of coins he'd made on the bar, stacking them by width. Two-pound coins first, then fifties, then twos. Then tens, twenties, ones, and finally, fives. He tried to pick them up and invert the pyramid, but they scattered across the bar instead. Si put the glasses down and poured drinks for waiting customers, keeping an eye on Arthur as he sat in front of the Guinness tap, trying to push a fifty-pence piece into the ice built up on the metal pump.

"Fucksake, Arthur," Si hissed. He finished serving a collection of wines and gins to a group of waitresses from the Italian restaurant down the street and leaned over to snatch the coin from Arthur's hand. "One of those lasses did nothing but smile at you, but you're away with the fairies."

Arthur picked up another fifty pence and lifted his head. "Did she take off her dress now?" he asked and grinned.

Si couldn't help but smile back.

"No, mate."

"Who was it?"

"That girl over there. The one with the black hair and the tattoo poking out of her shirt. Get a grip, mate."

Arthur looked for the girl and found her sitting at a round table with her friends, staring right at him. She smiled. He smiled back.

He stood up.

The room span.

He stepped towards her, then changed his mind. The song continued in the background.

I just can't look; it's killing me!

"I need a smoke," Arthur said to no one in particular, slumping back onto his stool and shaking a cigarette out of the packet next to his wallet. Si snatched it away as he put it to his lips.

"Outside, dickhead."

"Spoilsport."

Arthur wobbled unsteadily off the stool and headed to the door. He mumbled an apology to a young man in a red tie as he stepped around him, then pulled at the big brass handle. It slipped, and he caught it on the second go, then walked out into the crisp evening air, which hit him like a slap in the face.

He breathed deep and shook his heavy head. Slowly, so it didn't fall off. Behind him, he sensed the man with the red tie staring, but he couldn't care less. His head felt heavier and hotter than he needed it to be, the skin around his temples prickled, and his stomach bunched into tight knots.

He was drunk.

Drunk, drunk.

He took a stock check, and apart from the head and lead weight in his gut, he came to the misguided conclusion that he was still in control. He hadn't started singing yet, anyway...had he? He just felt unwell, that's all. Bloated. Too much beer, that's what that is. Time for a change.

The fresh air will do you good.

He smiled as the voice of his mother echoed back through the years. *Good old Mum.* He took another drag of his cigarette and settled on one of the cold metal bike racks that lined the pavement outside the pub, enjoying the fresh air.

Arthur was drunk, yes, but he wasn't *a* drunk, and this distinction was very important to him. He counted his points on increasingly blurry fingers.

One, a drunk gets smashed at lunchtime. Arthur waited until the end of his shift. Not a drunk.

Two...he'd had food. Not a drunk.

Four...he thought hard and swayed a little with the effort. *Ah, sod it.* He gave up. He knew he wasn't *too* drunk. Merry, maybe, but not hammered. *Wendy would say tipsy, but Wendy wasn't fucking here, was she? So, she could fucking say whatever the fuck she liked!*

Arthur blew out a cloud of smoke and closed his eyes.

Breathe.

He was in control. Or he would be in a few moments.

In truth, Arthur hated being so drunk he didn't know what was going on, so he tried to keep a handle on it. He knew when he was pushing it too far, and he was smart enough to stay on the stable side of the fence. The other side usually involved memory loss, spinning bedrooms, bad kebabs, and vomit. It wasn't fun.

But drinking was.

He enjoyed drinking. It evened out the edges. Drunken nights out with the lads were some of the best memories he had. "Halcyon days," his mate Nick would say. He could never quite work out if he was taking the piss.

Arthur took a deep drag on his cigarette and exhaled slowly, blowing the smoke from between clenched teeth, watching as it rose into the air in a thin plume. His gaze followed it into the night sky as it spread and vanished.

Something caught his eye then—a quick movement on the rooftop over the street. He blinked and tried to stand, getting it right on the second go. The buildings at this end of town were only two storeys high, their dark shingles glistening in the light of the new moon. The streetlights winking to life just below the level of the gutter cast strange shadows above. Something moved along the rooftop, darting in and out of the pools of black. Arthur stepped forward, the cigarette between his fingers forgotten as he narrowed his eyes, willing the buildings to stop moving.

A sleek black cat peeled from the shadows and raced along the tiled roof of the bar across the street. It paused in front of the tall stone wall of the last shop, which stood a clear storey higher than the rest. Then, to Arthur's amazement, it leapt high and scurried up the wall before clambering over the edge and vanishing into darkness. Arthur shook his head, then cursed as the forgotten cigarette introduced itself to the soft flesh on the inside of his fingers.

A few minutes later, Arthur walked back into the noise and warmth of the pub, sucking on his tender skin. He smiled at the man in the red tie standing just inside the door. The man made to say something, but Arthur stepped around him and walked to the bar.

"Si, how high can cats jump?"

"What?"

Bar staff are used to being asked utterly random questions by utterly drunk people, but every now and then, someone comes out with a good one. Si shook his head. "No idea, mate. Why?"

"I just saw a cat jump from that roof," Arthur pointed out the window to the building opposite, "to that roof," he said. Si looked to where he was pointing, then looked back at Arthur.

"You sure?" he said, wiping a glass with a clean cloth. "It seems a bit high."

"That's what I thought! But the damn thing parkoured up the fucking wall!"

"What? Like Spiderman?"

"Exactly! But a cat! Spidercat. Catman! Scotch and coke please, mate," Arthur added, losing his train of thought as he sat heavily on his stool.

Si stared. Arthur seemed alright. He wasn't mumbling or slurring his words, although he had taken a strange sidestep on the way out of the door and stumbled again on the way back in. Other than that, he appeared fine. Well, not fine, but close enough.

Si poured the drink.

CHAPTER 2

There is a certain level of inebriation required by some people in order to approach the unapproachably attractive. Arthur's sweet spot teetered on a knife's edge between self-deprecating charm and wonky-eyed slurring. At the moment, he wasn't even close, having just enough self-awareness to be painfully self-aware. He chanced a shy smile at the tattooed woman, then quickly looked away when he realised she was looking directly at him. He was definitely still on this side of the fence. Arthur sank back in his seat and tried to make himself small.

Arthur stood out. He was attractively scruffy in a way some men spend a fortune trying to tease into existence, yet he managed it mostly by accident. The expensive dark blue suit and open-collared white shirt were a requirement for work, but everything else was pure, unadulterated Arthur. Dark hair, dark eyes, and a permanent five o'clock shadow held at bay by clippers, plus the fact he refused to wear any shoes other than Vans, meant that, though he dressed sharp, Arthur still carried himself like a man wearing a comfy pair of jeans and a worn t-shirt. The 90s had never really loosened their grip on him.

Smartly dressed and yet somewhat unkempt, Arthur got

noticed, although he never noticed people noticing, which only served to make them do it even more.

The young waitress with the glass of white wine and regrettable but attractive Chinese tattoo had been watching Arthur with interest. When he eventually staggered out of the pub instead of walking to her table, she sighed and turned back to her friends. But now that he was back, she found some wine-induced courage to say hi.

Arthur sipped on his scotch and coke slowly, enjoying the change from beer to spirits, and relaxing into the familiar noise of chatter and music. He noticed someone walking towards him and turned on his stool.

"Mind if I sit here?" the newcomer asked.

"No problem," said Arthur.

The man in the red tie sat down and gave a shy smile. He was pale and his hands were shaking. Behind him, Arthur noticed that pretty waitress again. She seemed confused as she diverted her path away from Arthur to approach Si at the bar instead. It was odd. Perhaps she was drunk? He didn't have time to think about that too much as the man, now sitting beside him, drew back Arthur's attention.

"Thanks. I—I didn't think you'd see me."

Arthur blinked, not sure if he'd heard right.

"Pardon?"

"I noticed you noticed me, though."

"I'm not sure what you mean, mate," Arthur said, turning back to his drink and catching the barman's eye. He shook his head and smiled slightly, rolling his eyes. Si didn't respond, and instead just stared.

"You've never noticed me at work," continued the newcomer. Arthur turned in his seat.

"We work together?"

"Yes," said the man. "I see you every day." He ran his tie nervously through pale fingers and couldn't meet Arthur's gaze.

"At the City Council?" Arthur asked.

"Yes."

"*York* City Council?"

"Yes!"

"Which department?"

"Planning."

"But I'm..." Arthur paused. "Is this a wind-up?" he said with a short laugh.

Arthur worked in the planning department of York City Council on St. Leonard's Place. It was a large, spacious office but his department only had twelve people in it. Three in one room, three in another, and six in the main area. Then there was the basement where they kept all the old maps, a hidden toilet, and a janitor's closet. That was it; that was the whole department. Three rooms, twelve people, and a basement. Arthur looked closely at the man, leaning in slightly to get a better look at the downcast face.

"I'm sorry, mate, but I've never seen you before in my life," he said.

"But you can see me now," said the man lifting his head in a sudden blaze of confidence.

His eyes were blue. Deep blue and shining, rimmed with tears. He stared longingly at Arthur with something like desperation and reached out a trembling hand towards his knee.

"Arthur—" he said, but Arthur pulled away and stood up.

"I'm sorry, mate. I think you've got the wrong idea," he stammered.

He downed the rest of his drink and tilted the glass to Si who was talking to the tattooed waitress. They were both staring at the yammering drunk with wide eyes.

No doubt having a good laugh, Arthur thought.

"See you, Si," he said and flashed a smile at the waitress before briefly locking eyes once more with the blue-eyed man in the red tie, gathering his things, and moving toward the door.

"That was a bit odd," the girl said to the barman quietly as Arthur passed. "It was, wasn't it? It wasn't just me?"

"No, that was weird," agreed Si.

"Do you know him?"

"Who, Arthur? Yeah, well, sort of. He's a regular."

"Arthur," she said, repeating the name. Then she sighed, "Ah, well. Shame. The cute ones are always crazy."

Outside the pub, Arthur leaned against the bike racks once more and lit another cigarette. He felt cold suddenly, which was strange because the night was warm, but he shivered and pulled his jacket close. He had an odd feeling he couldn't shake like something had gone wrong. It was the feeling you get after a night out when blearily thumbing through your phone, trying to work out if you've sent any messages you shouldn't have. The conversation with the man in the red tie had unnerved him. Not because he thought the guy was coming onto him— that didn't worry him at all. Quite flattering, in fact. It was because he said they worked together. That couldn't be true, could it? There's no way he wouldn't have noticed another guy working in the same office. Sure, there were two other men, but both were in their sixties, and this guy had been late twenties tops.

He must have been mistaken, Arthur thought. *But then, how had he known my name*?

There was a perceptible change in the atmosphere, then, as a strange stillness settled over the great street of York. Traffic slowed as though driving through treacle and car engines cut to emit no sound. The revellers that had appeared in the last hour or so lost their voices and it was as though they had stepped into the great Cathedral of York Minster and were cowed into awed respect. A cold breeze lifted leaves and discarded crisp packets gently into the air so they could make no noise as they danced across the street. Arthur felt it. Deep within him, he felt it. The stillness burrowed inside and intruded on his spiralling thoughts. He felt eyes on him, watching, and he began to slowly turn toward the prickling gaze.

Then all at once, time caught up.

A sudden scream and a screech of tyres shattered the night,

and Arthur spun in the direction of the noise. Just down the road, beneath Micklegate Bar—the medieval southern gateway to the city illuminated by the streetlights and stars—a car sat skewed across the broken white lines in the centre of the road. A group of drunk women staggered around it, banging on the roof and bonnet while the driver hung out the window shouting at them all. A robustly built redhead in leather screamed back at him. Arthur shook his head and turned to start the long trek home when, for the second time that night, something caught his eye.

There. Just behind the parked blue car and the angry redhead stood a boy. He was at the foot of the stairs leading up onto the city wall, half in shadow, but even at this distance and in the dark, Arthur could tell he was crying.

Arthur stepped forward, and their eyes met, the boy's widening in fright, the whites showing against the grime of his face. Then, with a barely perceptible shake of the head and a gasp, he was gone, turning to flee up the stairs. It all happened in an instant, but Arthur had seen the fear—seen the bare feet and tattered clothes. He flicked his cigarette into the gutter and ran towards the city wall.

Micklegate Bar, like the other great gatehouses of the city, closed every day at dusk, primarily to prevent drunken tourists from falling off the walls in the early hours of the morning. So, it was unusual that Arthur could pull open the heavy iron gate barring the stone steps leading to the wall and the gatehouse. He might have paused to wonder about this had he been in the correct frame of mind—or any other frame of mind than the one he currently inhabited. He might even have paused to wonder how a young boy could race up these stairs without opening the gates. However, he wasn't, and he didn't.

Instead, he jogged up the steps and turned up the narrow passage to emerge on the city walls. On his right stood the imposing gatehouse tower with a solid, impenetrable oak door barring entry. To his left, a series of steps lead onto the wall proper, the only way for the boy to go. Arthur took the steps two at a time and stopped at the top. The wall stretched away like an uninterrupted ribbon of moonlight before him. He shivered and took a few steps forward, peering over the edge of the wall to his left. It was a straight drop down to a dark tangle of bushes and old wooden crates. Nowhere to hide. Beyond the scrub was a broad stretch of neatly tended grass that ran parallel to the wall. This, too, glistened in the silvery light of the evening, standing clear and proud and utterly devoid of boy.

Arthur caught his breath and leaned against the cooling stone of the city walls. What the hell was going on? He shook his head to clear it; he seemed to be doing a lot of that in the last hour or so. Perhaps Si had been right; he shouldn't have had another pint. And then another after that. Certainly not the scotch and coke.

He wasn't sure what had compelled him to chase after the boy. Now that he thought about it, he'd probably scared the shit out of the poor kid. Some drunk in a suit legging it across the road after him. He'd have run away too.

"Are you okay?" he shouted into the evening, a hint of pleading on the edge of his voice. "I just want to know you're okay. I'm not chasing you," he added, knowing as he did so that this was the calling cry of perverts and stalkers the world over. The night replied with judgemental silence and a cool breeze.

Bugger, thought Arthur, and he looked around. *Alone, on top of the wall. Again.*

He'd been here before. He'd done this before. Well, not precisely, but *close*.

Years ago, on Valentine's Day, Arthur had booked a table at Wendy's favourite restaurant in the city. It was notoriously busy, and he'd had to book it months in advance. To complete the evening, he planned a romantic walk along the city walls before sunset, complete with flowers and even a dodgy poem he'd composed in a fit of inspired romanticism.

As they walked down these same steps, something caught

his eye; a bundled shape squeezed into a shadowy nook against the wall. They'd walked on, but he couldn't get it out of his head. A while later, the couple took their table from a harassed waiter with a terrible fake Italian accent, which he presumably thought would get him more tips, when the intruding thought of the bundle of rags became too much for Arthur.

It was a freezing cold night, and the more his mind's eye replayed the scene, the more it seemed that the bundle may have been a child. So, he excused himself, raced out of the restaurant, dashed across the road and up the steps, and pushed past the angry man trying to lock the gates for the night.

It wasn't a child.

It was a bundle of rags.

Arthur had been embarrassed, so he paused to have a cigarette on the wall before the elderly gatekeeper tsk-ed him to the street below. He meandered back to the restaurant to find Wendy waiting for him outside. The waiter had been rude about his departure, so she had walked out. "Sod him," she said and linked her arm through his. It hadn't been the romantic Valentine's date Arthur had anticipated, but they had a nice night. They had gone to the pub and gotten takeaway on the way home.

He forgot all about the poem.

High above the brooding man in blue, atop the south-facing round turret of Micklegate Bar, two eyes gleamed in the darkness between the stone crenelations. A black cat rubbed its sleek body against the stone as fingers only it could feel scratched it between the ears. It peered down at the strange human on the wall and purred. The sound was not pleasant. It rumbled across the night sky and rolled down the stonework with all the warmth of a rusty dentist's drill, reaching for the man standing on the ribbon of moonlight.

. . .

A coldness spread across Arthur's shoulders, and prickling electricity rose up his neck, interrupting his stroll down memory lane. His body shook as he took a deep drag of his cigarette, startled by the unsteady fingers and a sensation he couldn't quite explain. He felt...*something*. A presence. Something watching him. It is the feeling you get in a dark room when you know there is someone else there. Inexplicable—an ancient instinct of self-preservation, perhaps? Whatever it was, he knew he wasn't alone. He turned slowly, not sure what to expect.

"Have you seen my keys?"

It wasn't that.

The woman stood against the stone wall of the bar just within the now-open door to the gatehouse. Her face was in the shadows, but what little light there was gave her away. She wore a long dark cloak that buttoned beneath her breasts and billowed over wide skirts. It was a plain-looking garment but oddly enticing, with a hint of barmaids and Oktoberfest, only without all the frills. It stopped above her ankles to reveal a pair of sturdy leather boots. Forgetting the boy and the invading sense of being watched, Arthur looked the woman up and down, pausing for a moment along the way as the lady breathed heavily. Arthur realised he was staring even as he failed to stop.

"Excuse me," said the woman, one hand moving to a hip with dangerous intent, "I said, have you seen my *keys*?"

"I, oh god. I'm sorry, love. Sorry. No, I haven't," said Arthur, suddenly besieged by guilt and embarrassment. He prided himself on being a gentleman—neither a letch nor a perv, but a nice guy. He had been known to stare fixedly at one spot in the middle distance until his eyes watered with pain rather than sneak a peek that might not be welcome. It seemed his drunken eyes had momentarily forgotten this.

Traitors.

Arthur lifted his head quickly as the woman stepped from

the shadows. He gasped and then coughed as he choked with embarrassment. He didn't realise people actually did that. But she was gasp-worthy beautiful. The kind of beautiful that would make a priest drain the communion wine in one go and rip his dog collar in two. Her appearance was simple—no makeup, no jewellery, no adornments, dark hair held back with a simple scarf, one stray lock tracing a curl around her smooth cheek—but devastating. Arthur found a spot behind her on the stone and stared at it like his life depended on it.

After an uncomfortably long silence, the woman stepped closer, wringing her hands in distress.

"I need to find my keys," she said with an edge of desperation. "My dad—" but whatever she was going to say was cut off with a sob and a flash of such sorrow that Arthur quickly reached out a hand.

"Hey, it's alright," he said, not quite willing to touch a strange woman in the dark. Even in his drunken state, he knew that such a thing might be unwelcome, but it was an effort. Arthur was a natural hugger—the first shoulder to cry on, Wendy used to say—but he wasn't a dickhead.

"I'll help you look for them," he said. "Where do you think you lost them?"

"I don't know," replied the woman, looking up at him with big brown eyes filled with pain and longing. He realised now that she was a lot younger than he'd first thought. Perhaps nineteen or twenty. Her clothing had made her seem much older. Probably an art student—the city was full of them in their homemade clothes or charity shop specials. They went one way or the other: total extravagance or a distinct lack thereof. Also, nearly all of them were nocturnal.

Arthur stepped back and spoke softly.

"It's okay, we'll find them," he said. "Did you have them here on the wall? Maybe someone found them and handed them in?"

"I don't think so," she said, shaking her head and wringing her hands. "My dad works here. He'd have them already." She stooped low and began to frantically search the steps, turning and heading into the dark open door of Micklegate Bar. Arthur blinked, and she was gone, swallowed by the deep dark of the gatehouse.

"Hey, erm...hey. Excuse me," he stammered, "I'm not sure you're supposed to go in there."

There was no reply. No sound at all. Nothing to indicate anyone had been there, everything swallowed by the black opening in the wall. Arthur let out a nervous laugh as he stared into the opening and felt it look back. He looked behind him. The moonlit ribbon of wall stretched away into the distance. There was nothing there, though the feeling of being watched had returned. Glancing upward, he noticed shadows on the stonework swaying above him, moving in the night. Still, they were no more real than a doorway that could stare back.

"I say, excuse me?" he tried again, a bit louder this time.

What the hell was that? You've never said "I say" in your life. God, you get more British when you're nervous, he thought, embarrassed by the cold shiver that ran down his spine and his own reluctance to follow the woman inside.

His brain suddenly thrust a bit of sense through the alcoholic sludge, and he reached into his jacket pocket for his phone. Fumbling in the dark, he tapped it a few times until bright light illuminated the floor at his feet, the stones shining white in the sudden glare of the torch. Then, in a moment shared by drunken idiots the world over, he turned the phone over and looked directly into the light.

"Shit. Idiot!" he snapped at himself as green and purple lights danced in his eyes. Laughter rang through the night, then, high and slightly manic, echoing oddly from inside the gatehouse as it bounced around the stones and out onto the wall. Arthur turned the light towards the sound and moved forward, one hand holding the phone and the other searching almost blindly in front for the edge of the door. He felt cool stone turn to wood under his fingers and moved through the opening into the room beyond.

It was so dark the torchlight barely penetrated to expose the bare stone walls, and Arthur blinked to clear his vision. He was sure there was a museum in here, something about one of the Richards, or was it a Henry? But a sweep of the torch told him the room was empty. Although that wasn't quite true. He could feel a presence and he was certain now that he wasn't alone.

"Where are you?" he asked, quite pleased with how little his voice wavered. He had to remind himself that there was nothing to be afraid of, but he was cursed with an excellent imagination and a brain swimming with alcohol. It wouldn't take much to lose his footing in the deep end.

"Here," whispered a voice beside his ear.

That did it.

"Fucking shit!" he yelled and stumbled forward, dropping the phone and plunging the room into complete and total darkness. Laughter peeled out, and Arthur turned around, arms flailing, jumping again as he backed into the wall.

"I'm sorry," came the voice of the young woman, choked with laughter, "but that was really funny."

Arthur was thankful for the darkness; it gave him the privacy to compose himself. He leaned back and took a few deep breaths, waiting for his heart to stop racing and his eyes to adjust. The woman was still giggling in the dark. Arthur looked around and saw a faint rectangular glow on the floor near his feet. He reached down to pick up the phone, and white light splashed into the world, illuminating the laughing woman. She giggled again and looked his way, squinting to avoid the light,

"Sorry," she repeated.

"It's okay," said Arthur. "What's your name?"

"Sarah." She smiled, and her eyes flashed in the torchlight.

"Arthur," said Arthur. He knew she wouldn't be able to see his face behind the glare of the torch, and he took the opportunity to have a really good look at her. She was beautiful for sure, but there was something strange he couldn't quite put his finger on. The clothes were...wrong, somehow. Not just art-student attire but something else. She looked like she'd stepped out of the pages of a history book.

"Why—" he paused, "why are you dressed like that?"

The woman wrinkled her nose and looked down at her clothes, pulling the skirts out on either side. Arthur tilted the torch so that it illuminated them both. She looked at him.

"Why are you dressed like that?" she said.

"Work," he shrugged.

"Same," she replied with a soft smile.

Well, that made sense; there were plenty of places in the city where people were expected to wear period clothing of some description. Arthur had even spent one memorable summer dressed as a Roman soldier handing out leaflets. He lost track of how many photographs he had posed for with smiling tourists and how many Hen's parties had tried to find out what Romans wore under their tunics.

"So..." he said, unable to take his eyes off her smiling face—she really was beautiful. "Your keys?"

The change was instant. It was as though Arthur had struck her open-handed across the face. The smile vanished, and all the humour left her eyes.

"The keys!" she yelled and resumed her frantic search of the stone floor. She spun and waved her arms around as though pushing through long grass like she was trying to drive away the very darkness itself. Arthur was shocked and lowered the phone. He reached out to her again,

"Hey, it's okay," he said, but she was frantic and couldn't hear him. She wept and mumbled to herself as she searched the empty room.

"The keys, the keys. I hid them, but I can't remember. I'll find them. I must find them. Don't worry, Daddy. I'll find the keys. I'll find the keys. Then it'll all be okay. It's my fault, my fault. I'll explain."

"Hey, hey," said Arthur with a hint of nervous pleading in his voice. "It's okay. I can help." And in his mind, he unknowingly echoed the words of the waitress, *why are the good-looking ones always crazy*?

"It's my fault, my fault. Daddy won't speak to me. My fault."

"I'm sure—"

"My fault!" she screamed at him, full in his face, her features a mask of madness illuminated by the glow of the phone's torch. Arthur stumbled away from her, and she ran then through the open door and out into the night.

By the time Arthur composed himself and stepped back into the moonlight, she was gone. He looked around at the still empty wall taunting him and laughed nervously.

"I need a drink."

CHAPTER 3

Si folded his arms across his broad chest and looked down at Arthur, who was trying his best to look nonchalant...and sober. He was failing at both. It is a very special level of drunk when a seated person can stagger. Arthur was one step beyond even that.

"Mate, you're wasted," said Si. "Go home."

"I'm not that drink," Arthur slurred in response.

One raised eyebrow was all he got in reply. The pub was emptying, and Si was very tempted to call time. The restaurant staff had already left, and he was pretty sure he wouldn't see the dark-haired girl with the tattoo again. She'd only had eyes for Arthur and barely said a word after he left, finishing her free drink in two mouthfuls and scurrying out the door. Si was not in the mood for any of Arthur's shit.

The guy used to be so well-adjusted, Si thought. He seemingly had it all together, but lately, he'd just been falling apart. He shouldn't have let him back in. Si stood up straight and made to walk around the bar, ready to escort the drunken regular to the door, but then Arthur swayed once more and giggled. There was no joy in the sound, and Si paused, indecision creasing his brow.

It was the curse of the barman; you grew to like the people

you served, and you actually encouraged their consumption even though you knew it was probably to their detriment. But, well, you had to make a living. Sometimes, though, it was all a little too sad. Si was a good man, and so he made an effort to quell the frustration that rose inside him. He reached for a pint glass and filled it with lemonade. He added ice, fruit, and Angostura Bitters. Then he tossed in a Berocca and some orange juice before giving it a stir and setting it on the bar in front of Arthur. He knew the lad, and he knew a good bloke when he saw one. Si also knew that Arthur was in here every night because it reminded him of better times and that when he did eventually go home, he'd be heading off to a flat that contained a giant Wendy-shaped hole. She'd really done a number on him.

The split had shocked Si. He really hadn't seen it coming. No one had. They were the golden couple that made it through university, the pair that everyone else envied. Young, good-looking, successful, and annoyingly likeable. But you never know what happens behind closed doors. It was over six months ago now. Si had made every effort to make Arthur feel welcome at the pub, as always, but now he was worried it had gone too far. Arthur had made himself exceedingly welcome...every single evening after work. And most of the weekend. He was too young to be a barfly.

"Drink up, mate," he said softly. "Then on your way, yeah? I'm closing up soon anyway." There was no response. Arthur's eyes had a far away, glassy look that Si was all too familiar with, but the hand reached for the pint of juice, and so the barman left him to it. The restaurant staff had left a right mess. Typical.

~

It wasn't just the alcohol that was causing Arthur problems. Though he had drunk enough to give a giraffe vertigo. He was swaying and glassy-eyed because his mind was in turmoil, trying to make sense of everything that had happened in the last hour or so. So much about it didn't seem right—didn't add up.

It was the cat.

The bloody cat had freaked him out, setting the tone for the following events. There was no way in the world a cat could make that jump. The roof was simply too high, and whenever Arthur tried to focus on the memory, it always came back to him in a strange sort of slow-motion.

The cat ran up the wall.

Wasn't there a nursery rhyme about that?

The bloody thing didn't skitter about and scramble up like it was struggling to find purchase. No, it ascended the flat brickwork as smoothly and steadily as if walking along the rooftop. Arthur was sure of it. He was also sure that cats couldn't do that. The unsorted file system of his mind kept flashing images of David Bowie in a leotard walking up and down walls in the movie Labyrinth, bulging codpiece on display. That was enough to make anyone glassy-eyed.

And then there was the boy with no shoes. Why on earth was a kid of that age out at this time of night without shoes on? Plus, what shabby clothing he did have was nothing more than rags clinging to his emaciated frame. More than anything, it was the look in the kid's eyes when he saw Arthur—complete shock and something else. Fear, perhaps? The boy had been terrified, and something deep within Arthur made him worry desperately that he was the cause of that fear. He couldn't handle the thought. It gnawed at him, picking at his tired mind, asking him to do something about it. Arthur knew he hadn't done anything wrong, but what, then, had caused such fear and distrust?

It was a bundle of rags on a cold Valentine's night.

On top of all this was the student, Sarah, and her missing keys. Arthur couldn't help but smile. She was crazy without a doubt, but it was a craziness that had sown a seed of something within him. There was something about her, something unique and unpredictable. She was at once both completely sure of herself—telling him off for staring and playing tricks on him in the dark—and completely unhinged. Dangerously so, by the look of it. How important could a set of keys be anyway?

He knew nothing about her, yet he couldn't shake the image of her face from his mind nor the curve of her form as she stood half shrouded in darkness like something from a movie. It was a still frame in his mind that had taken up residence and refused to be evicted. He closed his eyes, and there she was again, dangerously close in the dark with smooth skin glowing in the streetlight and eyes dark and deep. She was the type of girl you dreamed about meeting. The one you'd stay up all night with, and by the time the sun rose, you'd know each other better than you know yourself.

Arthur sat up straight. He had no idea how, but he was determined to see her again—to see if the illusion could be made real. Someone that unusual and unique would undoubtedly stand out in this small city. Someone must know her. He stood up too quickly and stumbled, steadying himself on the bar.

"You alright, mate?" Si asked.

"Champion!" said Arthur, fumbling to put everything in his pockets.

"Are you off home then?"

Arthur grinned at him. "Gonna see a dog about a man...a man about a...a woman! Gonna see a woman!"

Close enough.

"There's no dog," he added and steadied himself on the door.

"Mind how you go, lad." Si smiled.

"No, you!"

Christ.

~

Sarah Brocklebank ran headlong through the dark churchyard on Micklegate, passing in and out of large, withered trees and leaping over dense tufts of grass and thick scrub. At this time of year, the churchyard quickly got out of hand, growing faster than the old volunteer caretaker could cope. The front lawn was a mass of wildflowers and weeds, a copse in the middle of the city. Nature encased in stone. It was creepy enough in the day, but at this time of night, when the light from the streetlamps barely filtered through the knotted, reaching fingers of the canopy, it was the stuff of nightmares. Dark shades and shapes chased the young woman through the grounds; they hid behind stone and wood, clinging to grass and walls. Seen but unseen. Sarah had no choice, though she had tried here many times before, so she searched. She knew the keys must be somewhere close. They weren't at the wall, so where else could they be?

Dappled orange lights danced across the church's stonework and the low wall surrounding the yard. They moved like fireflies over the rotting trunks of the old trees as a gentle breeze shifted the verdant leaves above. Sarah shivered. She was tired. Deep down tired within the very core of her being. But she couldn't give up. Those keys meant everything, and she had to find them. Tonight was her last chance. Without the keys, her father—her family—lost everything. The young woman wiped her brow, wondering when she had last eaten. She was so hungry, but there was no time to stop. No time to spare at all. She felt thin, not in form but in spirit like an old rope pulled and torn too many times, ready to break.

An image of the handsome young man in the strange suit flashed in her mind's eye, and she smiled in the dark, a moment of relief from her torment. He had been sweet. It was good to talk to someone. It seemed like such a long time since she had spoken to anyone other than her father. Even that seemed an age ago, now.

"Find them, or we're done."

His final words, given with a look that broached no rebuttal. And he didn't just mean the family, she knew. If she didn't find them, then he was done with *her*.

Some instinct made Sarah lift her eyes to the arched entrance of the church, steeped as it was in shadows at the bottom of the square tower, the weak light unable to penetrate the depths. Sarah stepped quickly behind a tree to hide, though she couldn't say why. Something about the atmosphere of the churchyard had changed. A chilly danger seeped across the sorry grass and clung like mist to the trunks of the trees and the skirts of the suddenly nervous young woman. She peered carefully around the boll of the oak and stifled a surprised gasp.

A woman had appeared from the shroud of night. Tall and graceful and dressed entirely in white, she strode purposefully across the churchyard beneath the shadows of the stone building. This time the darkness failed in its task, for though she passed through deep pools of black, the lady never went out of sight as she made her stately way toward the east end of the building. She appeared to glow from within, a soft, ethereal light emanating from her skin and clothes. Sarah carefully moved around the trunk, positioned the tree between the mysterious figure and her, and peered back toward the building. The woman paused at the corner of the church and beckoned to someone Sarah could not see. A small child appeared, a girl, crying and shuffling her feet, slowly following behind the person Sarah assumed to be her mother. But the girl paused, hesitant and clearly scared of moving forward. A third figure, a short, round woman, swept swiftly to the child's side, wringing her hands and pleading. But the girl simply would not budge.

The tall woman stood with her hands on her hips and tapped one foot impatiently on the ground, increasing the urgency with which the older of them begged. Still, nothing would move the child. Nothing, that is, but her mother, who threw her hands in the air and marched back the way she had come. Sarah noticed the older woman shrink away from the domineering form as the first lady grabbed the child's wrist and dragged her around the building and out of sight. They both vanished as the shadows finally enveloped them.

Sarah leant against her tree in the still grounds of the church with no one but the old lady and the neglected gravestones for company. The night had fallen into silence, an oppressive blanket of quiet that settled over the world and stifled everything. The world held its breath. Sarah watched as the old lady took a tentative, furtive step towards the corner of the church, clearly afraid to follow. She clasped her hands to her bosom as she slowly approached the tall stone wall and leaned forward, peering around the corner. Sarah could see her shaking, but then the shoulder's slumped in defeat, and the bent frame also disappeared into the dark, following the others. This time, Sarah truly was left alone.

It grew a little lighter in the churchyard of Holy Trinity as the trees gave up some of their oppressive hold over the world, but a primal fear had taken hold of Sarah, and she couldn't bring herself back from the edge. It was like the memory of losing your balance at the very lip of a high cliff. Safe now...but what if?

A car horn shattered the silence of the night and a loud curse uttered by a gruff voice emanated from the street before the vehicle roared away. Sarah looked up and saw the man in the blue suit walk out of sight down Micklegate, heading towards the river, talking and gesticulating to a man in a red tie who was scurrying to keep up. She lifted a hand to hail a greeting, but something caught her eye before she could speak. A glint of metal flashed for a moment in the glare of the car's headlights, blinking like a star in the overgrown grass. She turned.

CHAPTER 4

"What did you say your name was, mate?"

"I didn't. You never asked."

Arthur sighed. There are people in the world for whom a normal conversation was to be tackled like an obstacle course, an obstacle course covered in ice. The man in the red tie had been waiting in the street outside the pub and had completely ignored all the usual cues that should have made it clear to him that Arthur did not want to talk. The drunk man had tried everything from slowly smoking a cigarette to taking a fake call on his phone. Now he had resorted to the power march. Sorry mate, I've got to be somewhere. Would love to chat, but you know how it is. Busy busy. The man in the red tie did not take the hint. He slowed down to wait, stepped away politely for Arthur to take his call, or, as now, walked with a strange gambolling skip to keep up with the taller man. When Arthur jogged across the road, and the man followed him out in front of traffic, Arthur realised for sure he wasn't going away. He slowed his pace as Micklegate began its curved descent towards the river and shoved his hands deep in the pockets of his blue trousers.

"Sorry," he said. "So, what's your name?"

"Steve."

"Hi, Steve. I'm Arthur." He held out his hand for the other man to shake, but instead of the expected greeting, Steve clasped his hands to his belly, gripping the red tie and twisting it through his fingers. He shook his head slightly. *Great, a proper weirdo.*

He looked up as they passed a nightclub, the heavy bass bouncing into the street, the sound of laughter spilling into the evening, and he thought about popping into the enticing, purple-lit entrance for another drink, but he knew Steve would probably follow. He sighed and kept walking, making his way down to the crossroads at the bottom of Micklegate, his new companion seemingly happy to walk quietly beside him.

"Well," he said as he paused at the traffic lights, "This is me. I'm heading over the bridge." He looked at Steve. Steve looked back.

"I expect you'll be wanting to get home," he tried. It wasn't a question. Which was good because Steve didn't answer.

"Right."

Arthur headed towards the bridge, and Steve followed. They made their way over the wide river as the lights from the buildings lining the bank sparkled in almost perfect reflection on the glassy surface. A cool breeze floated above the water, but it was barely enough to kick up a ripple before it flowed under the bridge and climbed over the railings to caress the two men. Arthur shivered. Steve did not.

The silent pair passed two Japanese tourists huddled together by the edge, leaning back, holding a mobile phone at arm's length to take a photo with the lights of the city twinkling behind them.

"Would you like me to take a picture for you?" asked Arthur, anything to distract from the awkward silence. The couple looked at him without comprehension, so Arthur pointed to their camera and mimed taking a photograph. The dark-haired Asian man smiled broadly and bowed his head quickly, handing the phone over without hesitation. Arthur took a few snapshots, taking his time with the hope that Steve would get bored. No such luck.

He handed the phone back to the grateful couple, who insisted on taking a photo of Arthur in return. He laughed. *Bloody ridiculous, but where's the harm?* He wondered how many photos he'd been snapped in over the years living in York, how many times he was in the background of treasured memories from tourists. He pictured the Asian couple showing their friends and family back home. "And here is the drunk man who stopped to take our photograph on the bridge. And here is the weird guy standing next to him that just couldn't take a hint."

Arthur looked at Steve, still fidgeting with his tie, and in a hazy moment of camaraderie, he flung his arm over the man's shoulders and grinned for the camera. Why not? The tourist began to laugh before bringing his eye close to take the photo. He nudged his girlfriend and peeled off a babble of something unintelligible to Arthur, and she joined in the laughter, pulling out her phone and happily snapping away. If Arthur was confused by this, he was utterly baffled when the man clapped his hands in quick applause and tried to give Arthur a fiver. Arthur took his arm from around Steve.

"No, no, mate. Don't be daft. You keep it," he said.

"No. You are funny. You keep it. Thank you," bowed the tourist.

The neatly folded five-pound note was pressed into his hand with such conviction that Arthur found he couldn't refuse. So instead, he awkwardly returned the bow and, with a little wave of the note to Steve, said, "Well, I guess we can get a pasty or something if you like?"

This brought another round of laughter from the tourists and some more bowing. *Jesus Christ, I must be hammered*, he thought, having absolutely no idea what the hell was going on. *Perhaps food wasn't such a bad idea?*

High above, sitting with graceful poise and a complete disregard for heights and precipices, a lone black cat watched the scene unfold on the bridge. Being a cat, it had absolutely no understanding of the social conventions of humans, or mobile phones and photographs, but it was all too aware that one of the men was going to be a problem. The cat stretched languidly and slowly licked a long forepaw. *Not my problem*. Proving, once again, that cats are self-absorbed twats.

"I've got a theory about photographs," Arthur said when he realised his silent companion would remain precisely that. "Back in the day, people used to distrust their reflection because they thought it stole their soul or something. I mean, in some religions, you aren't even allowed to create pictures of living things because of that, right? So, there are all these societies and cultures and stuff who reckon that creating an image of a person sort of, I don't know, *dilutes* who they really are. Now, fast forward a few thousand years and improve technology to such a state that everyone has one of these in their pocket." He brandished his mobile phone, which had run out of battery because he'd left the torch on and was now a useless black brick taking up space in his jacket. "We've all got one," he said. "I'm sure you've got one, right, Steve?" he looked at his companion and got absolutely nothing in reply.

"Yeah, course you have. Well, we know damn well that every teenager in the world seems to have one. And they're taking selfies, mate. Selfies, all the fucking time. They take photographs of themselves with their new hair, new clothes, with their food. I've got a mate who's a teacher, right, and he says they take about twenty photos just in the tutor group in the morning. Proper narcissistic stuff, right. Well, what if that constant photography is sort of, I don't know, leeching the soul out of them, you know? What if all these complaints about us millennials being self-absorbed and shit are because we've actually become kind of diluted by these things?" He brandished the phone again. And again, got no response from Steve. "Maybe we're getting trapped, mate? Maybe we're slaves or something? Like, the truth of the world is hidden from us because we're too busy taking photos and looking at porn and cat videos!"

He grinned at two young women who laughed at this last exclamation as they walked past him on their way to one of the many student clubs open in the city. They were on Coney Street now, a place Arthur normally avoided at all costs. It was the beating artery of the city's shopping district, but at this time of night, it was a quiet, cobbled thoroughfare from one end of town to the other, from one pub to the next. At the far end of the street, before it opened into St Helen's Square, there sat a small bakery that stayed open until the early hours, and right now, it wasn't even late. At this time of night, everything would be fresh. Arthur could almost taste the Cajun chicken panini with his name on it.

"Do you want anything?" he asked his silent companion as they approached the shop. Steve looked through the window with such longing that Arthur felt a strange sense of compassion for him. He looked so incredibly hungry. "I'll get you something," he said and ducked inside, blinking at the bright light. He smiled at the cute girl behind the counter.

"Two Cajun chicken paninis, please, love."

The girl gathered his order, took his money, and gave him his change without a word.

"No. Thank *you*," he said with heavy emphasis that did nothing but raise a bored eyebrow from the girl. *God, I can be a cock sometimes,* he thought and walked back out into the dimly lit cobbled street holding the two warm paninis.

"Here you go, mate," – he started, but Steve was nowhere to be seen.

"Fucksake."

Arthur finished the second Cajun chicken panini and crumpled up the paper. He was feeling much better. The blurred edges were evening themselves out, and the world appeared to be turning at something approaching normal speed. He leaned back against the wooden bench in the centre of the square, lit a cigarette, and let out a contented sigh. He really loved this city. There was something about it, something special. He'd felt it on the very first day after stepping off the train and walking through the centre to get to university. It was far enough away from home to be his own domain and yet close enough that he could always go back should he want to. He never wanted to. Not even when all the lads started to drift away, all heading off to hometowns or to start careers in new places, but Arthur had no desire to leave, certainly not to go back home.

He had become himself here; he was safe here. He knew the cobbled streets so well he could probably find his way around blindfolded if he had to. Arthur hunched forward, rested his elbows on his knees, and took a long drag of the cigarette. He'd only started smoking when he came here. His mum still didn't know, and he was twenty-six! Everything that was his, and his alone, belonged to this city. This was home.

Then, in the stillness of the late evening, with the noise of the pubs filtering through the night and the soft breeze gently catching his cigarette smoke and lifting it into the sky, his mind turned to Wendy.

As it always did.

To say her leaving was a shock was like saying Hitler was a tad naughty. He hadn't seen it coming. It wasn't just the heartache of the woman he loved leaving him but the shock that the future he had seen so clearly suddenly no longer existed. It had been so solid—so real—and then, on one blustery day, it was all gone. She said he was stagnating, that he had no ambition or drive, which made absolutely no sense as he'd just been promoted. She reckoned he was going nowhere. He'd laughed at that. Where was there to go? He had everything he wanted right here. The last thing Wendy said before she turned her back and headed towards the waiting red and silver GNER train was, "You could do anything you want, but you're doing nothing. I can't let you stop me too."

What the fuck did that mean? He was doing exactly what he wanted to do. He'd called and called, but those words had been the last she ever spoke to him. Six years and that was it. Game over. He still didn't want to leave, but the only problem now was that the town he loved was full of memories of the woman who no longer loved him. Even in his slightly addled frame of mind, he knew he'd picked this very bench because it was the bench on which they had shared their first kiss. Well, fuck it, and fuck her! This was his city, and he wasn't going to sit and feel all maudlin about something he couldn't change. And anyway, hadn't he spoken to two beautiful women tonight?

Sort of.

Arthur angrily stubbed out the cigarette on the faded red paint of the bench and stood up, happy to report that he didn't sway this time, and the paninis stayed exactly where he'd put them. That was something, at least. He breathed deeply and felt like he'd turned some mental corner. He knew he was fed up with wallowing in the past, creating ghosts for himself of a life that no longer existed. The Welsh had a word for it. He'd seen it on a meme on Facebook or something, "*Hiraeth,*" they called it. Homesickness for a home you can no longer get back to, for a home that no longer exists. The only thing you can do in that situation is to create a new home for yourself.

A new home.

Wendy was my home.

I need a woman.

Sometimes the minds of men are terrifyingly predictable.

CHAPTER 5

As fate would have it (if you believe in that sort of thing), Sarah Brocklebank ran into the square at that precise moment. She was laughing and whooping loudly as she left the mouth of Stonegate and raced across the cobbles with her skirts hitched up in one hand and a shining key grasped tightly in the other.

Sometimes the world likes to play tricks with the minds of men. It is embarrassingly easy.

High above, perched atop Betty's Tea Room's rooftop, the cat didn't laugh. As a species, they have never mastered the art, and anyway, this one just wanted to watch the show. Cats are easily entertained, though they aren't the type to leave reviews.

Arthur intercepted the manic woman just before the entrance to Lendal Cellars—the famous bar that exists entirely underground and is a great place to drink until the river Ouse bursts its banks. It was still a great place, but when it was underwater, not so much.

"Hi!" he said.

"You!" exclaimed the beautiful dark-haired woman as Arthur stepped in front of her. She smiled quickly then her gaze moved past him, her dark eyes darting back and forth. He stepped sideways to catch her eye, trying to shift her focus to him. Even as he did so, he realised how needy that seemed.

"Yeah, me," he said, in what he hoped wasn't a creepy tone of voice. Arthur was conflicted and struggling to make sense of things. He was painfully aware that, at the precise moment he had wished for a woman, one had appeared. In the lost romantic recesses of his mind, he thought that might mean something, and he wanted to share it with her. He had no idea if it was fate or providence or if those things even existed, but he knew Sarah was attractive and enticingly weird and absolutely nothing like Wendy.

He also had no idea if she wanted this information to be shared with her, but there was only one way to find out. The alcohol had stopped turning the world in circles, but now it drove Arthur in a specific and potentially risky direction. He didn't need to worry, though, as Sarah's attention was entirely focused on something behind him.

She went to push him aside, barely even acknowledging he was there, but his own dodgy behaviour had filtered through the sludge, and he stepped smartly out of her way instead. Sarah moved around him and up to the large wooden gates set inside the stone archway of Mansion House, a stately home that made up most of the southwest border of St Helen's Square.

Arthur knew next to nothing about the place other than he'd once thrown up on the steps of the main entrance a few feet away. It had a grand central doorway with a small flight of stone steps leading to it, and large windows on either side were guarded by spiked iron fences. The gate Sarah pounded on, however, must have been an old side entrance for horses and carts, perhaps leading to a central courtyard. Arthur had no idea; he'd never been through to the interior, though he had seen cars slowly negotiate the press of tourists and vanish inside. Big cars. Black ones. The kind of behemoth driven by men in suits who wore sunglasses no matter the weather or time of day. It was weird then that Sarah banged on those doors, shouting at the top of her voice. Something told him that this was probably not a good idea.

Arthur positioned himself between Sarah and the green-painted doors. She stopped with her fist raised. A light from inside Mansion House flickered on above them, spilling out onto the street from the strange circular gap at the top of the gates. Sarah looked at him, and Arthur couldn't believe someone such as her could exist in his world. She was so beautiful, with an air of innocence and yet, at the same time, strangely seductive. Though there was a spark of madness there, deep in her eyes, and it stirred a brief note of warning within Arthur. It was a warning he knew full well would be entirely and wilfully ignored at every given opportunity.

Sarah focused on Arthur for a split second, her eyes searching, hoping, before she again glanced away.

"Dad!" she screamed. "I have the keys! I found them! Let me in!" She became frantic, shoving Arthur out of the way and banging on the green wood, crying with desperation. Arthur had no idea what to do.

"It's okay, it's okay," he tried to soothe her, but she ignored him completely.

"Father!" she wailed. "I've got them."

The light from inside Mansion House intensified for a moment and focused on the girl like a roving spotlight. She paused in her exclamations as the yellow glow rested upon her face. She lifted her head to it as though basking in the sun before it faded slowly and turned to the side, finding Arthur. He stood in a panic, transfixed and unable to move, held by an invisible force. The light pulsed quickly and flashed a vibrant purple for a moment before suddenly blinking out.

In fact, at that moment, all the lights in St Helen's Square went out.

Darkness descended over the world, and Sarah Brocklebank began to cry.

Arthur fumbled for the woman in the dark, but the world

swirled around him, blurred edges melting and bleeding into one another. He blinked to clear his eyes, struggling against the ripples in his vision. It was akin to the moment one steps from a hot summer's day into a dark room—shapes and colours leapt like a kaleidoscope across the world, all blues, greens, and purples. There was something in his eye, but more, there was something...in the way.

Arthur couldn't see.

He couldn't see the cat on the rooftop as it padded closer, curious. Nor see the black shapes in the dark places turn their heads towards him. He couldn't see the ethereal purple mist that now encircled him. And he certainly couldn't see the man in the shadows with the book and the blade.

This was probably a good thing.

Arthur raised his hands and knuckled his fingers deep into his eye sockets until it hurt. He blinked and blinked, green lights and tears mixed before him. Slowly, one by one, the buildings of the square swam back into existence, the stars in the night sky and the bright streetlamps of the town went from moving lines of light to single pinpricks, winking back to life. He held onto the iron railing of Mansion House to steady himself and shook his head. But as the world shifted back into itself, he realized that Sarah Brocklebank had disappeared. He was alone. In fact, there was no evidence that anyone had been there or that any of the events of the past ten minutes had even occurred. Except for Arthur, the square was empty.

CHAPTER 6

The thing about being in an entirely empty space is that even the least observant human would notice movement in the tableau before them. So, when a black cat walked steadily down the sheer wall of Betty's Tea Room, tracing one of the bright white columns towards the ground, even Arthur's recent traipse with sightlessness couldn't prevent him from noticing. It hopped nonchalantly onto the stone pavers and then vanished into the shadows. Some part of Arthur's mind closed down, shut the image away for future contemplation and filed it under *Things That Did Not Happen*.

The shaking began in his arms and quickly spread across his chest and down through his legs. Uneasiness tightened its hold on him, and he felt as though he was hanging over a dark void, teetering on the edge of a terrifying drop into darkness. Sarah had been standing right in front of him. He knew it. He could practically hear the echo of her voice as she shouted at the door to rouse her father. Her disappearance had been instant. There was no one in St Helen's Square, and there was nowhere she could have run without him hearing something. Arthur had only rubbed his eyes for a second. He was sure of it.

And what was the deal with the damn gravity-defying cats?

Rationality and logic bombarded Arthur with potential answers, but he knew deep down that none of them were satisfying: The door to Mansion House had opened, and she'd gone inside. She had simply walked away, and he had missed it. She ran down the alley to Lendal Cellars.

That last one seemed the most plausible, and so Arthur made his way down the sloping alley that ran between Mansion House and the Post Office. When he descended the steps into the dimly lit bar, it was clear Sarah wasn't there. There were only one or two customers at the tables, and the barman was adamant no one had come or gone in at least thirty minutes. Arthur turned and headed back up the steps, jogging swiftly out of the alley and back into St Helen's Square. It was still empty. Deserted. But there was something about the silence that seemed unnatural and oppressive. Arthur's hands shook; from adrenaline or cold, he couldn't tell.

And someone moved in the shadows.

At the far end of the square, there in the mouth of the long Victorian street that leads directly to the towering Minster, a shape detached itself from the dark. Arthur blinked, worried he was seeing things, no longer trusting his own eyes, but the form became more apparent, more substantial. At the entrance to Stonegate, the street that connected St Helen's Square to the biggest gothic cathedral in the Northern Hemisphere, at the exact spot from which Sarah had emerged, there stood a small boy dressed in rags.

As before, the dark brown orbs of the boy's eyes widened in fright when they met Arthur's, and he turned and fled down the narrow street. Bewildered, Arthur jogged after him, quickly crossing the cobblestones that lined the square. He no longer felt drunk. In fact, he felt entirely sober, dangerously so, perhaps more sober than he had for a long time. The line between reality and...the alternative...was bleeding, and Arthur was no longer sure which side he was on.

He slowed at the mouth of Stonegate and peered down the

long, cobbled street with a mounting sense of unease. It was empty. The towering buildings loomed on either side, somehow wider at the top than at the bottom. They were a cramped collection of the old and new, a conglomeration that made Stonegate a street lost in time. The mixture of antiquated wooden beams crossing whitewashed walls and modern, glass-fronted facades merged in an uneasy alliance. The road kinked and curved slightly in the middle, suddenly revealing the grand, picturesque view of the Minster about halfway down. During the day, you could barely move for the press of tourists, but right now, Arthur had the street to himself.

Light spilled from the windows of the various pubs and shops, caressing large flagstones and dancing across small pebbles like the refraction of moonlight on still water. Soft music flowed from The Punch Bowl, a pub on the right-hand side. Revellers enjoyed a few more drinks before the clock struck eleven, at which point the street would no doubt fill once more as they made their way home or searched for one of the many bars that stayed open beyond normal hours. It was never entirely dark in the main streets of York. So many beautiful buildings remained illuminated throughout the long hours of the night, and Victorian-style streetlamps cast warm, circular pools of orange light across walls, footpaths, and roads. Arthur felt safe here. He always had. The city was an open and welcoming creature that never caused him to worry about walking through her alone, no matter the time of day or night.

So, the irregular pounding of his heart and the heavy reluctance of his legs to move further into the depths of Stonegate were even more unnerving. Why was he so scared?

He stood still, as an increasingly familiar, albeit frustrating, feeling overtook him—the invisible force that had gripped him so tightly as he gazed up at the light of Mansion House. Fear. Arthur was too petrified to move, and he stood silently in terror as the sounds of the pubs and people around him, so comforting just a moment before, melted into the dull hum of his terror.

CHAPTER 7

It began like a dark mist inside his mind and it spread into the real world like a shadow growing beyond the bounds of its host. Oily tendrils leached from the buildings and gathered in the low places where brick and wood met ancient stone. The lights dimmed, washing away and retreating from the encroaching darkness. The warmth and safety of St Helen's Square lay just behind him, almost within reach, like the sun on the back of a diver about to enter a cave, but some strange compulsion held him fast. He couldn't remember the last time before tonight he had been genuinely terrified, but the taste of fear crawled across his flesh now, and had been following him for some time. Something deep, primal, and otherworldly.

It was a feeling he recognised and greeted like an unwelcome visitor from childhood nightmares as it escaped the locked vault of memory. All children knew it, but few remembered the sensation when they grew into adulthood, the absolute certainty that the darkness held monsters.

It did.

Hundreds of pairs of silent dark eyes bore into the lonely man standing in the last pool of light on Stonegate. Figures coalesced in the gloom, moving on unseen winds, some thick and fully conceived, others wavering, insubstantial, and broken —clinging to the memory of form. They watched, and they waited.

Above them all stood the man in black, his book in one hand, his blade in the other. He watched those watching Arthur.

Arthur shook himself, determined not to be cowed by phantoms of childhood fear. He was simply remembering a nightmare from when he was just a young boy, indistinct shapes and shadows reaching for him in the dark until he woke up screaming, unable to help himself. It had seemed so vivid and real to him then, and waking didn't help—didn't put an end to it. If anything, it made it worse. They were in the room with him. He knew it. His dad had rushed in at his screams and held him, stroking his hair, soothing him, whispering that it wasn't real, that it was all in his head, that if he concentrated really hard on something else, it would go away.

It was a memory as vivid in his mind as it would be if it had happened yesterday. His dad had stayed with him all night, talking to him in the dark. He told Arthur that he would always be there for him, but that he also needed to learn to handle these things by himself. That's what a man did, he'd said. It had seemed to Arthur, even at such a young age, that this put a time limit on the comfort that would be offered in moments of fear. That didn't seem quite fair. But his father wasn't finished. He had gone on to say if ever the nightmares got too scary and the imaginary creatures got too close, all Arthur had to do was laugh in their faces and tell them to fuck off. Arthur had gasped in astonishment and childhood glee. He had never heard his father swear like that before. It was like their own silly little secret, but the power it held for the young boy was unmistakable. The young Arthur fell asleep in his father's strong arms, listening to his deep breaths as they became shallow, chest rising and falling in steady rhythm. He had never felt safer.

In the morning, they woke before his mum and made hot

chocolate. It was one of the happiest memories of his childhood. He'd almost forgotten about the nightmare that preceded it.

Until now.

Arthur closed his eyes, took a deep breath, opened them again, and began to walk. His father wasn't here. He was a man himself now, for god's sake!

He wondered when, if ever, he would feel like it.

A noise like roaring fire rolled through the alley, and then a child screamed in the dark, the sound bouncing off the close walls and filling the street with a chorus of wails before fading away into deathly silence. Arthur stopped, his heart pounding, his skin prickling, his mouth dry, the urge to run rising within.

But he didn't run.

He stayed where he was and, swallowing drily, turned to the invisible creatures in the dark.

"Oh, fuck off!" he said with a nervous laugh, the sound echoing down the dark empty street, bouncing off the walls and rattling towards the Minster.

Silence again descended upon the town.

The man in black would have held his breath, if he ever did things like that.

And, unbelievably, the spell broke. The shadows retreated—as did the shapes teasing the edges of Arthur's vision—the world returned to normal and Arthur sighed, his shoulders sagging.

Good old Dad.

But as this wasn't a childhood dream, the creatures in the shadows didn't vanish at the memory of well-meaning advice from a loving father. They just retreated slightly. The watchers still watched, and they waited as the man in the blue suit walked quickly down the centre of the long street, staying as close to the middle as he could and trying his best to appear nonchalant and at ease. He was neither. They knew it, and he knew it. To say Arthur was on edge would be an entirely disappointing and overused cliché. He wasn't *on edge*; he had already fallen off. He was currently hanging on with a single hand as, one by one, his fingers lost their grip on the crumbling ledge and his legs dangled over a metaphysical precipice far below. So, when two black cats leapt silently and suddenly to the cobbles in front of him, the noise that escaped his dry mouth was not one he would look back on with pride.

After the echoes of what Arthur would later recall as a manly scream died away and he finally opened his eyes, he looked up to see a familiar black sign stretching across the street above. *Ye Olde Starre Inne.* He sighed and bent over, resting his hands on his knees, taking a deep breath of the cool air as he did so. He looked at the two dark figures resting nonchalantly on the cobbled streets in front of him.

"Arseholes," he said.

Two pairs of yellow eyes regarded him with utter indifference and, in the way of cats everywhere, ignored him completely as they turned and vanished down the narrow alley leading to the pub, tails high in the air and arseholes on display like twin eyes of Sauron.

Arthur sighed.

"Don't mind if I do," he said and followed the cats to the pub.

The entrance to the Ye Old Starre Inne often surprised newcomers to the city, and Arthur remembered the first time he and the lads had stumbled across the hidden drinking hole on one of their many trips into town. Few people seemed to realise that the sign crossing Stonegate was associated with an open and thriving pub. Tourists often regarded it simply as one of those throwbacks through time, there to be pointed at and photographed. Those who took a moment to look around saw the narrow opening between two shops, little more than an alley and often overlooked as one.

Another sign hung on the wall above the entrance, but if you weren't looking, you'd miss it in the press of people that usually crowded the narrow street. Arthur grinned to himself as he remembered how they had first discovered the pub many years earlier. One of the lads, Graham, had tripped on a cobble while making eyes at an attractive American tourist and stumbled through the gap. His grinning face soon reappeared and beckoned them into the whitewashed alley. It ran for about ten metres between the buildings, and they were all laughing as they crammed in, shuffling forward with heads lowered.

"Where the hell are you taking us?" they asked as they grinned and stepped into a small yard.

Beer barrels lay propped against the wall, and, as ever in this city, the Minster gazed down at them from high above. They were standing in front of what appeared to be an old house. Colourful flowers in boxes were nestled beneath lattice windows and into one corner of the small clearing, and a door of frosted glass and wood opened into the beautiful old pub.

Arthur, shaking off the dust of recollection, paused at the mouth of the alley. Lights glistened from inside the pub, and people milled about outside, laughing and smoking, huddled together in the late evening, completely ignoring the two black cats that trotted side by side between the small outdoor tables and vanished into the shadows. Noise, music, laughter, life. Arthur felt some tension lift from his shoulders. He could definitely do with another drink.

The warmth of the pub washed over him as he opened the door and stepped inside. A loud bell announced his arrival and clattered again when the door closed behind him. Heads turned for a moment, then turned back. Shining glass, polished wood, brass signs, and leather seats, the smell of beer mingling with the cigarette smoke from outside, the chatter of customers in various nooks and snugs, and the low hum of music from behind the bar all filled Arthur's world. He smiled at the familiarity of it all, shaking his shoulders and pulling at the collar of his blue blazer. Yes, life and laughter. Just what he needed to help the shadows in his mind retreat.

Arthur propped himself against a large wooden barrel that served as a table and rested the small glass of scotch he retrieved from the barman on its smooth surface. He leaned comfortably against the tall pillar that stood between the entrance and the long bar with its polished brass taps and felt the last dregs of tension fall away. Fruit machines flashed their bright colours into the room, and for a moment, he fumbled for loose change in his pocket but thought better of it. Mobile phones and fruit machines. What did people do when they sat in bars by themselves other than play on screens and digitally gamble away their spare coins?

Arthur decided he'd do neither. His phone was flat, and he'd lost count of how much money he'd wasted chasing lines of bells and cherries over the years. More than that, he didn't want to be one of *those* guys. He was already acutely aware that, of the lone drinkers in the pub, he was by far the youngest. It was the reason he had chosen this perch instead of sitting at the bar or beside the welcoming fire with the other customers. Arthur liked people but wasn't in the mood to strike up conversations with the local barflies. They always seemed to give across an odd sense of camaraderie, which some might welcome, but only served to pick at the scab of Arthur's loneliness.

I'm not one of you.

Not yet.

He lifted his glass and peered at the glistening contents shining like gold, clinging to the inside in an oily slick. He sniffed appreciatively, the smell of woodsmoke clear in the sharp tang of the scotch. He had decided to treat himself. And why the hell not? It had been a long and crazy night. A couple of single malts before he headed back to his empty flat would take the edge of whatever the hell it was that had happened outside.

Two large scotches later, and Arthur had almost managed to convince himself that the evening's activities had all been in his head, or at least that there were perfectly rational explanations for those that weren't. He was buggered if he knew what they were, but that was a problem for future Arthur. Let him deal with that. Memories of the night flashed through his mind as he nursed his drink. Brown dresses and dark eyes—black cats and red ties. And one mustn't forget the shadows. Strange shadows everywhere. It was all there in an odd jumble of images like a bag of blank jigsaw pieces that wouldn't fit together. Of everything, though, it was the boy that stood out. The boy with frightened eyes. It worried Arthur deeply that a kid might be lost in the city somewhere, dressed in rags and barefoot.

He promised himself he would go out on his lunch break the next day and ask...someone. He wasn't sure yet, but he was certain there must be plenty of charities for the homeless. At the very least, he could go into one of the many charity shops on Goodramgate and ask there. But it wasn't enough, was it? He slammed the glass, shocking an old couple who had emerged from the snug and were putting on their coats, ready to leave. It wasn't enough when the boy was out there *now*, at—he looked at the clock on the wall and squinted—nearly eleven o'clock.

As if to emphasise the time, a bell rang from the bar, and a strong voice called out, "Last orders!" Arthur shook his head. What could he do? What could he do except wander around the streets looking for a kid that would run away at the first sight of him? At least when he got home, he could charge his phone and call the police. That was something, he thought. That was a sensible idea. That was a grown-up thing to do.

But one more drink first.

The grey-haired old man opened the door for his wife, and the bell set into the wood above the frame clattered loudly. The old lady winced as she wrapped a shawl around her shoulders.

"What a racket," she muttered and gave Arthur an accusatory look as if the noise was somehow his fault. The couple disappeared through the door, and it slammed behind them, rattling the bell once more. Arthur grinned as he heard the old lady comment on it again, and her husband told her to stop chuntering. It was a phrase he hadn't heard for a long time. One of his mother's favourites.

Arthur had nearly finished his third and final scotch when the noises began. Low at first, like scratching on the edge of his hearing. He wiggled his finger in his ears to try and clear them, but it soon became apparent that the noise was not going away. He spun on his seat and looked around. Only one or two customers remained, plus the two bar staff, a young man and woman so deep in conversation at the end of the bar they hadn't even begun to clear up.

The last few minutes had been a constant refrain of people leaving and the bell announcing their departure. It was beginning to get on Arthur's nerves. He guessed the ringing in his ears was causing the strange scratching noise, and the cacophony made him irritable. One of the customers stood to put his coat on and nudged a sleeping dog with his foot. Arthur blinked in surprise. He'd assumed the dog was stuffed—a local oddity of the pub—but the creature stretched and shook itself, then padded after its master as they moved past Arthur and toward the door. The wrinkled man pulled a flat cap over his head and touched the tip to Arthur, who smiled back and reached down to pat the dog, a silky Border Collie, between the ears. But the dog was having none of it. Its lips pulled back over glistening white teeth, and its black coat prickled as the docile pet transformed into a ferocious hunter. Arthur snatched his hand back as the dog growled, somewhere deep within its throat, a sound of primal warning and threat. The animal's eyes had widened so that the black orbs were ringed with white.

"Hey, hey, come now," said the old man, clicking his tongue disapprovingly at the animal, "there's no need for that." He smiled at Arthur apologetically, but there was also a hint of suspicion there—a there-must-be-a-reason-my-dog-doesn't-like-you sort of look.

The animal continued to growl, and Arthur grew nervous, standing up slowly from his stool and stepping away. The dog didn't follow his movements. Arthur and the man looked at each other, bewildered. The animal was growling at the pillar.

"That's strange," said the old man, smiling at Arthur with genuine apology and warmth this time. He stepped forward and grabbed the dog by the collar, "Come along, girl," he said. "Don't be daft."

Arthur opened the door for the man and his dog, shaking his head as he turned back to his drink while the bell faded away into the scratching and ringing in his ears.

Bloody weird night. He went to sit back down on his stool but changed his mind, eyeing the pillar suspiciously and moving to the other side of the barrel to take a seat on the cold leather. He laughed at his own nervousness, but it had indeed been a *very* strange night, and the sound! It was relentless, just on the cusp of hearing, trying to break through. It was definitely time to go home.

He picked up his glass and drained the rest of the scotch. The noise suddenly amplified as though it had moved closer. Screams, he was sure of it, but coming from a long way off. At first, he thought it was the mournful mewling of a cat, but the pitch seemed to shift into something more human.

There must be trouble in town somewhere, he thought, dismissing the shouts for drunken revelry. Funny for a Monday, though.

A loud cry of such pain and anguish shattered what calm he had dredged from the bottom of his glass, and Arthur stood up in shock. He stumbled back and bumped into a tall figure.

"Mind yerself, boy," came a gruff voice from above him.

"Sorry, mate. Sorry." Arthur said, spinning and then staring up in surprise at the man he had bumped into. "Did, did you hear that?"

"Hear what?" said the man. He was an imposing figure, a good foot taller than Arthur and broad across the shoulders and chest. His dark hair was long and tousled beneath a large beaver hat that added another completely unnecessary foot to his towering stature. Arthur gulped. The man was of the sort that caused an involuntary backward step from those who met him if only to move out of his shadow.

"The—the screams," he said.

"Aye," nodded the giant, removing the hat for a moment and scratching his head, "I hear the screams."

His voice was a deep rumble, gruff but strangely quiet—a rockfall heard from far away. He replaced the hat and crossed his thick arms over his chest, the split sleeves of his red doublet opening to reveal a faded white shirt beneath. His trousers were old breeches that, on any other man, would gather to flare above the knee-high leather boots, but this man's legs were simply too big, his muscles bulging against the fabric. He was a mountain in period clothing. Arthur couldn't help but stare. What were the odds of meeting two actors in one night? Regardless, he wouldn't like to meet this guy on a battlefield, even if the weapons were fake.

"Do you reckon it was a fight?" Arthur asked.

The man snorted and looked down his nose. "Where have you been, boy?" He looked away, a weariness coming over his face for a moment. "There's no end to the fighting."

A bit melodramatic.

Arthur couldn't say that he'd come across much in the way of violence in the city. Oh sure, all towns had dodgy areas, but everyone knew where they were, so they were pretty easy to avoid. Arthur never went out of his way to find trouble. In fact, he wasn't a big fan of confrontations at all, especially drunken ones. He avoided them at all costs if he could. Drunk people were capable of doing things they wouldn't even dream of when sober.

Arthur hiccupped.

An uncomfortable silence stretched between the two men. Arthur looked down at his feet and then glanced nervously at the giant who remained silent and impassive, his eyes and thoughts focused on something Arthur couldn't see.

"Well, erm, I best be off," he said with another hiccup.

The giant looked down at him, seemingly forgetting Arthur was there, and then tipped his hat. "Mind how you go," he growled.

Opening the door to the cool evening air, Arthur grimaced as the bell chimed right above his head. He closed the door behind him and stepped, head swimming as the fresh air hit him. He blinked rapidly, trying to push away the bleariness of the evening's drinks *just* enough to find his way home.

It would take a lot more than a bit of blinking, he realised, as he took an unsteady step forward and stumbled. Arthur leaned against a wall and fumbled for his cigarettes. Two left. He put one to his lips and lit it, looking around the small courtyard as his vision swam in blurry lights. He closed his eyes tight, then opened them again, taking in the white brick walls and barrels.

Something about drinking made Arthur nostalgic, and a strange sensation rose within him. He felt like he could be in any moment in time, the courtyard of the pub a lost remnant of a world gone by—an odd place with very little in the way of modernity to advertise the twenty-first century. This was why he loved this city.

Why would anyone leave?

Arthur took a last drag of the cigarette and watched the end glow bright orange before flicking it to the floor and grinding it under his foot. Time to go home.

"Boy!"

"Fuck!"

Arthur spun around, wary. The giant man in old-timey clothes stood in the courtyard, looming in the darkness. The two black cats had reappeared and were preening against his leather boots. *Where the fuck had he come from*? Arthur looked behind him to the door. It was firmly closed, and no bell had rung.

"Boy, come here," said the man.

Arthur instinctively looked down the narrow alley that led to Stonegate. People passed by the opening at the other end, leaving the various bars and pubs closing across the city. He felt the urge to run and join them—to slip into the safety of the masses and flee from the giant—but there was something about his voice that tugged at Arthur's curiosity.

The giant man stepped forward slowly, hesitantly. If anything, he seemed incongruously shy. That was what Arthur had heard in his voice, a nervousness that was completely out of place, falling as it did from a mountain of muscle.

"Are you okay?" Arthur asked.

"I—I don't know," said the man, removing his great hat and scratching at his head.

He looked at Arthur with something akin to wonder and stepped forward again, lifting a giant hand towards him, not unlike Steve had done an hour or so before. Arthur blinked and stepped back. The giant lowered his hand, clutching the furry hat tight to his chest. Pain and confusion creased the rugged face, and for a split second, he looked utterly lost. A powerful sorrow roared from the depths of his eyes and reached toward Arthur. It touched him like a melancholic frost for just a moment, and then it was gone, the memory of pain lingering in Arthur's chest as he caught his breath. He had felt what the man was feeling—pain, loss, longing. The giant's eyes widened. He'd felt it too. The connection. The link between the two men. The giant shook his head suddenly and set his jaw against his torment. He forced the hat back onto his head and, with shoulders back and head high, he became the entirely imposing figure he had been before. He glared at Arthur.

"I know you," he growled, stepping forward with intent. Arthur backed away in urgency. The shadows of the night closed in around them, and the cats at the giant's feet slunk down to their haunches, stealing forward as though on the hunt.

"I know what you are," said the man with something like wonder. Arthur stepped away, but the giant filled the world. They moved slowly into the narrow alley, the wall brushing Arthur's shoulder as they did so. Reluctant to take his eyes from the dangerous form in front of him, he ran his hand along the cool brickwork to guide his retreat.

"They'll all know what you are," said the man, bearing down on him. "There's no hiding now, no running away. Everyone knows."

Arthur couldn't reply. What could he possibly say? He had no idea what the man was talking about. Again, he returned to the idea this was all a bad dream, but the threat was far too real for him to entertain the thought seriously. He could only see one choice in front of him, so he took it. Arthur turned and fled down the alleyway.

The giant shouted a single word after him,

"Fetch!"

CHAPTER 8

Arthur burst from the alley and ran headlong down Stonegate, back towards the light of St Helen's Square, his black Vans pounding across the cobbles, the echoes of his footsteps bouncing from the narrow walls. The street was deserted and dark, a fact that failed to register in Arthur's panic and drink-addled mind. The people had vanished, replaced by shadows and creeping dark forms that once more swirled on the edge of his vision, never quite coming together to make themselves known but always there.

He felt like he was being chased—that he was surrounded with nowhere to go. Alarm rose painfully in his chest, and he glanced over his shoulder, forgetting for a moment to look where he was going. Arthur crashed into someone or something and stumbled awkwardly to the left. He lost his footing and fell to the cobbled street, hitting the ground hard. Still gripped by adrenaline, he scrabbled backward in an attempt to regain his feet. A shadowy figure moved above him, and he looked up in fright.

"I found them," said Sarah Brocklebank. "I found the keys!" Her dark eyes were wide and filled with the frothing madness of a deer in the headlights, they flitted back and forth in her head as she reached for him.

Arthur tried to move away and instead bumped into something else. He yelped again and whirled around. A sad smile looked down at him from above a familiar red tie.

"I'm hungry," said Steve in a hollow voice that arrived in Arthur's ears as if from a great distance.

Regaining his footing at last, Arthur backed away from the two figures who turned towards him in the eerie darkness that had descended like a veil over the world. The terrified man lifted his hands in fear.

"Stay back!" he said, his heart racing and his voice trembling.

Something wasn't right. The world had all gone wrong. There was drunk, and then there was this—whatever the hell *this* was. Arthur's heart pounded painfully in his chest, each beat a sharp stab that sent waves of pain through his body. He felt sick, but he knew it had nothing—or at least only a little—to do with the scotch or beer. He shuffled backward and stared fearfully at the two figures in front of him. They didn't seem real. They were washed out, fading in and out of sight.

What the hell is going on?

Black tendrils of mist seeped from the shadows and crept across the street's surface, reaching and searching—coils of darkness seeking light to feed upon. They rose from cracks between the cobbles and the dark lines beneath windowsills, from behind drainpipes, and wherever the light failed to touch. The darkness grew and spread. A roaring filled Arthur's ears and his mind.

Someone must have spiked my drink, he thought. *I'm hallucinating. I need help.*

A final attempt at escape failed when his back hit the wall behind him. He turned his head, and the unmistakable red and orange glow of fire flickered against his face. Arthur looked through the window of the pub, scared to put his back to the two figures in the street but drawn to the sight unfolding within.

Through one of the small panes of glass, Arthur saw the pub engulfed in flames. The fire roared across the floor and licked at the ceiling, devouring tables, stools, curtains, carpets, and walls. Ravenous and insatiable, it attacked everything beyond the glass, moving through the room like a vengeful monster.

A woman ran screaming through the fire, the skirts of her long dress already alight, flames trailing up her body as she ran out of sight and into a back room. Arthur smashed his fist against the window, shouting for someone to help. He ran to the heavy wooden door, but it was locked tight. Kicking at it as hard as he could, the door wouldn't give. Instead, he was rewarded with a shiver of pain rifling up his leg from his heel to his knee. Even in his fear and torment, Arthur couldn't help but despair; the movies had lied to him again. He ran back to the glass and peered through, and that's when he saw him.

The barman.

The elderly gentleman with grey hair and a large belly walked through the flames as if they weren't there. The fire raged around him, but he continued on, wholly untouched and unharmed, even stopping to pick up a few empty glasses from one of the tables. The man turned, looked slowly around the bar, and then walked through to the back room. This would have been a perfectly natural occurrence if it wasn't for the inferno that raged around him and the fact that he didn't use a door.

Arthur stumbled back from the glass, aware suddenly that there was no heat coming from the blazing pub, nor was there any smoke. He turned, agape, to the two figures still standing in the street, his mouth working, trying to form the question that his brain couldn't process when the bawling of a baby tore through the night.

Reminded of a past he had been trying to forget and a last addition to a mad night that kept getting madder, Arthur snapped.

Once more, he ran.

CHAPTER 9

Headlong through the night, he ran with all his might back the way he had come. Back towards Ye Olde Starre Inne and aiming beyond it to the Minster, his only thought to reach the safety of the magnificent building—the one remaining bastion in a city gone mad. He raced through the pressing darkness with his blue jacket billowing behind him. Arthur was fast. He had always been fast, but he hadn't always drunk or smoked this much. Within moments he could feel his lungs bursting as he pushed his body onward, his thighs aching with effort before he'd covered half the length of Stonegate.

Why he had chosen to go back this way, he wasn't sure. He had just started running away from the fire, and the Minster had been there, a towering presence in front of him, forever present and welcoming.

It didn't bear repeating, but the thought came to him again just the same—something was most definitely wrong this night. He needed a doctor or the safety of a church, and the church was closest. None of this made much sense as Arthur harboured no real belief in God, gods, or the supernatural, but rational decisions were beyond his reach as he hurtled down the street in his desperate need to get away. He almost didn't see the giant man standing in the hidden entrance of the Ye Olde Starre Inne, and he jumped in fright when the figure stepped forward, hands like shovels reaching into the street, long fingers curling and pointing,

"Fetch!" cried the man, and the two cats appeared at his feet.

Arthur gasped and dodged away from the grasping hands. He veered across the street and stumbled into a dark alley opposite the entrance to the pub. Searing pain bit his shoulder as he crashed into a metal gate and rolled away. His footsteps and panicked breath bounced back at him in the narrow confines of a small tunnel, and he bent his head as he ran, ducking beneath a low roof.

Bursting abruptly into an open space, the sky opened above him as he clattered into a small courtyard surrounded by tall white buildings crisscrossed with a lattice of thick wooden beams.

He spun on the spot, desperately searching. *Where is the way out*? He knew this place, but couldn't see the exit, just dark pools of shadow piling up against the wall. He bent low, hands grasping his knees for support, trying to calm his breathing and frayed nerves by taking long, steadying breaths. He peered back down the passage, knowing his pursuers, if there were any, would come that way, but the alley simply stared back at him, mocking his fear. There was nothing there. No cats. No giant man. No reaching figures in the dark. He was alone in a hidden square in the narrows behind Stonegate.

Arthur looked up at the open sky above him. The stars twinkled brightly in the night but failed to penetrate the blackness cast into the square by the tall buildings. A wooden staircase climbed up one wall, leaving an impenetrable patch of shadow beneath. He backed into it slowly, his breath coming in sharp, ragged bursts. Better to let the shadows take him and hide him than face whatever was coming in the night.

Pulling his jacket tightly over his white shirt and lifting the collar, he sank further back, allowing the darkness to swallow him completely. The only sound to be heard was that of his breath and the pounding of his own heartbeat as blood roared in his ears. He felt certain that anything creeping into the courtyard would be able to hear it, but nothing came. Nothing followed, though he couldn't shake the feeling he wasn't alone. Arthur never really felt alone in this city, but for a multitude of reasons, that thought wasn't as comforting as a person might think. Not tonight. He shivered in the dark beneath the stairs, friendless and terrified.

Arthur's breathing became less ragged, and his heart slowed to something near normal. He crouched beneath the staircase like a cornered animal and, with shaking hands, pulled his last cigarette from the packet, fumbling in the other pocket for the matches. Willing his hands to still as he searched, he was struck with the heaviness of realisation—he had no fucking clue what was happening to him, and worse yet, no idea how to get it to stop.

With trembling fingers, he grasped a match and struck.

The sudden spark of flame illuminated the pale features of the boy in rags sitting quietly in the shadows beside him, big eyes reflecting twin pinpricks of flame.

The noise that escaped Arthur's lips was an entirely unprintable combination of every curse word he had ever heard jumbled into one elongated yet quietly terrified syllable. It came out in a desperate breath of surprise. A breath that extinguished the match and plunged him and the boy once again into complete darkness.

CHAPTER 10

It's at this point in the tale that a protagonist finally grasps the thing that any outside observer would have figured out a long time ago.

"You're a ghost," said Arthur.

There we go.

The boy nodded, his eyes wide, his body poised to run. He was like a horse at a glue factory, every sinew ready to flee from the oncoming double-barrelled shotgun. Arthur himself was in the exact same boat, though he had almost convinced himself he was going mad. It seemed easier that way. But sure, here he was, sitting in the dark, talking to the ghost of a small boy. Why not?

Arthur lit his last cigarette after another series of fumbled attempts and sat back on the cold stone, hugging his knees and taking small, sharp drags on the smoke. "You're a ghost," he said to himself. "Of course you're a ghost. Why wouldn't you be? Perfectly natural."

"Not really," said the boy. "Nothing much natural about this." He leaned backward until his head and shoulders vanished into the wall behind them, leaving just his torso and legs on the stone beside Arthur. A little of the boy's chin still poked through the brickwork and the grey arms lifted to give two thumbs up, which the terrified man thought was entirely unnecessary. Finishing the cigarette in one deep drag, Arthur let the smoke out in a long plume that shimmered in the night air. He tried not to notice how it passed through the boy's body as he sat back up.

"Please, don't do that again," Arthur said in a weak voice.

"Sorry, dude," the boy said with a grin.

Silence spread as Arthur stared incredulously at the boy. Of everything that had happened to him this evening, the ghost of a small boy saying "dude" struck him as ridiculous. It took a long moment to stack the deck of his jumbled thoughts into anything even remotely usable.

"Dude?" he managed, his voice one tiny strain away from cracking and bringing his newly assembled house of cards tumbling down around him.

"Dude," the boy grinned.

"How old are you?"

The boy looked at him. "Eleven."

"Yeah, but I mean...when did you, you know...?"

"Oh, you mean when did I die?"

"Yeah."

"I don't really know, man, but it was when this place was being built," he indicated the square they were sitting in.

"But this has been around for hundreds of years!"

"Nah, not really," the boy said. Some of his initial hesitation seemed to be falling away as he, for want of a better word, *warmed* to Arthur. This drunken man had scared the boy twice tonight. People didn't usually scare him. How could they if they couldn't see him? But Arthur had. The ghostly child wasn't sure why he had run, but it had seemed like the smartest thing to do at the time. When Arthur burst into the square, the boy realised he wasn't the one being chased. In fact, it looked like the man himself was running away and was probably just as frightened. That changed things.

"Look, I can't be sure," the boy said. "Time is, well, sort of a bit funny. You don't exactly have a bedtime when you're dead, and birthdays are, well, you know, a bit shit. So, time becomes kind of meaningless."

"What year was it when you died?" Arthur asked.

He was staring at the boy's clothes. Grey rags, he had first thought, but now that they were close and his eyes were adjusting to the lack of light, he was seeing them differently. They were tattered and old, that was certain, but there was a strange familiarity to them as well. Something he couldn't quite place.

"I don't know," answered the boy in a quiet voice. "It's all sort of muddled up. I shouldn't be here," he said with a sudden sob of such sorrow that Arthur instinctively put his arm around him.

The boy flinched and seemed ready to run, but then he felt a squeeze that brought him in close, and the boy gasped, shuddering with emotion.

"I miss my mum," he sobbed into the strange man's chest.

The strange man who could see him.

The living man who could touch a ghost.

This realisation seemed to be slowly dawning on them both.

I'm touching a ghost.

Arthur leaned back slightly, torn between his need to comfort the young boy and the strange sensation of this ethereal figure beneath his arm. He patted the lad's tousled hair and tried to focus. *Hair. Well, it felt like hair.* He could feel the contact of the boy leaning against him. The pressure. He knew he was there. *Of course he was there. Look at him.*

But...

But he wasn't entirely sure his own body knew it. The cold sensation of touch seemed to arrive directly in Arthur's mind without the intervening need for skin or nerve endings. The harder he concentrated, the harder it was to hold onto. Literally. The boy began to sink into Arthur. A coldness entered his body, and he felt his heart slow and sit heavy in his chest as their bodies began to merge. He gasped and moved away, clutching at his chest and breathing heavily. The boy looked at him with wide, fearful eyes.

"What's wrong?"

"You're dead."

"I know."

"But you're dead!"

"Yes. Totally."

"Then how—?"

The boy shrugged.

"Are you a zombie?"

The boy gave a small laugh. "No. Zombies aren't dead."

"What?!"

"They're just the bits that are left over."

Arthur chose to ignore this. One massive life-altering revelation at a time.

"How can I touch you?" he said softly, leaning forward and poking the boy in the forehead.

The boy rocked back with the touch though Arthur wasn't entirely sure his finger had actually made contact with anything more substantial than air.

"I don't know," said the boy, settling back. "You're the first person I've met who can. You're the first person I've met who's seen me more than once," he added.

"Why did you run away the first time?" Arthur asked.

He looked at the boy's clothes again; there was something on the edge of his vision that just wouldn't fall into place, something he couldn't quite see.

"I was scared."

"*You* were scared? But you're the ghost!"

"I know. But I didn't know what you were, though," said the boy.

"What do you mean?" asked Arthur. His mind was reeling. It was taking all his concentration to keep the world from spinning, the ache behind his eyes was getting heavier, and now a sharp swirling sensation filled the pit of his belly. He knew the feeling. Everyone who had ever drunk a lot of alcohol and then inexplicably decided sprinting was a good idea knew the feeling. The pressure behind his forehead grew, as did the deep ache in his stomach. It was too late. Before he could stop it, a violent plume of hot vomit erupted from his mouth and hit the boy.

Or rather, it went right through the boy and splattered on the floor, a sight that Arthur knew would be forever scorched into the dark recesses of his mind. Another rumbling spasm hit his belly, and he threw up again. The boy stood up in horror. Before Arthur could say anything, the grey figure turned and fled from the square, disappearing down a small tunnel in the corner, an opening in the wall that Arthur had previously mistaken for shadows.

He reached out a hand to shout for the boy but vomited instead. Sledgehammers pounded behind his eyes, and tears rolled down his cheeks as he heaved bile onto the flagstone floor. But Arthur had seen something as the boy turned his back and ran, something familiar that should not have been. He needed to get up. He needed to get it together and go after the spirit—he needed to talk to him again.

The ghost of the boy wearing a grey *Teenage Mutant Ninja Turtles* t-shirt.

CHAPTER 11

Arthur didn't get far. It was just a few feet before he had to rest in the dark tunnel beside Barley Hall. He bent over and tried desperately not to be sick again, but there was nothing left to give. He leaned against the wall and registered the strange sensation as his body touched glass instead of stone. That's right. He remembered now. Barley Hall had a full glass wall in this tunnel that allowed people to see the medieval dining room inside.

He turned and rested his forehead against the cool glass, the smooth surface like a wet washer on his brow, and moaned as waves of nausea assaulted him. He blinked at his own reflection staring back at him from the darkness—the whites of his eyes filling the world in front of him, obscuring the shapes of grand tables and chairs on the inside of the building.

A window into another world, Arthur thought, having no concept of just how close he was to the truth. *Get yourself together, man. There's no time for this.*

He leaned back and looked at himself. Even in the dark glass, he could see the rough, pale skin, clothes in disarray, and bloodshot veins spidering across his bleary eyes.

"Get it together." He chastised his reflection, which, to his horror, smiled back at him.

Arthur staggered back from the glass. The reflection didn't move or copy his actions as it was supposed to. Instead, it stared straight at him, then, horrifyingly, tilted its head slightly as though regarding a novel curiosity. It lifted a hand.

Arthur looked at his hands just to be sure—both remained by his sides.

The apparition clenched a fist in front of the glass and knocked.

CHAPTER 12

By the time he stopped running, his mind a blur of twisting streets and narrow alleys, of jostling bodies and angry shouts, Arthur was completely lost and more than a little fed-up of legging it through a city that was supposed to be his home. He had run full-pelt out of the glass-walled tunnel, smashing his head on a low beam as he went. His vision filled with agonizing lights, and blackness threatened to take him as he staggered into Grape Lane before stumbling down Back Swinegate.

He ran straight into a group of late-night drinkers dressed in a bizarre array of clothing, from Viking warriors and nuns to Roman soldiers and witches. Many had open wounds or bleeding sores. Arthur screamed a scream that a B-movie horror star would envy and bolted into the dank, piss-stained passage of Nether Hornpot Lane. The group of actors from York Dungeon stared after him as he fled, one or two laughing but others wondering if they should call someone. By the time they reached for their phones, Arthur was long gone.

He burst out of the narrow brick lane and emerged into a forest of barren trees, the leafless nubs of cut branches reaching toward the night sky with the plaintive cry of silent amputees. Arthur swerved away from the terrifying forms and crashed into

Three Cranes Lane, where he ran headlong into a wheelie bin and fell to the ground amidst the ear-splitting crash and crack of glass bottles. A mural of Queen Elizabeth looked down her nose at him in silent judgement.

Some instinctive part of his body had decided to put as many twists and turns between him and his potential pursuers as possible. Three Cranes Lanes spat Arthur out onto the broader artery of Church Street, and he ran northeast past the old church on one side and The Golden Lion on the other. A sleek black cat jumped from a window and landed in the centre of the road in front of him at the entrance to Goodramgate. It stood smack in the middle of the 'o' of a *No Entry* sign painted in large white letters on the road and hissed at him. The sight of another black cat caused the already panicked man to panic again, and he grabbed a lamppost and swung himself down Low Petergate. Everything was closed. No pubs, no people, no cars. He ran on through the quiet night, slowing as his legs began to shake, and ducked into the relative safety of another of York's snickelways before finally resting in the darkness there.

He felt awful. His whole body was a fire of nausea and dull pulsing pain, and the less said about the taste in his mouth, the better. The world spun as he tried to catch his breath, and he retched loudly in the cramped alley. Arthur lowered himself to the floor between two wheelie bins, sobbing with fear and exhaustion.

He would have sobbed even harder if he realised he'd just run in a circle, for despite all the twists and turns and zigs and zags, Arthur was little more than a few hundred feet from where he had started. The woman watching him from the shadows found it all very funny. She even did a little dance.

~

"Who are you?" Sarah snapped at Steve, who backed away from her sheepishly.

She was marching down Stonegate, heading the way Arthur had gone, tracking his passage, and the man in the red tie shuffled nervously along behind her.

"I'm Steve," he said in a small voice.

"Well, why the bloody hell did you say you were hungry? You went all...all *ghost* on him!" She spat the word like she was chiding a small child for being a small child.

"I *am* hungry," he mumbled in reply. "I'm always hungry."

"You scared him!"

"*I* scared him! *You* scared him with your creepy reaching hand and your mad eyes!"

"Sorry," he added when she paused and rounded on him. He stepped back and looked at his feet. "It's been a strange night," he mumbled.

"The nights are always strange in this city," Sarah said in a distant voice before laughing maniacally.

"See! Now you're doing it!"

Sarah sighed, her shoulders dropping, "Sorry," she said. "Force of habit."

The pair paused in the middle of Stonegate, in the middle of York—one of the most famously haunted cities in the country—and regarded each other.

The spirits of the dead—let's not beat around the bush, for spirits they are—see one another in much the same way as the living. There is not a lot in the way of evidence to suggest that the person you are talking to is cardiorespiratorially-challenged, other than a lack of breathing of course. But some spirits, especially the recently deceased, find habits hard to break. Like ex-smokers who hold pens between their fingers and absentmindedly place them to their lips, the dead go through the motion of breathing, even going so far as to gasp, sigh, and on occasion, yawn. It's best not to think too hard about it.

Some ghosts are much easier to spot than others. The headless ones are a dead giveaway, but Sarah and Steve were about as normal as you or me, in appearance at least. Each of them had been inexplicably drawn to Arthur, and as they stared at each other in the ethereal grey ghost-light of York's long thoroughfare, they began to understand.

"You thought he was dead, too," whispered Sarah.

Steve nodded. "I don't get it," he said. "He saw me. He spoke to me. I even touched him! He felt real!"

"He is real."

"No, I mean—" he halted, the right words leaping just out of reach. "Not *his* real," he managed. "My real. *Our* real."

"Have you seen him before?" Sarah asked.

Steve nodded, "I see him all the time at work. He—he works where I—where I used to...Where I live."

"Where you haunt," corrected Sarah, and then regretted it when she saw the look of pain flash across Steve's features. She looked at him closely. His baggy, long grey trousers, creased white shirt, scuffed shoes, and red tie. His hair fell on both sides of his face in curtains that he peered from beneath like a scolded child. Her eyes widened in surprise.

"How old are you?" she asked but was interrupted by a gruff bark from the shadows.

"Halt!" came a voice like gravel. A giant form detached itself from the building and stood before the strange couple. "State your business," rumbled the officer. "There have been strange things afoot this evening." Steve recoiled and stepped back like a startled puppy, but Sarah lifted a hand to steady him.

"It's okay," she said. "I know him. Lord Acaster!" she called, turning to the giant man. "It's me, Sarah." Then, in the middle of the street, she dipped into a polite and elegant curtsey.

"Forgive me, madam," the giant man rumbled as he, in turn, descended into a deep bow, removing his beaver-skin hat as he did so. "I did not recognise you, and I am unfamiliar with your companion," he said.

"This is...Steve. Sir Steve," Sarah Brocklebank introduced the man by her side.

"Sir Steve?"

"Just Steve," Steve said, slightly embarrassed.

"A strange name," rumbled Lord Acaster. Steve didn't feel in any position to argue.

"Tell me, Just Steve, are you named for your daring do, for your gallantry, and for your ability to meter out the king's righteous justice?"

Steve opened his mouth and tried to form the words to reply but couldn't find any suitable, so closed it again.

"You *are* for the king, are you not, Just Steve?" The giant man peered at him intently. Then, leaning in and lowering his voice, he hissed dangerously, "Or are you a filthy traitor?"

This, of course, left very little in the way of options for Steve. "The king," he said in a small voice.

"Glad to hear it!" roared Lord Acaster, standing up and proclaiming to the world in general, "Those murderous, treacherous, villainous scum will never take this city while His Majesty lays claim, by the grace of God!"

A scream sounded in the night, echoing from the alley to the Ye Olde Starre Inne.

"I am needed," said Lord Acaster, turning on his heel. "But beware, Lady Sarah. There are strange happenings this night. I believe a Fetch is loose about the town."

Sarah gasped, "Are you sure?"

"Alas, the comfort of certainty eludes me, but I know not what other creature could cause such chaos among the denizens of the dark places. You remember what happened last time," he added.

Sarah nodded sadly.

"This is worse. I do believe our fellow knows not what he is."

"By any chance, is the man you speak of dressed in blue?" Sarah asked.

"I know not, lady. The pleasure of colour deserted me long ago."

"Sorry, Lord Acaster," she bowed. "Thank you."

"Farewell, Lady Sarah and Sir Just Steve. Travel safe."

Lord Acaster bowed and walked towards Ye Olde Starre Inne, not bothering to use the alley but rather passing through the wall of the shop next door. Sarah and Steve watched him go, and Sarah noticed the shudder that ran through Steve as he watched the giant man vanish through the bricks.

"Just how old are you?" she asked again as they crossed Stonegate and turned into Coffee Yard.

They were following the trail Arthur had left. It was completely invisible to the likes of you or me. Perhaps we would notice it as a shiver or the strange sensation of déjà vu, but for Sarah and Steve, the passing of Arthur was marked by a faint wisp of delicate blue light hanging in the air. As they made their way to Barley Hall, the smoky tendril seemed to grow thicker. A hint of a thought was nagging at Sarah, something important she couldn't quite grasp. She needed time to think—to piece it all together.

"Thirty," Steve replied.

"No, I mean—" she paused and turned, eyes wide. "Wow, you really must be young," she said in a stunned voice.

Steve stared at her blankly, and she stopped in the narrow alley. "When I ask how old you are, I mean how many years since you died," she explained.

"Oh, well, I'm not really sure, to be honest. It all sort of blends together after a while, doesn't it. I think...I think maybe I died quite recently. A few years."

"So young," said Sarah, and Steve realised she wasn't lamenting the loss of a man only just out of his twenties, but rather, she was marvelling at how young this new form of his was.

"How old are you?" he asked as they continued down the narrow alley.

"Oh, I've been around for a long time," Sarah replied. She ran her hand through the solid stone wall as though it was water. "Long enough to get used to this anyway," she said, pulling her hand out and wiggling her fingers.

Steve shuddered, "I don't think I'll ever get used to it."

"What I don't understand," said Sarah, "is how you can wander around the city like this."

"Like what?"

"Well, it doesn't seem to be causing you any discomfort at all," she said.

"Should it?"

"I'm not sure," she admitted, reaching into the pocket of her skirt and gripping the metal key she had placed there. "I just know that it hurts me. I feel sort of...I don't know...stretched thin...when I venture too far away from where I—" She let out a manic little laugh, a high-pitched giggle in the dark. "...Where I died."

"Where did you—?" Steve began to ask, but as they entered the courtyard of Barley Hall, the question died on his lips. To Arthur, the courtyard had been nearly empty, but to the two ghosts, it was as crowded with apparitions as Stonegate could be crowded with tourists.

"What happened here?" asked Steve.

He stared in wonder at the multitude of ghosts and lost souls that filled the area, passing in and out of walls as they paid no attention to the boundaries set by the living. He guessed there must have been a massacre or a plague of some description for so many ghosts to be congregated in one place.

"They rebuilt this place a few years ago," Sarah said. "I remember it well. That was when everything changed. It had been boarded up and all but forgotten, but then they started to piece it back together again, bit by bit."

She gripped the key again tightly.

"Why was that such a problem?" Steve asked.

Tugging at his tie, he tried not to look too closely at whatever two big brown rats were nibbling on beneath a wooden staircase. Ghostly feet passed through the rats, stepping on them and through them, but the creatures did not stir from their feast.

"Whenever they rebuild something or move something, it plays havoc with the associated spirits of the dead. Look there," she said, pointing as two Roman soldiers marched through the square, appearing from one wall and vanishing through the opposite. "They don't belong here, but there will be something in the building that has drawn them to this spot. I dare say they march through here over and over, never really knowing where they are or why. Or maybe..." she trailed off, lost in thought.

"Would Arthur have been able to see them?" Steve asked. "I'm guessing he was here."

"I, I don't know, to be honest," Sarah replied. "I don't think whatever ability he has is quite settled yet."

"What do you mean?"

"Nothing," she said. "Just a feeling. If he is...if he is a Fetch, there is really no knowing. He'll be drawing ghosts from all over the city, though."

"Like them?" Steve asked, nodding his head to a group of injured people who appeared from the tunnel.

"They're alive," Sarah said.

"Really?"

"Yeah, they're just dressed up. Watch."

The group was still talking about the strange man who had run into them and screamed at the top of his lungs before darting away down one of the alleys. They paid no attention to the gathering of ghosts in the small courtyard and walked right through many of them, knowing nothing other than perhaps a small chill on the back of their necks or raised hairs on their forearms. Most were convinced the man had been playing some kind of practical joke.

"He was having a laugh," said a witch.

Steve knew it was a witch because of the green skin, the giant wart, and the pointy hat, all of which he got to inspect very closely when she walked right through him. The sensation was not pleasant. Of course, he couldn't feel anything, but that didn't mean he enjoyed the experience. He whimpered and gripped his tie even tighter, trying to fade into the background.

"You really are new to all this, aren't you? Where did you die?" Sarah asked.

"At work," Steve said in a small voice.

"No, I mean, where?" The idea she had been working on was swirling and leaping about, taking form, wanting to get noticed. She was close.

"The council building on St Leonard's Place," said Steve. "In the toilet," he added and wished he hadn't when he saw Sarah's expression.

"And you don't feel any...well...discomfort, being this far away?" she asked. "It doesn't hurt you? You don't feel a pull? An urge to go back?"

"I guess so," said Steve quietly, twisting the substance-less cloth through ethereal fingers, an action Sarah did not fail to spot. So close. So very, very close.

"Your death," she said slowly, "was it violent?"

He nodded. Only once.

"I knew it," she sighed. "Violence or passion. Rage or Love. That's usually always how we end up like this. Although some just miss the boat, so to speak."

"What do you mean?"

She shrugged, peered under the stairs at the rats, and turned back, not liking what she saw, "I don't know all the rules," she said, "Although I'm sure there are some. Well, I hope there are."

She looked at the scared young man and made a decision. She could have done with someone around to talk to her in the early days; it would have made it all a little easier. Not a lot, but a little. She pulled the metal key from her pocket and showed it to Steve.

"This key," she said, "is linked to my death. As long as I keep it on me, as long as I hold it, I can go wherever I want. But every night..." she went on, and her eyes—against all biological basis—misted with tears. "Every night, I lose it, and then I'm trapped again. Trapped between home, between the places I think it might be, and between where it needs to go. And I forget where it is. Every night, I have to find it again."

"Every night?"

Sarah nodded and wiped ineffectually at her eyes. Steve gripped his tie even tighter, then readjusted the knot around his neck, loosening it and pulling it tight again.

"I...I have something similar," he whispered. "I can be wandering around the city, then I close my eyes for a moment, and I'm back there." His eyes filled with such pain that Sarah felt compelled to be gentle, as though approaching a child that might spook.

"I thought so. Have you ever wondered why you didn't pass over?" she asked.

Steve shrugged and let go of his tie.

"Pass over to where?"

"To the other side. To...to...heaven. Or hell? Whatever is there."

"Not really," he said. "I just figured this was it."

Sarah gasped, "This! You thought *this* was the afterlife!"

"Well, it is *after* life," said Steve, although even he was disappointed by his lack of conviction.

"If that's the case," said Sarah with her hands on her hips, the tide of spirits swarming around her, "where is everyone else?"

"What do you mean?"

"Come here," she said, and taking hold of his hand she walked them both through the wall of Barley Hall. If the courtyard was full, then the hall itself was overflowing. The pair had to squeeze their way through a swirling press of bodies, gripping tightly to each other so as not to be separated. Dancers and musicians skipped through tables crowded with revellers, a lord and lady lounged on a raised dais laughing along to the antics of a belled-up jester, and everywhere there was food. Every surface, every tray, every plate, every sideboard, table, and bench that didn't contain a ghost was stuffed with dishes of every kind, though no one was eating.

Steve's mouth fell open, and he felt a hunger close to physical agony if he had anything physical with which he could feel agony, but Sarah didn't pause. She dragged them through the far wall into a restaurant kitchen, through an alley, then a cleaning cupboard where a mouse shivered as they stepped on it—the small creature deciding then and there never to nibble at rotting apples again. They moved on through an empty bar and finally out into the quiet of Grape Lane, the evening sky opening above them dotted with stars. The gentle wisp that was Arthur's trail floated off to the right, but that was it. The world was silent.

The night was still.

The spirits gone.

The streets of York lay in peaceful slumber.

"If this was it," said Sarah quietly. "If this was the afterlife, wouldn't the world be crowded? If every person who ever died came back, there would be no room to move. Anywhere. It would be like it was in there. Imagine plague victims, war, the elderly, the young. They'd all be here."

"Then...then why aren't they?" stammered Steve.

"Wrong question," said Sarah. "What you should be asking is, *why are we*?"

"Well?"

"Well, what?"

"Why are we?"

"I have no idea," she said and cackled to herself in the street. The laughter turned to a heavy sob, and she gripped the key even tighter and giggled.

CHAPTER 13

Less than two hundred metres away, a man in a blue suit sat between two wheelie bins and groaned. The alley smelled of piss. His stomach hurt. His head hurt. He spat thick phlegm onto the ground and then nearly shit himself when a voice in the darkness called out, "Charming!"

For a moment, Arthur considered running again, but then he simply sighed, resigned, and turned his head toward the newcomer. *One more visitor in a night of madness, what's the difference?*

"Sorry," he mumbled and rubbed his face with his hands, trying to drive some life back into the sallow skin. "So, who are you?"

It was rude, he knew, but he was past caring. Something ridiculous was no doubt going to happen, and as long as he didn't have to run anywhere, he really didn't care. Arthur just wanted the pain behind his eyes to go away and to finally make it home.

"I'm Alice," the newcomer said, a dark shape in the alley that Arthur couldn't quite make out.

"Well, it's nice to meet you, Alice. I'm Arthur."

"I'm Alice."

"Right."

"I'm Alice,' came the voice again, giggling, "Alice, Alice, Alice. A-lease. A-lice. Alice."

"Fucksake," groaned Arthur under his breath and slowly climbed to his feet, gripping the wheelie bins to steady himself. "Let me guess," he said, turning in the direction of the voice, the realisation that he had managed to run so far and yet travel such a short distance dawning on him. He knew exactly where he was and who he was talking to. "Mad Alice, right?"

The shape in the shadows cackled gleefully.

Every resident of York knows the story of Mad Alice, as do many tourists. At the very least, they know about the snickelway named after her, Mad Alice Lane. The narrow entrance had become a regular spot for tourists to clog up Low Petergate while taking photographs of the unusual sign fastened to the wall above – *Lund's Court (formerly Mad Alice Lane)*. It was a fair guess that any woman caught beneath the sign pulling a daft face for a camera was probably called Alice. Arthur often wondered if they knew the reason for the name.

Alice was a murderer. She had poisoned her cheating husband after catching him with another woman, and the violent act drove her to madness. In the end, it was for the crime of being insane that she was executed at York Castle in the 1820s. Arthur always found that oddly fascinating, being executed for the "crime of insanity."

Well, we're all criminals tonight.

"I don't suppose you smoke?" Arthur asked and laughed at the ridiculousness of asking a ghost for a cigarette.

Madness—it was contagious.

"Smokey, smoke, smoke," sang Alice and stepped forward. "Normally, they run away," she crooned. "The people run!"

The woman capered upon the edge of the shadows, in and out of the light, mumbling to herself, glancing at Arthur, and quickly looking away. She was fascinated by him. He was different.

"You're different," she said, a crooked finger pointing at him accusingly.

Arthur wasn't different. Not in that way, anyway. He was terrified, and he really wanted to run, but his body simply wouldn't let him anymore. So, he stood up as best he could to face his fear. He looked at Alice and forced a smile. She wasn't what he expected, and that made it a little easier.

For reasons he couldn't quite explain and didn't want to think too closely about, Arthur had always pictured the famous Mad Alice as being young and attractive, like a sexy but dangerous femme fatale in a detective show or the impossibly good-looking women usually accused of witchcraft in made for TV specials. What he wasn't expecting was someone who looked like his gran.

Alice grinned at the young man, and her face creased into a mass of wrinkles. Her silver hair was combed straight and tied neatly with a headscarf. She wore a plain, tidy dress behind a clean apron with big pockets and looked like she'd just stepped out of an old-time bakery. The only thing missing was a rosy complexion and a smudge of flour on her cheek.

Arthur blinked in surprise. He realised that it wasn't just her hair that was grey; all of her was. She resembled a character from a black-and-white photograph—washed out and over-exposed. If he concentrated really hard, he could make out the pattern of the brickwork through her body. He quickly decided not to do that. It made the back of his eyes itch.

"You look...different," he said, throwing her words back at her. "Different from the others, at least," he added.

"What others?" she asked with a tilt of her head.

"The other ghosts."

Ghosts. Fucking hell.

He closed his eyes and took a deep breath. Hopefully, the memory would be purged by the colossal hangover he expected in the morning, but for now, he was in the thick of it. His very own ghost story.

"Ghosty, ghost, ghosts," Alice said, her wrinkled eyes flashing as she skipped from foot to foot. A strange thought flashed through Arthur's mind. She reminded him of those old ladies on long-haul flights who stand near the toilets—bobbing up and down on the balls of their feet, jogging in place to keep the blood flowing.

Blood flowing? Do ghosts even have blood?

There were so many questions.

"You *are* a ghost, aren't you?" Arthur asked, starting with the basics. There was something about Alice, something in the way she looked at him, something that didn't add up. It was right there, but he couldn't quite grasp it. He felt like he was waiting for his eyes to adjust. It was as though he was thinking more deeply about things, which was astounding considering how drunk he still was.

"Well, I think so," she sang, lifting a hand in front of her face and dancing a little jig. Her eyes widened suddenly as though seeing her hand for the first time, then to Arthur's horror—and no help at all to the state of his stomach—she pushed her fist through the centre of her face, turning around and giving a little wave from the back of her head.

"Think so, thinky, think," she said, completing the circle and flashing Arthur a wicked smile as she pulled the hand back through her face.

He tried to swallow, but his throat was too dry. His heart had either stopped or was beating so fast he couldn't tell the difference, and frankly, he didn't care anymore. His body shook involuntarily as he tried to think of something, anything he could possibly say that didn't involve screaming.

"I—" he began.

Then he passed out.

It was a valiant effort.

~

Waking up beside a stinking bin in a dank alley is not the best way to arrive back in the world of consciousness. Neither is it particularly helpful if the thing that caused you to pass out in the first place—in this case, the face of a deranged old lady—is inches away from your face as your eyelids flutter open. Arthur finally let out the scream that had been threatening to make itself known, and it was a good one if he did say so himself. It rattled down the alley and burst into the city.

Dogs howled, cats yowled, and rats scurried away. Late-night couples held each other tight and stared fearfully into the shadowy places of the quiet streets before deciding it was best to call that taxi after all. As screams go, it was the very definition of blood-curdling. Alice nodded. It was nice to be appreciated.

All across the city, creatures invisible to you or me ceased their various nocturnal creeps, lurks, haunts, and hunts and looked up at the noise. It is perhaps best not to describe them.

One such creature waited nearby, gathering strength—feeding on the fear in the air.

In the shadows of the Ye Olde Starre Inne, Lord Acaster bent down and whispered to one of his big black cats, who butted her head against his riding boots and darted away into the night. At the same time, on the roof of the city hospital, the man in black turned his head and lifted his face to the air.

Arthur sat up slowly, and Alice shuffled back to give him space. She had been kneeling on the floor beside him, staring in fascination at his breath as it whispered from his nostrils. It's funny the things you forget about when you're dead. Nostrils. Amazing things.

Arthur ran his hands through his hair and rubbed his face again. Alice stood up and plunged her hands deep into her apron pockets, taking a step back and biting her lip with an odd expression on her face. Arthur groaned and pulled himself to his feet.

"So," he said out of a desperate need to hear his own voice—something familiar and real—"You're Mad Alice? I'm talking to *the* Mad Alice."

"Indeed."

"Do you, do you live here?"

"Live here. Heredy, heredy, here."

"Stop that."

"Sorry."

The lady looked to the ground, and the suspicion that had been niggling quietly away at the back of Arthur's mind suddenly knocked on the door and made itself known. Something about this whole situation wasn't right. Well, *nothing* about this situation was right, but there was something else going on, something extra. Something that Arthur just couldn't quite grasp.

It was like there were thoughts in his head that weren't there before. Or places of his brain that had been dormant but were now waking up. It felt like déjà vu, only he knew for certain that he hadn't experienced these things before. There was knowledge teetering just on the edge if his mind, like a vision in the corner of his eye. When he reached for it, it vanished, but when he looked away, he knew it was there.

He could sense it. Arthur looked closely at the woman, and she looked away quickly with a flash of, what? Embarrassment? Yes, it was embarrassment. And suddenly, the cards fell into place, and Arthur understood. The thought landed in his mind fully formed, and he knew it to be true, though he couldn't say how he knew.

"You're not actually mad, are you?" he blurted before he could stop himself. What a strange thing to ask a person you've just met. Then again, were there any normal things to say to the spirit of a deceased woman who had just taken face-palming to a whole new level?

"Of course I am!" Alice snapped, a look of fury flashing in her eyes, the embarrassment vanishing in an instant. The shadows in the alley deepened, and the strange old lady loomed larger before him. But it was no good. Arthur had come to a realisation, and though he didn't know it now, it was going to change his entire life. He did the only thing he could think of and followed the advice of his father.

"Oh, fuck off!" he laughed. "That's a neat trick, though. I'll give you that," he added.

This, however, turned out to be a mistake.

"I. Am. Mad. Alice!" spat Alice, each word slashing at Arthur like a scythe.

"But you're not, though, are you?" he said softly. "I mean, you're no madder than anyone else around here."

Alice, wringing her hands deep in the pockets of her apron, did a frantic little skipping dance, turning away and then turning back, biting her lip. She lunged towards Arthur suddenly and screamed in his face. Mouth wide open, her eyes vanishing behind a mass of wrinkles, she roared as though all the demons of hell were tormenting her, but Arthur didn't flinch. She was just an old lady playing a part.

Alice tucked her fingers up under her chin and pushed them through the substance-less flesh, wriggling them like worms in her open mouth. Again, to no reaction from the man in the blue suit. She stamped her foot, turned away for a moment, and then spun back with triumph shining in her eyes. She lifted a spectral hand to her cheek and began to claw at her face, pulling at the flesh and peeling away long pieces of dead grey matter.

"Mad Alice, Mad Alice!" she sang, flicking ethereal skin at Arthur in the dark of her namesake alley. They passed through him like cold drafts, and that absolutely did the trick.

For the second time that night, Arthur vomited directly

through a person, and Alice nodded in satisfaction. A job well done. It didn't matter that Arthur had discerned a strange truth. No epiphany—no matter how important or life-changing—can stop a gut reaction when someone lobs a load of dead skin at you.

"Jesus Christ!" he said and spat bile and phlegm onto the stones. "Stop that, will you. You're good, I'll give you that, but there's something else going on here, isn't there? What is it? I want to know."

Arthur looked at her, and the dark patches of missing flesh on her face slowly closed over, filling themselves in from inside, just as smoke billows into a glass, pressing against an invisible barrier. The strange pieces of ghost flesh at his feet vanished.

Alice looked sheepish and refused to meet his gaze. She seemed abruptly nervous and brought to Arthur's mind the image of a shy young girl. He knew he was onto something.

"Is your name even Alice?" he asked softly.

She shook her head. Only once.

"Who are you?"

A sob escaped the lips of the woman, and suddenly she seemed very old, very frail, and very tired. Arthur stepped forward impulsively and put his arms around her. He couldn't help himself. It was like watching your gran cry. The whole atmosphere of the tunnel changed around them, the darkness easing away, the night becoming less oppressive—less close. The walls themselves seemed to step back respectfully as the man and the old lady's ghost held each other in Mad Alice Lane.

"It's okay, it's okay," Arthur soothed, once again trying not to pay too much attention to the fact he was hugging a ghost. "What's your real name?" he asked. "I really am Arthur if, that helps."

He almost told her his surname but stopped, knowing enough to know better. That wasn't going to help matters.

"I don't know," sobbed the woman. "I can't remember."

"You can't remember your name?"

"No."

"But it's not Alice?"

"No."

"I don't understand," said Arthur, stroking her ethereal hair and concentrating hard on not concentrating too hard at all. The lady who wasn't Alice pushed him away gently and patted his cheek with a cold hand.

"You're a nice boy," she said. "You shouldn't be here."

"What about all the stories?" he asked, ignoring her, "About Alice? Are they true?"

"It depends on which ones you mean, my love. There are so many. Do you mind if we sit, dear? I like sitting. It reminds me of the need to sit."

"What do you mean?" asked Arthur, who, considering the amount of alcohol he'd consumed, was following along quite well.

"I'll show you," said the lady, nodding to the floor between the two bins.

Arthur pushed one of the bins away slightly and sat down. The lady lowered herself beside him onto the cold stone...and then kept going. Her legs and hips sank into the earth, and she sighed, just like she was lowering herself into a bath. She giggled and wriggled her feet, the toes of her shoes sticking out of the earth where her outstretched legs ended.

"It's all to do with memory," she said, looking at Arthur, who looked equal parts terrified and utterly confused. She patted his leg gently. "Memories and names. There's a lot of power in a name. Yours means courageous if I'm not mistaken."

Arthur nodded, vaguely conscious that doing so made him look like a right arrogant prick. "'S just a name," he said and hiccupped.

"No, it's more than that, dear. I don't understand it all, but I'll do my best to explain. You see, I'm sitting on the pavement of Mad Alice Lane," she nodded to her toes, giggling again. "They changed the name, but it's still Mad Alice Lane. And what I'm sitting on is the Mad Alice Lane *I* remember, not the one you're sitting on. They've added to it over the years, of course, and built it up. Actually..." she paused, lifting a finger as if to test the air for the thought she'd just had, "I'm not even sure it was called Mad Alice Lane then. It can't have been, now that I think about it."

"But you did live here?" asked Arthur, who was beginning to form some of his own opinions. "And that's why you...you..."

"Haunt it?" she finished for him.

"Yes."

"I guess so."

"And did you—" Arthur wasn't sure how to ask the next question, but he wanted to know the answer.

"Go on, dear, you can ask."

It was strange. Here he was, sitting beside a little old lady in a dark alley in the middle of the city, a lady who, only moments ago, had thrown parts of her face at him, but Arthur knew instinctively somewhere deep down that she wasn't dangerous nor was she mad. He could almost sense it around her, her true essence. She was full of sorrow and incredibly lonely, but she wasn't mad. Arthur had no idea how he knew these things, but he was convinced they were true. So, asking the question was even harder. He took a breath and asked,

"Did you really kill your husband?"

There was a long silence as the lady beside him looked down at her lap, which to Arthur, was below street level. A group of students ran along the opening of the lane, a quick and noisy snippet of the living world—Plato's cave with a traffic cone. Students always find traffic cones. The echoes of their passing filled the alley for a moment, and Arthur nearly missed the whispered answer.

"Yes."

The word was so soft and quiet, barely a breath. Arthur wasn't sure she had spoken, but when he turned to the lady and saw the expression on her face, he knew he had heard her right. She stared straight ahead and spoke softly,

"I put arsenic in his ale and added sugar so he wouldn't taste it," she said, then laughed. "I can't remember my name, but I can remember that! And that, that *devil* crying out for a 'physician of the body, not a physician of the soul.' Devil!" she spat.

Alice looked at Arthur's uncomprehending face and explained, "I sent for the priest, not a physician. I used enough arsenic to know what he really needed. I thought he at least might wish to confess. But no. He just wailed for a doctor. Cried and begged, he did, but it would have done no good. The man was a monster! So, I made sure. Needed to be sure. Surety, surety, sure."

She began twitching beside Arthur, her legs shaking beneath the stones, sometimes visible as she was wracked by convulsions. Then, gripping her knees and clenching her jaw, her eyes grew wild and staring. Arthur put his arm around the trembling form and held her. He didn't need to focus this time. Instead, he just sat with her until the shaking stopped.

"How did you end up here?" he whispered. He'd always found that asking questions and listening to the answers worked wonders. It was amazing how many people in the world didn't actually listen when that was pretty much all anyone wanted. Including, it would seem, the dead.

"They hung me at the castle. I remember that. They took me there on a sledge, and then I watched them take me away again on the same sledge, only I *wasn't* me. I wasn't there. There was a strange blue light, and I followed it to...a door. Beautiful, it was. Huge and round and just sitting in the middle of the city, clear as day, wreathed in purple flame. But no one paid it the least bit of notice. Not the living, mind. Others were passing through—others like me—but when I got close, it vanished. It just vanished." She sobbed once, then she sighed. "So, I made my way back home, and I've been here ever since. I lived here as a little girl. It was safe. It felt like coming home. But now I can't leave. I'm stuck."

Arthur couldn't help but feel for the woman, a feeling that really made him wish he had a cigarette and, despite all the evidence to suggest it wasn't a good idea, a drink.

"I'm sorry," he said. "I'm really very sorry."

"It's okay, young man." She reached up and patted his cheek; it was oddly comforting. "I'm used to it. I guess this is my lot. Thou shalt not kill," she said wistfully, "And I did. Oh, but I did."

"But he deserved it," said Arthur softly.

"Who are we to say who deserves to live or die?" said the woman.

~

At the far end of Lund's Court (Formerly Mad Alice Lane), a figure detached itself from the shadows on the opposite side of the street and peered into the inky black hole of the tunnel. It raised a sightless face and caught two faint but distinct trails on the soft breeze that blew down the lane.

The creature slunk low to the ground. It seemed to taste the air as it moved closer to the gaping mouth. If it had been capable of smiling, it would have done so. But it had no mouth with which to smile nor a tongue with which to taste, but it knew its prey was close. It leapt up the wall and skittered silently to the top of the tunnel, effortlessly crouching upside down on the arched ceiling. The creature moved its head slowly left and then right as if checking the pulse of the street below. Then it crawled one long limb at a time into obscure darkness.

~

"So why the Mad Alice thing?" Arthur asked. "Is it all an act?"

The lady formerly known as Mad Alice laughed, though there was absolutely no humour in it.

"I tried to talk to people," she said, "in the early days. Oh, occasionally, someone would come along—a bit like you—who could see me or hear me. For the most part, the living don't want to know some of us are still here. And it was hard work. The first time I really made someone notice me was when I lost my temper and screamed at a young girl. She saw me. Oh, she saw me, alright. She saw my screaming face on a dark night in a poorly lit alley, and she ran raving to the local priest. I think I damaged that poor girl. I never saw her again, though I heard plenty of talk about her from the little children who would creep up and dare each other to run the length of my alley. 'That's the place that sent Alice mad,' they'd say as they urged each other on. There was even a song for a few years. I quite liked it. *Alice, Alice, Alice, A-lease, A-lice, Mad Alice. She lost her mind. It's hard to find. The old lady scared our Alice!*"

"So, the girl was called Alice!" said Arthur, whose foggy mind was slowly keeping up.

"You're sharp," she replied with a wry smile. "Yes, the girl was called Alice, but now the title is mine to bear. And I'm stuck here. As far as I can tell, the spirits of the dead only vanish when there is no one left alive who remembers them. In some horrible twist of fate, I'm now stuck with a name that's not my own but holds enough power to keep me bound."

"I don't understand."

"Over the years, dear, I've seen spirits come and go. And I think they only get *released* when you lot forget about us. Or they fulfil some kind of purpose, or something takes them. I'll never be forgotten about," she said. "Mad Alice is famous. Got my own sign and everything. And I have no idea what my purpose might be."

"But you're not really Mad Alice!"

"But the name is now mine!"

"That's not fair!"

"Names have power," she said simply.

"What can we do?"

"Nothing," sighed not-Alice, though she was impressed at the man's use of the word "we."

"I can't even remember my own name, and I'd say it's a fair bet that no one else does either. That means I'm stuck as Alice." She laughed, another humourless chortle. "I'd need someone to remember who I really am."

"And then forget you," finished Arthur.

"Good luck," hissed a voice from the darkness. Neither Alice nor Arthur had spoken. They looked up in unison, and they both screamed.

~

Over on Goodramgate, Sarah Brocklebank and Steve heard the screams and began to run. It was the second time this evening they'd heard a shriek such as this—the first they had tried to follow, but the sound bounced around the narrow streets and came back at them from all over the city. They couldn't hope to find the source without losing the faint trail they were following, and though neither wished to say it, both were struggling with the distance.

The deep internal instinct that drew them back to their place of haunting was pulling them away, and the further they walked, the harder it got to ignore. Now that Steve was aware of it, he wasn't sure he could ever be unaware. The blue wisp had veered off Church Street and into Low Petergate, and it was as they turned that corner that they heard the scream. No sooner had they started running than they saw a familiar figure burst headlong from the cluster of buildings and head their way, a dark and evil shape close behind him, skittering along on all fours.

CHAPTER 14

Arthur didn't dare look back. When the thing spoke from the darkness, he had screamed in fright, but Alice had shrieked a challenge. She rose to face the monster on the roof, the tunnel growing darker and colder as she shouted at Arthur to run. He did.

He ran out into the world as fast as he could, desperate to put as much distance between himself and the nightmare as he could. But it was right behind him. Whatever it was, it was coming, and Alice had barely slowed it at all. He didn't have time to worry about her in his need to get away. He could hear it behind him, gaining; a skittering scraping noise like a dog with unclipped nails racing over tiles. There were no other noises in the night save his own heavy footsteps (*Too slow, too slow!*) and the skittering of the creature chasing him (*Too fast, too fast!*). Arthur thought his heart would burst in his chest, and he felt the heavy build-up of lactic acid in his legs. His hands were already shaking. Hot sweat prickled at his skin, and he forced his leaden limbs to move faster. He had been the fastest kid in school! He could move quicker than this! School days were a long time ago, and the buildings on either side slowed as though he jogged through treacle. He thought he saw two people in front, but he blinked, and they were gone. He was alone except for the *thing* moving ever closer.

You're going to have to fight.

The thought arrived in his mind like a bullet. He knew it was true. He also knew he wouldn't be one of those people in the movies who turn in the darkness, scream once, and get ripped apart without so much as a struggle. He refused to go out like that. Even though he was scared beyond all reason, he would go down swinging. It was his only chance.

He let out a strangled sob and skidded to a halt, turning as he did so and raising his fists in front of him. A shiver ran down his spine as though he stood in an icy draft, but then he saw the creature and the cold seeped deep into his bones, gripping his very being with frigid claws. His whole body shook with adrenaline, cold, mortal dread, and a significant amount of instantly metabolised sugar.

The creature checked its run and came to a smooth, controlled stop a few feet from Arthur. It slunk low to the ground, long black limbs poised to spring like a wild cat or wolf on the hunt. The blank face was almost human in shape but devoid of eyes, nose, and mouth, a featureless mask of grey that turned to Arthur's left and right before settling on him. The thing rose to its hind legs, and Arthur took an involuntary step back as it unfurled itself to tower over him, growing all the time—six, seven, eight feet tall, stretching thin like elastic as it grew. Then it began to change, its form flowing like thick oil. The head lowered, the shoulders filled out, the sticklike legs and arms became broader, and dark patches appeared on its face, spreading like ink over fabric, shifting to resemble a mouth, nose, and eyes. Arthur staggered back and nearly fell.

He was looking at himself!

The thing that was Arthur and yet not Arthur opened its mouth in a vast, horrifying smile filled with sharp, jagged teeth. It snarled and lunged forward, a hunter towards its prey. Arthur was ready. There was no way out, no one coming to help. Not Wendy. Not his parents. None of the lads. No one.

This was it.

He clenched his fists. *Once more unto the breech.*

"Come on then, you fucker!" he snarled. "I've been fighting you my whole goddamn life!"

The creature snarled back at him, pulled back its lips, and leapt.

So did Arthur.

It was then that the cat hit.

It came from nowhere in a scream of fury, hitting the doppelganger mid-leap and slicing a great gash across the flesh of its neck. In the moment before they connected, Arthur saw his own throat cut, his own eyes flash in surprise and agony, and then they crashed into one another and tumbled to the ground. Arthur hit out in blind fear and rage, grabbing, punching, pulling, and pushing. He managed to scramble out from beneath the creature as it thrashed and screamed, and he turned to face it again.

The beast somehow managed to get to its feet, and the cat hit it once more, scratching and clawing at the face in a dark whirlwind of ferocity. The noise was tremendous! Amplified by the close buildings of the street, it was deafening and maddening all at once. Arthur stepped forward and threw punch after punch, screaming as he did so. He staggered and kicked out as the creature managed to push him back and throw the cat to the side. It had been utterly unprepared for such an assault, but it composed itself quickly as the cat skidded on the ground and hissed, yellow eyes flashing, body coiled and ready to spring. The cat leapt at the creature again with barely a pause, but the beast was prepared. An impossibly long hand darted out and caught the animal under the jaw. With the other hand, it shoved Arthur away.

The creature rose before Arthur, holding the hissing and spitting cat at arm's length in one giant fist while the other clamped about its own neck, blood spilling from between the fingers. Ignoring the scratching and kicking from the savage claws of the struggling cat, the creature looked at Arthur, grinning before clenching its fist with a sickening crack. The cat's body dangled limp and lifeless from the outstretched fist. When the fingers opened, the body dropped to the floor with a heavy thud. It was so disgusting—so violent and visceral and tragic that Arthur screamed in fury. He stepped forward, left foot first, right fist curling back, turning his hip and shoulder.

Arthur swung his fist with a roar of rage and terror that gathered all his strength behind it, and he punched "himself" right in the face.

It was a good punch.

Never in his life had Arthur punched anything or anyone in genuine anger apart from a boxing bag, and even those times, he had lacked true conviction. In his dreams, the punches he threw never connected—his fist travelled too slow, the knuckles never bunched in time as if held back by elastic, and he could never connect with the target.

This punch connected.

With all the weight of his terror, anger, and revulsion, Arthur's fist smashed into a face that looked exactly like his own.

The head snapped back, blood poured from the nose as he felt the bones crack, and the creature sprawled backward onto the cobbles. Before he could act, the thing of darkness that had stolen his form turned tail in the street and loped away on all fours, growing smaller and less human as it went before finally melting and vanishing into the shadows.

Sarah and Steve looked at each other and then stared at the heavily breathing Arthur as he knelt beside the still body of the cat.

"Arthur," Sarah whispered, but he didn't respond.

After a long moment of silence, the man gathered the cat in his arms and stood on shaking legs, turning in the dark street with his burden held close to his chest. Sarah and Steve watched in amazement as, with tears in his eyes and blood on his hands, Arthur walked right through them.

High on the sloping roof of a novelty gift shop overlooking the street of battle, there was a sound like a small thunderclap, or it could have been the sound of a heavy book snapping shut. Who knows? Things aren't always what they seem.

An hour later, Arthur sat on his couch and thought about closing his eyes. He wasn't sure he wanted to, though, because he couldn't be certain of what he would see when he did. The dead cat lay triple-bagged in bin liners on the front porch of his flat next to his scuffed and muddy black leather Vans. The mirrors in his home had towels draped over them, and not only had he locked the two doors—the front door and one leading to the fire escape—he'd also wedged chairs under the handles. Arthur had no real idea if that even worked, but it's what they did in the movies. He'd also checked every window, drawn every curtain, and turned every single light on in the two-bedroom apartment. The rooms blazed, and his eyes stung, but he didn't care about that.

He still wore the dark blue suit jacket, which he pulled tight about him as he shivered. He just couldn't shake the cold. He'd drunk three pints of water, thrown up two, and managed to choke down a few slices of leftover pizza. Now he was sipping on a Berocca and orange juice and enjoying the reassuring fizz as he used it to swallow two Nurofen. And then two more. He felt raw. And entirely sober. Soberer than perhaps he had ever felt in his life, and yet he could feel the alcohol's warpath in his system. He could feel the uncomfortable electric tingle of sugar beneath his skin and knew that no matter what he did, tomorrow was going to be rough.

No worse than tonight, though.

Arthur turned the television on and scrolled through Netflix for a few minutes before pressing play. He needed something comforting, something familiar that reminded him of his childhood. The opening theme of Blackadder hadn't even finished before he was asleep, the upturned glass of Berocca seeping into the fabric of the couch near his leg. Steve, who sat beside him, inched away even though he knew he couldn't get wet. Sarah Brocklebank rolled her eyes and settled in to watch her first-ever television program.

CHAPTER 15

Arthur woke up to a silent flat and the TV screen asking if he was still watching. He yawned and stretched, then rubbed his heavy eyes, blinking at the bright lights of his apartment, his brain not ready to make the connections just yet. He noticed the upturned, empty glass on the couch and the dark patch on the blue fabric and swore, though he knew it wasn't the worst that could happen. The other side of the cushion had a big round brown stain from where he'd fallen asleep eating Chinese takeaway. He really ought to get that cleaned.

Arthur stood up and groaned as his leaden head protested such treatment. He stretched again, turning to crack his back, and glimpsed the chair propped beneath the front door handle. He turned around and peered at the fire escape door. Same thing. The jumbled pieces of his memory sloshed about in his mind, not quite ready to float together. He opened and closed his dry mouth. Gross. A memory of being sick in an alley bobbed to the surface, and he walked into the kitchen to grab a glass of water. He didn't feel too bad, all things considered, though the blank patches were a little disconcerting. His legs ached. Had he been running?

Arthur opened the fridge looking for leftover pizza, but none was left. There was, however, a half-eaten roast chicken that he'd cooked on Sunday; some traditions are hard to break. He always had a roast on Sunday, even if he ate it alone. He leaned against the fridge holding the plate of chicken and ripped off a leg, tearing into it with his teeth and closing his eyes as he ate. His head was heavy, but by some miracle it didn't hurt. He saw the open pack of Nurofen on the small kitchen table beside the Berocca.

Good man Past Arthur, he smiled. *Good man.*

His legs were sore, his fists hurt, and he had what felt like a nasty bruise on his shoulder—*Oh god, did I fall over?*

Other than that, he felt fine. An unease was gathering at the back of his mind, though. Fragments of the evening swirled around him, tantalisingly close but just out of reach. Deep down he knew something was wrong. He immediately jumped to the same conclusion most drunk people do when they wake up with unidentifiable concerns about the night before. Arthur put the plate down and looked for his phone.

Damn. Who did I call?

It was on the coffee table beside the front door where he usually plugged it in to charge, though he noticed the cable lying loose on the floor like a forgotten shoelace. He walked over and picked it up. The battery was completely empty.

Fantastic. Now he'd have to wait for it to charge a bit before he could figure out what he'd done. *Oh god, please, not Wend*y.

He groaned. He'd been so good lately. He hadn't drunk-messaged her in a few months, and it was ages since he'd called her parent's house. That's real progress.

But he knew she had been on his mind last night. He always knew.

Suddenly, a loud voice barked from the corner of the room.

"We black monks hate sin!"

Arthur jumped and spun around, his heart racing. On the TV, Rowan Atkinson cowered behind bed sheets as the Bishop of Bath and Wells leered at Molly, the reasonably-priced prostitute. Arthur let out a nervous laugh.

Bloody hell! Just Blackadder.

He walked over to grab the remote, which wasn't where he had left it. He stared at the small black object as it sat suspiciously at the other end of the couch. Wendy's end. He didn't put anything at that end apart from his feet and the occasional empty can of beer. *Strange.*

He shivered again. He would have to turn the heating up, but he could do that when he got home from work. Arthur looked around for the clock, forgetting once again that it had been Wendy's, and her dad had collected it—along with many other things—the week after she moved out. Arthur hadn't been here. He'd gone to the pub. When he came back later that night, most of the nice things in the apartment were gone, and there was a bare space on the wall where the clock used to be.

I really should buy a clock, he thought, not for the first time that year.

Arthur yawned and walked over to the window. He gripped the curtains and pulled them aside, expecting the usual morning sunshine and what the estate agent had laughably called 'Minster views'. You could see part of the north tower, if you stood on a chair. But the world outside was black. Arthur gasped. What bloody time was it? He felt like he'd been asleep for hours.

Oh no, have I slept right through the day?

He closed the curtain again, completely missing the yellow eyes that peered at him from outside. He padded across the room to see if his phone had enough juice to power on. It did.

Three-thirty, and no messages. None were sent, or received, and no calls were made, either. Well, that was something. Arthur sighed, put the phone down, and stared around the empty apartment. It never *felt* empty. He always expected someone else—Wendy—to be here. He still felt uneasy about the missing events of the evening and the faint tickle that there was something he was forgetting, but the thought that he might be able to squeeze in five hours of sleep if he used his flexitime and started work at ten was an enticing one.

With that in mind, he stripped off his clothes and walked naked across the front room to the bathroom. Suddenly, he shivered and spun around, cupping himself, certain someone was watching. There was no one there, but it seemed as though there were whispers on the very edge of his hearing. He laughed at his nervousness and against the pressure of some forgotten memory trying to push its way to the forefront of his mind.

Arthur shoved away his unease, walked into the bathroom, and turned on the shower. The room quickly filled with steam, and he climbed into the tub, groaning as the hot water enveloped him.

The lads had asked why he stayed in this apartment after Wendy had moved out, and of the many reasons he couldn't give, there was one he could: the shower was too damn good. It battered his body and he felt the heaviness in his head and shoulders wash away with his worries as he shampooed his hair. He closed his eyes and let the water beat against his face as he washed his body.

Images flashed before him: a cute waitress, a glass of scotch, the city walls, and a dark-haired woman running. So, he'd definitely run, then? He massaged the back of his thighs.

Yes, seems that way. Wonder why?

Arthur tried to bring back the image of the dark-haired woman, and she slowly began to take shape among the swampy recesses of his mind. He saw her more clearly as the figure in his memory walked toward him, moving out of the shadows. He smiled. That's right. He had met her on the walls, and she had been gorgeous.

The thought of her face, dark eyes, and body close to his on the quiet Micklegate Bar rose in his mind, and he concentrated his washing on a particular area for a moment, dropping the sponge and using his hand instead. Why the hell not? It had been a long night, and he needed to relax. He closed his eyes tightly as he tried to bring her image to bear, to take whatever had happened and add a sprinkle of fantasy. He remembered her dress and her breasts, and he smiled.

She stepped from the shadows of his memory and leaned in close to whisper something in his ear, her full lips parting slowly as she moved closer to him. He let out a soft groan before, suddenly, the water turned ice cold, and the groan morphed into a gasp of shock.

Arthur stumbled out of the spray and opened his eyes, fumbling for the taps. He shivered and swore as he reached through the water and turned the shower off, his fantasies of the dark-haired lady forgotten. Arthur shakily reached for his towel, which, for some reason, was hanging over the bathroom mirror, and wrapped it around himself. The steam that filled the room settled quickly onto the mirrored surface, and he stared in shock as a word written on the mirror slowly came into view. It said, "Drink." Arthur stared at it for a moment before rubbing it away with a grunt.

I'm a funny prick when I'm drunk.

He padded into the bedroom with wet feet, too bewildered to notice that his reflection did not follow.

Arthur dried himself as best as he could be bothered, pulled on a pair of boxer shorts and a t-shirt, then climbed into the unmade bed. He kicked the covers out and shivered as the cool breeze floated over his body, raising goosebumps on his bare skin. He pulled the duvet over with a fist and wrapped his elbow into it.

He was asleep in moments.

~

Look at Arthur now, tousled hair slowly drying on the pillow as he snores. His eyelids flutter as visions of the night dance behind them—nothing concrete, nothing real. All diluted images of actual events. The mind builds walls to protect itself, and while Arthur sleeps, his mind protects him, trying to repair the damage of the evening. Surprisingly, alcohol helps. Look now at the knuckles of his right hand, and the way they grip the sheets. White and shaking. See him twitch and hold his breath. His mind might have its work cut out this evening. Zoom out and see the bed in the middle of the room and the two grey figures at its foot, like guards standing to attention. See how one can't look at the sleeping figure, and one appears to be shaking with laughter. But that is not important. Rise up further, through the roof and into the night sky. It is cold out here, unseasonably so. The bricks of the city shiver as the dark closes about them. The sun will rise soon but not yet.

It is always darkest before dawn.

Witness the wraiths of black mist swirl around the two-bedroom brick flat. Note the cats on the tiles—sitting, watching, waiting. Look closer at the shadows, and notice the figures dancing on the edges of reality, trying desperately to break through. Now notice the more substantial forms in the dark places—the people. The men, women, and children in a great ring around the house—standing, watching, waiting.

All waiting for Arthur Crazy, whose life is nearly over and yet only just beginning.

PART II

'THE MORNING AFTER'

CHAPTER 16

"Yes, that really is my name. I know...How can I help, sir? No, I've never thought of changing it. Yes, it is quite unusual. So, sir, your call? I know...my father—"

Arthur held the phone to the side of his face as he rested his forehead on the desk, his computer keyboard pushed unceremoniously to one side, and his eyes screwed tightly shut as he slowly banged his head on the smooth surface. Maureen patted him on the shoulder as she walked out for yet another cup of coffee. She asked if he'd like sugar in his, as she always did, and he put two fingers up—not unkindly. The phone call ended with the client laughing at having to liaise with Mr. Crazy at the council for the next month or so, and by that time, Arthur was ready for a cigarette.

"The chaps at the golf club are going to love this."

Oh, are they? Twat. He grabbed his coffee, thanked Maureen, who was clipping her toenails at her desk, and headed through the island of computers to the glass-doored stairs.

Once outside, he leaned against the cold bricks of what the office laughably called the bike sheds, two rusting bikes locked below a sagging, corrugated iron roof, and struck a match. He shivered at the memory of another struck match, but he didn't know why. He'd been like this all morning. Déjà vu on repeat.

Maybe I should quit drinking? he thought, then he remembered the message he'd left himself on the mirror last night. *Or maybe I should take my own advice?*

Today would have been his and Wendy's anniversary. Who was he kidding? He was definitely going to drink, and considering he felt so rough, the hair of the dog might be the order of the day. No one would mind. They probably wouldn't even notice.

Arthur found his new 'highly-paid and important' job, as Eileen, the sunbed-orange manager, insisted on reminding him, laughably easy. He oversaw the zoning for the council. If people had disputes about property boundaries, they called Mr. Arthur Crazy. Most of it was straightforward; a few taps on the keyboard, and he could tell Mr. Whitton that he did indeed have permission to cut down that eyesore of a tree. For it did not—despite protestations—sit in the land owned by Mr. Dawson, no matter what the miserable old bastard claimed.

Some cases were more interesting and required Arthur to dig a little deeper than the relatively new digitised database. Down in the basement, in a secure, climate-controlled room, stood racks of huge, delicate, sometimes hand-drawn city maps. Arthur loved those cases, the ones where he had to rummage around in hundreds of years' worth of history, and they were nearly always for a class of people beyond Arthur's everyday experience. The gentleman who had called earlier, the golf club man, was a genuine Lord, and, as Maureen excitedly whispered with her hand over the mouthpiece of the phone when she transferred the call to Arthur, "fifty-sixth in line to the throne!" It was all a far cry from the average life of the Yorkshire-born man.

The first thing Arthur had done when he got the job was to organise the maps into date and zone order. It took nearly two months, but he'd received a small bonus for a job well done, though what it actually meant was that he could now complete searches in a fraction of the time it had taken his predecessor. In fact, the man before Arthur had often taken a week to go through one case. Arthur averaged a day. He learned early on to keep this to himself. By completing three cases a week, he was a prodigy, Yet he spent most of his time watching Netflix on his phone in the basement toilet.

"You're so much quicker than Steve," Eileen purred, with an uncomfortable touch of Arthur's bicep. "Stronger too," she laughed in what Arthur presumed she thought was a coquettish giggle. It wasn't. But he could tolerate it for the money and the infinitesimal amount of work he actually did.

Steve.

The cigarette dropped from Arthur's open mouth, bounced off his black shirt, and fell, forgotten, to the cracked and weed-strewn ground.

Fuck.

"Maureen, can I talk to you?" Arthur said, trying to catch his breath.

He'd sprinted back through the office, nearly crashing into the awkward intern who was being 'kept busy' delivering internal mail. Though, because of the efficient intranet system and the fact everyone had a phone, it primarily consisted of people writing notes to each other to keep the intern busy.

"What's up, dear? Girl troubles? You can tell your Aunt Maureen."

Arthur repressed a shiver. Maureen was nice enough, but she championed herself as everybody's aunty, the shoulder to cry on, the go-to lady of the office. What she was—and it was for this reason that Arthur had sought her out—was an incurable gossip. Every office had a Maureen; they traded secrets like currency, and the word "confidentiality" meant only to lower your voice slightly. She leaned forward conspiratorially, placing a hand on Arthur's shoulder as he crouched beside her desk.

"What was the name of the bloke I took over from?" he

asked, noting the look of disappointment that flashed across Maureen's face.

She was obviously expecting something a bit juicier, a bit more personal, but she rallied magnificently. Disappointment faded into a morose sadness. She could have been an actress.

"Steven," she said. "Poor, poor Steven." She actually sobbed.

Arthur was a little bit impressed. He moved her box of tissues across the desk, and she delicately pulled a single sheet free, folding it carefully and dabbing at her eyes with a sharp corner though there was no need.

Arthur caught Nigel's eye, one of the older men whose desk sat in the corner of their office, who shook his head with a small smile and went back to his computer, tapping entries one finger at a time.

"I knew, you know," she said in a whisper. "I knew he was unhappy. He talked to me a lot; called me Aunt Maureen."

There was a perceptible change in the atmosphere, and Arthur shivered. Something tugged at his mind, but he couldn't quite grasp it. He thought he heard a laugh or a snort, but it was nothing more than a whisper on the edge of comprehension. He glanced at Nigel, still tapping away, his tongue poking from the corner of his mouth, completely oblivious to their conversation. Nigel had worked in the same space as Maureen for nearly a decade. He'd learned to switch off.

"What happened to him?" Arthur pressed Maureen, and she dabbed at her eyes again, glancing away, staring into the middle distance. Definitely an actress.

Arthur's memory of his introduction to the office was hazy. As far as he could recollect, no one had told him about his predecessor when he received the promotion. For all he knew, the man he took over from had simply left. Perhaps retired? He never thought to ask. The truth was, someone may have told him, but his first day in the office was the same day Wendy hopped on that train. He wasn't really paying attention. He'd grasped just enough to get the job done and then worked in a frenetic daze for the next few weeks, his mind in turmoil, life as he knew it in ruins.

When he surfaced again, sometime around Easter, as yellow daffodils covered the city, he was a well-worn part of the office furniture. But the name *Steve*; it rattled around his mind like an itch he couldn't scratch. It was important, wasn't it? Another déjà vu, perhaps? The morning had been full of them.

"Please, Maureen?" he asked, but she was in full flight, having coaxed a few real tears to dampen the tissue.

She lifted a hand to stop him as if it were just too painful and then fanned her face, staring at him with wide, sad eyes.

"I can't—" she mouthed and ran out of the office sobbing.

She fled not through the side door, Arthur noticed, the one that led to the small kitchen and the privacy of the toilets, but right down the centre of the crowded office towards the glass doors, heads turning as she ran.

Arthur looked at Nigel.

"Pub?" the older man asked. Arthur looked at Maureen's pink glittery clock on the wall—noon.

"Why not." He shrugged.

Two hours later, Arthur sat, dozing, in the end stall of the downstairs toilet, his mobile phone propped on the toilet roll dispenser showing Saturday's *Match of the Day*. He'd eaten a beef and gravy roll and chewed his way through three pints of Guinness. Not his usual choice, but Nigel had insisted. The older man had enjoyed the company. His daily lunchtime two pints of the black stuff tasted much better with a pal, he announced. So much so that he bought a third, which had to be necked in a matter of minutes so they could get back to the office without Eileen tutting at them for the length of their break.

As soon as they got back to the office—now with no Maureen—Arthur declared he needed to check the maps for Lord What's-His-Face. It was a job he completed in less than half an hour, and so, more than a little bit tipsy, he made his way to the secret toilet, the entrance to which was hidden down a long tunnel that ran beneath the offices of St. Leonard's Place.

The building was another of York's regularly photographed features; a curving Georgian terraced street of white-bricked townhouses that held a variety of council departments and offices. The once beautiful facade of York's answer to London's Royal Crescent now slumped on the edge of the city like all municipal buildings do if you leave them out in the sun too long. It sagged under the weight of bureaucracy, but it did contain one or two interesting secrets.

Down in the basement, through a painted door half-hidden beside the map room, lay the entrance to a catacomb of white-washed tunnels. Arthur had discovered them out of sheer bored curiosity. The flaking paint of the door crumbled behind tall metal shelves, home only to dusty files and the dried husks of dead flies. They moved easily, swinging into the room and kicking up dust, the paint on the edges of the door cracking open like a seal to reveal a drafty underground tunnel.

Electric lights fixed to the walls were connected by thick wires that had also been painted white, the decorators not bothering or caring about edges down here. Splash it on; get it done. But the lights still worked and illuminated a tunnel that ran twenty feet underground before taking a sharp right turn. Another few feet and a door opened into a forgotten toilet with a wide trough, three sinks, and six cubicles. The long strip lights were still operational, and so was the plumbing. For as long as Arthur had been coming down here, which was every day for almost half a year, he'd had it to himself. And he had no intention of sharing.

A few messages to the lads, a bit of social media scrolling, and a cursory check of the news later, and he was almost ready to fall asleep while Gary Lineker quietly commented on the football. Arthur put his feet up on an old milk crate he'd brought down for just that purpose and closed his eyes.

CHAPTER 17

Arthur's eyes snapped open with a gasp, his heart beating painfully in his chest as an almost electric terror prickled through his veins. His flesh stung with goosebumps, the hairs on end, his body poised, ready to flee. He was immediately alert and yet completely confused. His dreams had been full of dark shapes leaching out of shadows, terrifying, unseen forms chasing him through narrow tunnels, the walls shrinking as he ran, twisting and turning, never quite sure of what he was running from.

And voices. Voices everywhere, on the very edge of hearing. Whispered, unintelligible words hissed at him from invisible mouths. It took him a moment to catch his breath and work out where he was. He clutched his pounding chest and tried to quell the panic. Arthur reached for his phone, but the screen was black, the battery spent streaming unwatched football.

He stood up, laughing at his own nervousness, stretched, and groaned at the stiffness in his bones and then he noticed the silence. It sat heavily over the wood and stone of the basement, the old building weighing down on him from above. Something was wrong. There were always noises down here, the crackle of the lights, the creak and groan of old pipes, the filtered and diluted clamour of the offices drifting down from above, but now there was nothing.

Reaching for the lock on the cubicle door, he paused with fingers resting on the cold metal, some instinct urging him to caution. Without really knowing why he moved the bolt back slowly, carefully, sliding it so it didn't make a sound that might disturb the unnatural silence. He pulled the door open, grimacing and pausing at the squeak of the hinges, and stepped around the edge to look out.

The lights flickered, dancing on the gently swaying body of a man hanging by his neck from a metal pipe. His arms swung limp and low by his side, the head tilted at a strange angle as whatever was wrapped about his neck pulled the body up and forced it to nod and dip. Arthur suppressed the scream that threatened to choke him and staggered back into the solid wood of the cubicle. The lights flickered again, and the body was gone.

As in his dream, Arthur ran headlong down the dark tunnel but unlike his dream, this tunnel ended. He crashed through the door of the map room raising a dust storm of ancient cobwebs and dead flies as he went. He turned and slammed the door shut behind him, dragging the shelves into place before racing upstairs. He didn't stop until he'd cleared the almost empty office and joined the throng of people outside St. Leonard's Place where he paused to catch his breath. Three pints of Guinness and a beef sarnie threatened to make an appearance if he didn't get his body under control. His hands were shaking.

What a fucked-up dream!

But it looked so real.

It definitely wasn't real.

But...

No!

Arthur gave a nervous laugh, embarrassed at himself as he argued in his own head about what he had or hadn't seen in the basement. Not for the first time that day he wondered if he might be going a bit daft. He had a habit of over-thinking things, after all. One thought would appear in his mind, a hazy memory of the night before perhaps—a did-I-really-do-that poking around his head—and then suddenly another voice quite independent from the first would answer.

No, of course, you didn't. Arthur assumed, or rather, hoped, that everyone went through this process, the strangest part of which being the realisation that yet *another* part of you is standing back and watching how the conversation plays out, probably eating popcorn. The devil on one shoulder, the angel on the other, and you stuck in the middle while they shout at each other. What was that song?

Clowns to the left of me, Jokers to the right, Here I am, Stuck in the middle with you.

Arthur shook his hands and paced back and forth. He'd had enough of being stuck in the middle, so he metaphorically put the popcorn down and took charge. Of course he hadn't seen anyone hanging from the bloody pipes! It was a trick of the light...*or the dark.*

He'd had weird dreams all night, a sense of déjà vu all day, and then a beer-induced nap on top of a pretty solid hangover. It's no wonder he felt bloody weird, especially considering his memory of the night before was so hazy. Now that he was outside and in the fresh air, he was already beginning to feel better. He ran his hands through his hair and took a deep breath. Then another. Slowly, he began to calm down.

York bustled about as normal, nothing unusual or out of place, just a hive of life as the city breathed in the early evening air. Buses and cars and the ever-increasing number of cyclists jockeyed for position on the crowded roads in a comforting, familiar way. Horns sounded, engines revved, heavy wheels rumbled along the road, and brakes squealed as the traffic stopped and started. Double-decker buses deposited long lines of people into the crowd and took away the same again. Across the street, the Theatre Royal blazed with colour and he saw people behind the great glass front laughing and talking and drinking at the brightly lit bars. Arthur laughed again but with more humour this time. He smiled to himself as he adjusted his jacket.

That'll teach me to fall asleep in the basement. Bloody spooky down there.

It occurred to Arthur that he didn't know what the time was, what with his phone being flat and his watch, no doubt, on the bedside table at home. So, he turned to a man standing next to the iron railings that ringed the council buildings.

"Excuse me, mate, do you have the time?"

The man didn't respond. He was facing away, waiting for a bus. Probably had headphones in. Arthur tapped him on the shoulder and the man jumped with shock, his chest and shoulders rising rapidly as he flinched away. It was such a strangely over-exaggerated movement that Arthur laughed and put his hands in the air to show he meant no harm.

"Bloody hell! Sorry, mate!" he said, "I just wanted to know if you have the time please?"

The man turned towards him, parted his curtained hair with a trembling hand and looked at Arthur through large, fearful blue eyes. His other hand gripped tightly onto a red tie, holding it out in front of him almost as if for protection. Arthur's eyes widened in recognition.

"Wait, I know you, don't I?" he said, as disjointed and formless memories floated about his head. Trying to hold onto them was like trying to hold onto mist, but finally, something took shape.

"Steve! You're Steve!" he said in triumph.

Steve's eyes softened and he nodded.

"Oh man, that's right. We met at the pub last night, didn't we? I'm so sorry, mate. I was hammered. I can barely remember a thing."

"That's okay," said Steve in a quiet voice. He was shaking.

"I didn't make a dick of myself, did I?" Arthur asked, reaching for a cigarette and his matches.

Steve shook his head.

"Right. Good," Arthur said. He lit a cigarette and shook the match out, watching as the curl of smoke floated away like calligraphy. "Actually, mate," he said, taking a drag and breathing it out slowly, "I was asking after you today. Do you want one?" he asked, offering the pack to Steve who shook his head again.

"You...erm. You said you work here, right?" Arthur nodded to the fading white building behind Steve.

Steve nodded.

Quite the conversationalist.

"Did I—" Arthur hesitated, unsure how to ask. "Look, mate, I'll just come out with it. Did I take your job? Like, what happened? I asked Maureen about you. I'm sure you know Maureen—everybody does—but she got all weird and dramatic. I'm really sorry," he went on, "I just can't remember how the whole thing came about. Those first few weeks were all a bit of a mess."

"I work here," Steve said in a flat voice.

"Right. Okay. Guess it was a promotion then?" Arthur offered the question to absolutely no response from Steve, who looked on the verge of tears. "Look, I'm sorry if I've ever ignored you or whatever. I'm not being rude. I just sort of live in my own little world, you know."

"Okay."

"Do you?" he started then paused.

You're not going to do what I think you're going to do are you?

"Do you fancy going for a pint?"

Fucksake.

But Steve's face lit up with such happiness that Arthur suddenly felt like he was filling in his good deed quota for the rest of the year. And anyway, it'd be nice to have a drink with someone for a change. First Nigel, now Steve. Getting the band back together.

Sort of.

~

Si watched the strange scene unfold at the end of his bar with a growing sense of unease. Arthur had arrived much later than usual and already a little frazzled. Si greeted him warmly and pulled a pint of IPA without having to be asked, and when Arthur ordered a second pint, he pulled that as well and sat it on the bar alongside the first without comment. His most regular customer was waiting for company. It would be nice for him to be hanging out with someone for a change. But no one showed up and Arthur sat there, sipping on one of the pints while the other remained on the bar completely untouched.

Si had seen this before of course, as had every barman at one point in their career. *And one more for absent friends.* Si wanted to ask but couldn't find the right moment. Arthur was clearly on edge, mumbling to himself, talking under his breath. The poor guy. What a shit year it had been for him. His mates all gone, his girlfriend left, and now a death to deal with.

If only it was as simple as that.

A death.

Arthur and Steve were each arriving at previously withheld conclusions like slow-moving trains entering a tunnel from opposite ends. It was taking a while, but they were getting there steadily and with all the inevitability of a derailment. Arthur knew there was something off about Steve, but he couldn't put his finger on it. For Steve, it had been a long night and an even longer day. He'd kept watch over the sleeping Arthur until the sun broke through the curtains and the shadows surrounding the small flat were chased away by the encroaching day. Sarah had remained by his side but vanished sometime before dawn. She hadn't uttered a word since they'd followed Arthur into his bathroom and witnessed, well, the events that transpired.

Steve couldn't find the words to explain to Arthur what happened. In life he had never been much of a talker, preferring to keep to himself, the anxiety brought about by simple social interaction sometimes threatened to overwhelm him completely and he was disappointed to learn that nothing changed after death. Though, thankfully, the opportunities to talk and be heard were few and far between. He didn't think he missed it, though, happy as he was spending his days hiding staplers and his evenings wandering the city streets. But then he met Arthur, and everything changed.

Steve had no idea how long he had been dead; he only knew that Arthur was the only living person he'd come across who could see him. Even touch him! He shivered at the memory of the touch, he longed for it again, his hand twitching across the bar, close to Arthur's, but, as in life, he never had the courage to make the final step.

Except once.

For Arthur's part, the last twenty-four hours were a stark reminder as to why he never touched drugs. Alcohol was bad enough. The one and only time he'd taken something more elicit he felt, well, not unlike he felt right at this moment. Shades and shapes of memories flashed in his mind, and he clutched at them ineffectually, never quite able to grasp something important, something obvious, something right in front of him. He knew he wasn't in control, and it scared him. He was seeing things, hallucinating, imagining things that weren't there or couldn't possibly be real. And he was pretty certain it all had something to do with a cat. He didn't like cats. He needed some air. The conversation was floundering, and his head was spinning.

And so it was that Arthur did something that would finally and irreversibly change his life forever.

"I need a cigarette," he said.

No, not that.

"Do you want one?" he asked Steve, and, in some fraternal show of camaraderie, he patted the other man on the hand. Or rather, he tried. Instead of the warm touch of flesh, his hand slipped right through the skinny fingers and patted the cold polished surface of the bar.

That.

CHAPTER 18

Arthur handled it remarkably well. He didn't leap off the chair or fall over. Neither did he scream or cry out. In fact, he barely flinched. A mild, curious raise of his left eyebrow perhaps gave some small hint as to the true nature of his demeanour but even the best poker player would be hard pressed to notice it as a tell.

Externally, Arthur seemed perfectly fine. Internally, not so much. He tapped his fingers on the bar and giggled slightly as they shared the same space as Steve's, weaving in and out of focus. A thought dashed momentarily into his head that it was simply blurred vision from too much alcohol and what he was actually seeing was his own hand, twice. The good old, how-many-fingers-am-I-holding-up trick. But that thought was unceremoniously shown the door by the realisation that he was not that drunk. And here we finally have the tipping point. The peak moment. The perfect storm in a pint glass. Arthur was precisely, and perfectly, the correct amount of *not that drunk.*

There are rules. There are always rules, even for the dead. Especially for the dead! If the spirits that didn't cross over —those unfortunate souls that 'missed the boat' as Sarah put it —could do whatever the hell they wanted, then all would be lost. It takes a lot of effort to be dead. Well, that's not entirely true, sometimes it takes very little effort at all, sometimes it's just a case of not hearing someone yell 'mind that bus!' but once you are dead and you find yourself *not* skipping through paradise with a cohort of the sexually inexperienced, or plucking at harps on clouds, or enjoying a toasty pitchfork or two, the effort it takes to maintain form is quite remarkable.

Ghosts require rest, which is why you rarely see them during the day, but they don't have the luxury of walking back home after a long night's work; they simply vanish and reappear at the place which holds the greatest resonance to whatever passes for their soul. As not-so-Mad Alice said, it is all to do with memory. Memory and names. A person is never truly gone while they are remembered. Which sounds nice but can be a bugger if someone writes a famous story about you. Arthur doesn't know the rules, and neither, really, does Steve. But together they are about to figure a few things out. The metaphorical trains are about to crash.

Cats.

Dark alleys.

Lights winking out.

A small boy.

A tall man.

A beautiful woman.

Fetch!

A hideous, horrible shape, reaching, searching, sneering.

Running.

Spinning. Sick. Laughter.

The monster!

Mirrors.

Dreams and toilet cubicles. Lights flickering. A body hanging. Hanging from the thick steel pipes in the intermittent faint glow of a single strip light, swaying in an unfelt breeze, head tilted, arms still, neck bulging around a thin, red, tie.

Arthur looked at Steve.

Steve looked at Arthur.

Arthur folded, almost gracefully, into a heap on the floor.

Si said, "Fuck!"

When he came to, Arthur was sitting where he fell but propped up against the bar. Si knelt in front of him, lips moving amid the red beard, but no sound reached Arthur's ears. He remembered everything. He even remembered new things. Standing above Si was Steve. The *ghost* of Steve. Steve, the man whose job Arthur took. Steve, the man who killed himself in the secret basement toilet of the office. Steve, who hung himself with his own red tie. Arthur remembered it all. But they weren't just his memories. They were Steve's. He felt the silk of the tie around his neck and the last second panic and dreadful, terrible hope.

"Are you okay?"

Si's voice filtered through, heavy and distant as though deep underwater. Arthur looked up.

"I've never seen underneath a bar stool before," he said, poking his finger at the bare wood on the bottom of his round stool. Sometimes it takes the brain a little time to fully engage.

"You're okay," said Si with relief.

"That coat-hook looks like a drunk octopus," said Arthur, pointing to one of the old-fashioned brass hooks that ran along the underside of the bar. "It looks like it wants to fight you," he grinned and put his fists up. Si laughed and pulled him up by the wrist.

"You sure you're alright, mate?"

"Fine, fine. Never better," said Arthur, who was looking at something just over Si's left shoulder. The barman turned round. There was nothing there. He sighed.

"Look, mate. I'm cutting you off tonight, alright. I don't know what's going on, but you need to go home, and you need to have some rest." He patted Arthur on the shoulder. "I'm sorry if you lost someone," he added, nodding to the untouched pint on the counter. "I know what that's like. Once you sober up, sleep it off a bit, come back in, and we'll have a few quiet ones okay. Just a few—you can't keep doing this every night. You're going round in circles."

Arthur looked puzzled. He turned to the bar then back to Si then back to the bar again. "Oh," he said, "Oh right, no. I get it now. Right. You can't see him, can you."

"Who?"

"Steve."

"Who's Steve?"

"Steve, the man in the red tie."

"What man in the red tie?"

"He's behind you," hissed Arthur, vague memories of pantomimes absentmindedly filtering into his thoughts. He giggled.

He wasn't *that* drunk, but he *was* drunk.

Si turned round. There was no one there.

"Arthur, mate. Go home. I'll call you a taxi."

"Don't worry. Steve and I will walk," he said. Arthur gave Si a little wave and opened the door. He held it open in his right hand and made a show of ushering someone out with his left. He grinned at Si and then walked out into the night to join his invisible companion. Si checked his watch, locked the door, flipped the sign, and walked over to the bar where he poured himself a quick measure of Laphroaig and downed it in one. Then he had another. He checked his watch again.

"Sod it, I'm going home," he mumbled to himself and put the green bottle back where it belonged, which was a shame really because if he'd kept drinking, who knows, he might have seen Arthur walking away from the bar with a man in a white shirt and red tie. He might. Who knows? There *are* rules but they get broken all the time.

The only problem with remembering everything about a horrific night on the town is remembering everything about a horrific night on the town. Arthur and Steve made it about ten steps from the bar before Arthur saw his reflection in the window of a parked car and it winked at him. The pit of fear he had closed away and pushed down somewhere deep inside came roaring back, memories of reaching hands, long-limbed creatures and changing faces. He felt his heart thump heavily, just once, then it settled back into a frantic hummingbird rhythm.

With ghosts come fear, it's only natural (sort of), we are talking about the spirits of the dead after all. If a person wasn't at least a little bit afraid in the face of a ghost then they're either lying, entirely insane, or they dedicated their formative years to a very particular brand of young adult fiction.

Arthur spun away from the car in fright and saw himself in a shop window. He noticed that Steve cast no reflection, but this fact did not get given the consideration it truly deserved because his own reflection waved at him, and he ran away with a yelp.

Ah, running again. This was familiar.

It seemed Si was right; Arthur was destined to repeat the same night over and over again.

Arthur sprinted down Micklegate and his reflection chased him across shop windows, glass doors, polished signs, and the sides of cars. It seemed to be having a great time. It was certainly smiling more than Arthur. He ducked between two parked cars and ran out into the middle of the road, leaping back from a screeching white van as it ground to a halt before him.

Stopping, he lifted his shaking hands and rested them on the bonnet of the warm vehicle, blood racing and fingers tingling as they brushed across the smooth metal. He looked at the driver who swore and shouted through the window. Arthur's focus shifted and his own unkempt hair and familiar close-cropped stubble screamed at him from the tinted glass then burst into silent laughter. His reflection cocked its head to one side and Arthur ran again, across the road, glancing around desperately in his haste to find a space in the city that did not contain glass.

Then he saw it. A dark patch in the middle of the street. A spot where the light didn't penetrate and not a single streetlamp glowed. He ran towards the dark and pushed open the heavy iron gate. Nature. That's what he needed. Trees and grasslands. Dirt and stone. He ran inside and let the quiet dark envelop him. He didn't stop running until he dropped to the cool earth beneath a large oak tree with low overhanging branches and hugged his knees close to his chest.

Looking up, the old stones of Holy Trinity church stood over him in a looming dark silhouette against the night sky—sanctuary. He'd never been much of a believer, but it's funny how one night can change things. Arthur rested his head against the trunk of the tree and closed his eyes. He was safe. He was drunk again and quite possibly losing his mind, but he was safe. The beating of his heart began to settle slowly, and he breathed deeply—in through the nose, out through the mouth—like his mum taught him. He could taste the soil and the bark and the moisture in the leaves. He could *feel* the earth. Perhaps that's what he needed, to get out of the city—go home for a bit; back to the country.

Arthur had almost settled himself when Sarah Brocklebank stepped up beside him and leaned down, her ethereal lips so close he could feel the cold,

"Hi."

It was no more than a breath but in his terrified state and with the build-up of everything that had happened the night before, it was enough to push Arthur over the edge. His body went rigid, and it would be nice to say he toppled gracefully to the warm receptive ground, but instead, he remained entirely upright as he lost consciousness, sitting like a corpse against an old oak in a graveyard.

It was this that saved his life.

Because once more, the world changed.

Silence flowed over the graveyard and spread like thick oil through a millpond. Inky black touched every tree, stone, and blade of grass, and Sarah Brocklebank shivered beside the still form of Arthur Crazy though she had none of the necessary features to facilitate shivering. She looked around, suddenly scared and on edge. Steve approached quietly from the other side of the inert form. He glanced nervously at the young woman who lifted a hand to stop him from speaking and nodded towards the church. There was something there; something was happening. They slunk down low on either side of their living yet entirely unconscious companion and watched.

The white lady appeared. Tall, beautiful, and stern. She walked across the front of the church with a purposeful gait and only paused when she reached the end of the building. There she turned and beckoned for her daughter and the nurse that accompanied her; this was their nightly routine—the pattern they were forced to replay every evening. But this time the daughter didn't appear and neither did the nurse.

Instead, a shadow detached from the stone and turned to face her. It was a man dressed in black. From the tip of his polished shoes to the small button on the top of his flat cap, he was covered head to toe in a black so pure he appeared like a walking hole in the fabric of the world, a silhouette of nothingness. He seemed, on one hand, to be as common as a coal miner but at the same time as noble as a Victorian Lord. The man lifted his head and touched the brim of his cap in what appeared to be a respectful salute to the lady. His face appeared momentarily, and although it was a flash of colour, there was no warmth there—a sharp chin and straight mouth, colourless skin pulled tight over pointy cheekbones, eyes twin sunken holes of black. He stepped forward with intent.

"Shadowman," gasped Sarah under her breath.

Steve looked at her. He had no idea who or what the Shadowman was but by the look on Sarah's face he decided ignorance was probably bliss. Sarah was terrified and if a ghost can be scared then it is safe to assume it's for good reason. Sarah looked frantically around the graveyard searching in vain for a place to hide. Steve reached for her, but she shook her head. Her eyes grew wide, on the verge of panic, and she looked down at the still form of Arthur resting as he was against the tree.

The tree.

She reached out, her hand pushing into the trunk of the old oak, then she grabbed Steve and pulled him with her. They vanished. Only Arthur remained, breathing softly in the blissful peace of unconsciousness.

The Shadowman strode purposefully towards the ghost of the tall woman and stood before her. He was taller than she was and peered down at her from beneath his peaked cap. She stared back, her face a mask of determination, unflinching before the strange man. Wordlessly, he pulled a book from somewhere on his person. It was dark, thick, and heavy with the type of cover that would make even the most avid reader think twice about trying to discover what secrets it might contain. He opened the book slowly and ran his finger down one page. When he had found what he was looking for, he tapped the page once, then closed the book. The two halves fell together with a noise like the lid of a sarcophagus slamming into place. The man lowered his hand and the book vanished.

The lady trembled. She made as if to step back but some force held her fast, perhaps even her own fear, for the mask had fallen and it was clear that, like Sarah, she was terrified. Her legs wouldn't move. Her ethereal form shook violently as the man's hand lashed out and grasped her around the neck. He raised her effortlessly off the ground so that the toes of her shoes scraped across the floor. He moved her face close to his own and sniffed her. First one side of her face then the other, then he tossed her disdainfully to the ground. The lady hit the floor and rolled against the wall of the church where she scrambled to her feet and ran around the end of the building, vanishing into the dark.

The dark man raised his strange gaunt face to the night sky and sniffed again. You could hear it hissing through the still evening air, more snakelike than human. It's enough to send a shiver down the trunks of the trees themselves. He caught the scent he was looking for and turned sharply to face the source. To face Arthur.

Inside the trunk of the old oak, the two ghosts shivered despite not having any of the necessary equipment.

"We shouldn't have left him," said Steve.

Sarah didn't reply. She felt the same; she was consumed with guilt and desperately trying to think of a way out of this. They were safe inside the tree, but Arthur lay out in the open and she was pretty sure it was Arthur the creature was coming for. She needed to do something, but what?

"What is that thing?" whispered Steve.

"Shadowman," she hissed the word again in a tone that suggested it contained everything Steve needed to know about the creature.

It didn't.

"That doesn't help."

"They're the things we should be scared of."

"I am."

"Good."

"But what is it?"

"Shh," hissed Sarah, desperately trying to think.

She leaned forward slowly and pressed her head through the tree, apologetically passing through sap, wood, and bark until she held herself just on the edge of the outside world. The

Shadowman had nearly reached Arthur. She pulled back quickly, shaking. "It's nearly got him," she said in panic.

"Surely it can't hurt him," said Steve with absolutely zero conviction.

"It's complicated," said Sarah.

"Then what—" Steve started but Sarah cut him off.

"They search for the living," she said, "the ones on the edge."

"Can it get in here? Can it walk through walls?"

"No. I don't know. I don't think so. They are shadow creatures. Hush now." Sarah had thought of something and shook her head slowly.

As ideas go it was pretty terrible and almost certainly wouldn't work. In fact, she was more certain that it might make things worse—much worse. But what choice did she have?

Slowly, she crouched down, being careful not to let any part of her body show in the world outside the tree. She closed her eyes and tried to picture Arthur leaning against the trunk outside, the position of his body, the way he leaned, slightly to the left. She took a deep breath (which made absolutely no sense) and pushed her hand slowly through the tree, hoping she had judged it right. Further, further, a little more. Moving her hand slowly she found what she was looking for.

Sarah Brocklebank held Arthur Crazy's beating heart between cold dead fingers and gently closed her fist.

The heart fluttered in wild panic and then slowed, the beats becoming weaker and more distant, then, with a final desperate spasm, it stopped beating altogether.

Inches away, the Shadowman paused in confusion. The scent was still there but the sound had gone. That beautiful, enticing, deafening roar of blood coursing through a living body...was no longer there. The graveyard sat in the night with only the familiar sounds of the dead, the whisper of wraiths, the susurrus of spirits. Nothing more.

CHAPTER 19

Look at the Shadowman.

Now he is so close you can see his eyes, or rather, the dark shapes where eyes should be. Enough form to fool a person from a distance or in the moment of a passing glance but if Arthur were to wake now, he would not see the windows of the other's soul looking back at him (the Shadowmen have no souls, not of their own anyway, so this is a moot point, but still nicely poetic). Instead, he would see bottomless pits of swirling black as full of nothingness as the clothes worn by the strange creature.

The Shadowman sniffed Arthur and paused, tilting its head almost as if listening, but there was nothing to hear, nothing to smell, nothing to taste. Just another dead human. The same as all the rest.

Somewhere in the darkness behind the church a cat screeched in the night and the creature turned his head away from Arthur. The hidden animal continued to yowl and screech, and the racket was immediately picked up by another cat, then another, and then another. From every direction, the noises tore through the night like a dentist's drill as more and more creatures joined in the song. It bounced from stone and tree and coalesced into a wave that could almost have been physical for the way it seemed to affect the Shadowman.

It was the song of the black cats and it held all the poetry and warmth of a mangy tom shagging a bagpipe. The Shadowman crouched down and rocked back on his heels, placing long-fingered hands onto the cool grass to steady himself. He was poised like an animal. He looked left and right but there was no telling where the sound came from. It was everywhere. His nose lifted and the dark mouth opened as if tasting the air, there was a brief pause, then he stalked away and vanished into the darkness beneath the tall stone building.

Sarah let go of Arthur's heart and did something she hadn't done for over two hundred years.

She prayed.

Outside of the tree, the two ghosts stared at the prone figure of Arthur. He was breathing, though it came in short, ragged hisses that Sarah thought couldn't possibly be healthy. She had never attempted anything like that before and had no idea if it would work. Now that it had, she almost wished it hadn't. Steve said nothing. He just gripped his tie and occasionally whimpered.

Arthur's eyes fluttered open slowly and he coughed. Sarah smiled. Steve tugged at his tie like a toddler tugs at his willy.

"What happened?" asked Arthur groggily. He looked around and a more immediate question took precedence. "Where am I?"

Sarah and Steve looked at this strange man who had entered their afterlives and couldn't find the words to explain things to him. They had no idea why he was so special, but they knew with unerring certainty that he was. It was why they were drawn to him. It was why they searched for him. It was why they stood guard over him all through the night. That had been an unspoken agreement.

For as long as they could bear, they had decided not to leave him, not while every spirit, wraith, ghoul, ghost, and ghast swarmed towards him like moths to a flame. The irony that they were exactly the same did not escape them, but, as Sarah put it, they found him first. And anyway, it wasn't the normal spirits they had to worry about. It was the dark ones. The shadow creatures. And now the Shadowmen had joined the fray. One at least. With his book and his blade. The Fetch had been bad enough but the presence of the Shadowman was a real problem.

Sarah looked at Arthur as he stared at her with wide unblinking eyes. He was scared, that much was sure, the security of his existence—the things he believed as fact, the certainties of his life—were all being challenged, and in some cases, ripped out from beneath him. It was not a pleasant experience, one Sarah had hundreds of years to get used to. Arthur had one night and a gutful of alcohol. Even Steve got more than that.

She opened her mouth to speak, but Arthur looked past her, over her shoulder towards the church, and his eyes opened even wider. She turned quickly, scared that the Shadowman might have returned but instead she saw the cats. All of them—small and large, male and female, flea-bitten and pristine. And every one of them black. They filled the graveyard, standing in the shadows and the dark places, yellow eyes glowing like a hundred fireflies in the night.

Arthur turned his head slowly. They were everywhere, standing on gravestones, in the branches of trees, and on the roof, ledges, and carvings of the church. If Alfred Hitchcock had filmed the movie *The Cats* instead of *The Birds*, this is exactly what it would have looked like. The only thing missing was a rusty child's play-swing creaking in a soft breeze.

The tall door of the church suddenly opened with an

ominous groan and wonderfully gothic timing, and Arthur turned his head towards it, already petrified of what he might see. But from out of the dark opening there stepped not a monster, but a small, grey-haired old lady. She was wrapped in a knitted shawl that seemed to cover her whole body, looping around her head and pulling tightly across her chest before falling to the ground. It put Arthur in mind of a child swaddled in an overly large beach towel.

The newcomer looked directly at Arthur and smiled. It was a smile that promised warm cocoa and Werther's Originals. It was comforting and homely. The old lady lifted a hand and beckoned Arthur towards her with crooked fingers. Without a word she turned and entered the church.

Without knowing why, without ever knowing why, Arthur stood up and walked after her.

~

"Let the Council of the Grey Ladies come to order!"

The voice that came out of the stooped old lady, the same one Arthur had followed into the church, did not fit her fragile form. There was nothing fragile about the voice. It boomed around the cavernous gathering with all the tenor of a field-marshal. This was a voice of power and authority, for whom wielding the former and never having the latter be questioned were simple matters of fact, as irrefutable as gravity and as incontestable as a Sunday morning parking ticket.

Arthur sat open-mouthed on one the pews at the back of the church, his mind in turmoil. He felt caught as if in some bizarre dream, but he knew deep down that what he was experiencing was real. All of it. However, it was a realness that was alien to him and frightening. Not for the first time in the last twenty-four hours, he seriously considered the possibility he was going mad.

Craziness had always fascinated him, with a surname such as his how could it not? His life had been a constant refrain of 'crazy' jokes, every person he ever met thinking they had the monopoly on some previously unheard comedy masterpiece. Don't be crazy, Arthur. That's just crazy, Arthur. You must be crazy, Arthur...or is it Arthur Crazy? Ha-ha...

Ha.

Oh, fuck off.

He'd heard them all, his family made most of them up themselves, they had to; it was self-preservation. His dad was the worst. Wherever they went he took great pride in introducing himself with a firm handshake, strong eye-contact, and a clearly enunciated "Hi, I'm Crazy." The length of the pause he left before adding the words Mister and Thomas depended on what kind of mood he was in. He took pleasure in asking for a table for the Crazies, and then, when they were shown to their seats he'd invariably say, "room for one more Crazy" before the last person took their place.

Every waiter that had ever served their family had to tolerate a sudden outburst of, "this place is full of Crazy people!" and a self-deprecating chuckle before a credit card or driver's licence was whipped out to drive the punch line home. So, it was of little surprise that the question of his own sanity swam around Arthur's pounding head. What if you could be crazy but you didn't know it? What if your normal was not the same as other peoples' normal? What if you did something and yet had absolutely no memory of your actions?

You could go crazy just thinking about it.

Arthur looked around to take stock.

He sat in a church that was as full as any he had ever seen. Every pew, seat, stool, and chair were occupied by similarly dressed, grey-clad women. Their ages varied from wrinkled and bent old crones to fresh-faced youngsters and everything in between. It wasn't the disparity in ages that stood out the most, however, it was the fact that some of them didn't have heads, others didn't have arms, and one he was almost sure—but did not want to look too closely in case he was proved right—had neither.

Arthur was unaware there were so many shades of grey. It was like looking at a church service in a black and white movie. If you concentrated hard enough, you could make a passable effort at guessing what colours might once have existed but as 'crimson' would have been the main feature this was probably not a wise move. The ladies had been chatting away in good spirits (for want of a better phrase) before the elderly one had stepped up to the lectern and brought them to order. Arthur watched in horrified fascination as a long-haired woman in front, who had been chatting to an armless girl of about fifteen beside her, turned to face the speaker, revealing the fact she only had half a face. He stared now at the front of the church *through* the space where the rest of her head should have been.

He stared hard.

He stared until his eyes watered.

"You may have noticed that we have guests in our midst," announced the elder.

Every head turned towards Arthur, who closed his eyes because the lady in front had turned *the other way*. Sarah Brocklebank and Steve sat on either side of him. Steve waved shyly to the crowd. One or two waved back. Most did not.

"Do not fret, ladies," continued the woman, "they are here at my invitation. Many of you will know Mistress Brocklebank," she nodded to Sarah. "Part of her haunt reaches into the graveyard here at Holy Trinity, although she has never deigned to join us at our meets, have you dear?"

The tone was polite enough but there was a weight to it that made Sarah shrink back in her seat. The lady moved on swiftly.

"The other two are strangers to us. And one—," she paused then, thinking about what she was about to say and the impact it would have on the assembly. The silence stretched on, and Arthur just knew it was going to be about him, he opened his eyes—she was staring straight at him— "And one," she continued, "is a Fetch."

Considering none of those gathered had the required apparatus, the gasp that filled the room was quite impressive. Some of the ladies stood up and one even attempted a swoon but thought better of it about halfway down. Some habits are hard to break. All eyes turned to Arthur and many of the ladies began to inch away, backing off with wide, fearful eyes. He glanced back and forth, his eyes darting across the crowd of women and the many black cats that filled the spaces like smooth pools of black ink. Even *they* seemed to be shrinking away from him, the usual haughty aloofness of the animals replaced by an electric wariness. Arthur realised that every creature in that vaulted space was poised and ready; fight or flight, to strike or run. And all eyes were on him.

He stood up.

"I—I don't know what is happening," he said, which, all things considered, was a good start. Might as well go with the truth.

"I've had a really weird day. And I—," he hesitated as some of the grey ladies backed away from him.

He turned instead to address the woman at the front, at least she didn't flinch.

"I don't know what a Fetch is, but I'm not one. I promise. I'm just an ordinary bloke. I think I drank too much and now I don't know what's happening. Maybe I'm going crazy I don't know—" Arthur giggled to himself then, which didn't really help matters. "But I just want to go home. If I've caused any problems, I'm really sorry, but I didn't mean it. I don't even know what is going on. What *is* going on?" he finished with a hint of desperation.

He had walked to the front of the church between the massed pews of grey ladies and tried not to notice as they leaned away from him. From Sarah and Steve's point of view, he looked like Moses parting the monochrome seas.

The elderly lady looked down at Arthur and then spoke in a soft voice.

"You are a Fetch, my child. Or rather, you will be."

"I'm—" Arthur started but the lady raised a hand to silence him.

"Have you seen yourself this evening, love?" she asked. Arthur hesitated. As questions go, it was an unusual one. Images of mirrors and reflections crossed his mind, and he touched his hair self-consciously, but the lady wasn't judging his appearance. She was asking a question, and suddenly Arthur understood. Dark glass tunnels, grey streets, towels over mirrors. Cars and vans and shining surfaces.

"I have," he said, slowly. "My reflection. It keeps...it's got a life of its own," he said.

"That is a Fetch, child," explained the lady.

She looked at him sadly and Arthur suddenly felt an overwhelming urge to cry. It was like watching your nanna get upset. He stepped towards her and then stopped as even she took an involuntary step back. They looked at each other and she spoke again.

"You have seen your own ghost," she said, and if that wasn't enough, added, "and it will come for you. You will die before the night is through. It is inevitable."

Arthur staggered back as if he had been struck. He didn't doubt the words of this strange lady, why would he? He knew the truth of it as soon as the words left her mouth. It was like hearing a diagnosis for terminal cancer that the doctor was meant to give you six months ago. His hand reached for his phone and then stopped. It was flat. What was the point and who was he going to call?

His breathing became laboured and heavy, and the pain that sat in his chest since he woke beside the tree intensified. A heart attack? Is that how he was going to go out? He was too young for a heart attack, surely? His thoughts floundered and his head spun. The rope had been cut and he was adrift. He fell sideways into the pews and the ladies there all panicked and shuffled away from him, allowing him to collapse onto the cold wooden surface.

"I'm going to die," he said, clutching at his chest.

"Yes," said the lady.

Arthur looked up at her and then further up to the tortured effigy of Christ hanging like a crucified Men's Health cover model from the ceiling.

"In a church," he said.

"It is fitting," replied the lady.

"But I don't believe in God," he said in a quiet voice.

"That is not important."

"Are you sure?" said Arthur. "It seems pretty bloody important!"

"It is better to die here than let your own ghost take you," said the lady. "We can help."

She was being kind. Arthur knew she was being kind, but the words struck him like an open-palmed slap.

We can help. We can help what? Help him to die?

All the kindness and gentle words sort of drift away in the raging sea of inevitability when you've just been told your number is up.

"Why?" he demanded. "Why is it better to die here? Why can't I go home and die in my own bed, or, or, or go to the pub and get absolutely shit-faced and die face-down in a gutter? Or run away and avoid all mirrored surfaces. If I don't see my reflection then the bastard can't kill me, can he...it...I?! I'm not fucking Dorian Grey!" he shouted.

"He is already coming for you. We must be swift," said the lady.

"But I can run! I'm a fast runner. Fastest in school, apart from Ben Warrior. No one could catch *him*." Arthur was babbling now, bordering on mania. Sarah and Steve appeared at his side and Sarah spoke,

"A word if I may?" she asked politely.

The lady looked at Sarah and then to Arthur who was mumbling something about Narcissus and not Dorian Grey. She looked back to Sarah and nodded.

"The Fetch came for Arthur last night," Sarah said.

She spoke softly but her words landed in the church like a hammer on an anvil. For those ghosts old enough to know, the implications were immense. For those too young, the shock of their elders was enough to leech away the chatter and bring the council to silence. The only noises to be heard were from Arthur himself as he mumbled incoherently and one cat at the back of the church who yawned loudly—they have absolutely no sense of occasion. The lady at the lectern stepped through the wooden dais and drifted down to Sarah.

"How?" she demanded. "You must be mistaken. If it came for him, it would have him, and this would be a very different council."

"He fought it off," Sarah answered, simply.

The lady was speechless. Nothing in her experience had prepared her for such a ridiculous notion. The living touching the dead...preposterous! It simply did not happen. It could happen the other way around, of course, a spirit could train itself to make some form of physical contact with the living but the effort it took was tremendous and those who tried it once rarely did so again. Poltergeists lost all memory of physical shape in exchange for the ability to throw crockery and turn on television sets. It hardly seemed worth it.

The ability of the living to touch the dead was a matter of legend, of myths and stories that guardian ghosts tell young sprites to keep them away from the world of men until they have complete control over their ethereal forms. Sarah looked at the expression on the elder's face and realised there was nothing she could say, no words that would make the old one understand and so she sat on the pew next to Arthur.

Sarah closed her eyes for a moment and gathered her thoughts. She had to prove it, and she knew how.

"Arthur," she whispered while bringing the memory of her father's angry face to the forefront of her thoughts.

She could already feel the emotions welling up inside her, the hysteria that was part of her existence now. It was easy to call upon but difficult to bear.

"Arthur, I need you. I don't know what I'm going to do..." she let the sentence trail off and sobbed.

Years of practice—of long nights spent searching for the keys, of appearing on the walls, in the churchyard and then in the city itself, of being held hostage by her own form of madness—added credence and weight to her performance. She might not have a central nervous system, but Sarah's emotions fired with electricity just as strong as any neuron. Arthur looked up. His eyes were wild and unfocused, but he shook his head and tried to clear them, to bring himself back. Sarah swam into his vision, and he saw the pain on her face and instinctively reached for her.

The first shoulder to cry on.

There was a collective scream.

Step back for a moment. Survey the scene. A full church. Dark but with ethereal light coming from god-knows-where. The smell of wood, the glint of gold. Packed pews crammed with women—young, old and everything else. Grey. Ghosts. Dead. And at the front, Arthur. The only living being in the building apart from the hundreds of cats—but they don't count—and he's holding a young woman in his arms. She needed comforting and so he comforted her, putting aside his own pain. He holds her now, not sure why. Tight to his chest, he holds her. She sobs and so he strokes her hair.

He is stroking hair that is not really there.

Patting a back as insubstantial as smoke.

But you can tell from the reaction of the young woman that

she feels his every caress, his every touch. And you can tell from the expression on the face of the elder staring at them in disbelief that this changes everything. She opens her mouth to speak. Profound words of wisdom, perhaps?

"Fucking hell!"

Almost.

CHAPTER 20

The Council of the Grey Ladies emerged out of a perceived necessity to "bring the dead together" and gave rise to lots of half-hearted jokes along the lines of "community spirits." But, as ghostly councils go, it is a relatively new organisation. In fact, in living terms, the group has only been gathering for the better part of ten years. It took one Irene Napier to gather the disparate ghosts and bring them together as a collective.

It was something Irene had a natural inclination towards. As president of the Museum Committee, the Neighbourhood Watch Alliance, the York in Bloom Committee, Treasurer of Holy Trinity Church, founding member of the Friends of the Walls, The Grey Street Cleaners, the Knit for Africa Club, Tuesday Coffee Mornings (everyone welcome, bring a plate) and Friday Bingo (everyone welcome, bring a friend), she was used to mobilising groups of women to champion a cause. Irene failed to see how a little detail such as death should stop her from doing what she was good at. Even the dead need organising. *Especially* the dead. It gave her purpose.

"Oh, it keeps me busy," she would say both before and after shuffling off the mortal coil.

Busy was a word entirely insufficient when used to describe

Irene Napier, and now that she didn't have the need for sleep, she was a force of nature in her own right. The fact her husband had died two days after she, and then entirely failed to join her on this plane of existence, is a testament to that. He couldn't live without her, but the thought of spending eternity standing in a corner figuratively holding the coats was enough to make him jump through the door at the earliest opportunity.

Irene—Mrs Napier to you—made things happen. She created a schedule to ensure hauntings were fair and even. She made committees and subcommittees of sprites, shades, wraiths, and every subclass of the mortally challenged so that they knew "who was who and what was what and where to go when."

She put the poltergeists into a cleaning rota and made absolutely certain that the gargoyles and grotesques were regularly fed. Tourists think there are a lot of pigeons in York. Thanks to Mrs Napier, there are a lot less. Right now, she was struggling with a notion with which she was very unfamiliar. She didn't know what to do. She wasn't going to let anyone else know this of course, but her mind was whirring with the possibilities and ramifications of what they were all witnessing.

Mrs Napier wasn't an elder in the sense of her time as a ghost, but she was an elder because *that is what she was.* The crowd of her ladies looked to her expectantly. She stepped back to the lectern and raised her hand for silence. She opened her mouth and hoped that by the time the words spilled over her lips she would know what they were going to be.

"Ladies! Let's come to order," she said, the rhythms of committee life giving her comfort in their familiarity. "We have been presented with a unique opportunity. It appears that we do indeed have a Fetch among us, but one entirely different to the legends we are all so familiar with. For those who do not know, allow me to explain."

Little more than twenty-four hours ago, Mrs Napier would have counted herself as one of those who did not know, but her girls had brought her messages from the black cats regarding this new and unfamiliar word and so she had learned. The thing about being dead is there are plenty of people with long memories to ask questions of. And Mrs. Napier always knew.

"A Fetch is a ghost of one who is living. They appear on the eve of their death. When one sees their own ghost, death is inevitable, just a matter of time. They hold immense power, and the living component of this creature shines brightly for a moment and draws all towards him, as you would know if you were out haunting the city last night or heard the tales of the black cats. Mr. Arthur Crazy here had quite a night."

She looked down at Arthur who was still sitting with his arm around Sarah Brocklebank. His head swam but he was keeping up, not that he believed a word of it. But there was nothing he could do. So, he stroked the hair of Sarah Brocklebank and listened as Irene Napier continued.

"A Fetch is half in and half out. A conduit if you will. There are some who believe a Fetch can allow us to finally cross over to the other side—"

She was interrupted by gasps and the murmurs of hundreds of voices trying to process what she had just said. Irene Napier glared at them all and tapped her toe. It was a glare that could halt a stampede. Silence spread back through the room.

"Thank you," she said, haughtily. "There is no evidence of this...this *myth*. Other than the chaos caused by those who believe it," she added. "The last time a Fetch was reported in the city the spirits collectively forgot themselves and allowed stories and fanciful notions to get in the way of their *duty*."

The word was said with an emphasis that bordered on the fanatical. Armies had mobilised under such enunciation.

"We must stick to our allotted tasks and our own haunts. We must not be distracted or go looking for trouble," she said this last part with a pointed look at Sarah Brocklebank. "We must not deviate from—"

"But he's touching her!" shouted a one-armed woman in the second row, interrupting Irene Napier mid-sentence.

Irene thought fast, she was getting to that, only she didn't know what she was going to say when she got there. The interruption would have been welcome if it weren't for the fact that absolutely no one interrupted Mrs Napier. She seethed inwardly and yet smiled warmly.

"If you'll be so kind as to let me finish."

The one-armed woman sank back into her seat and lowered her gaze.

"Now, if I may continue. Mr. Crazy here, as we can see, is somehow able to not only communicate with the passed-on (Mrs. Napier didn't like the word dead), but also make physical contact with them. If reports are to be believed, and I'm not sure why I was not informed of this sooner," she turned her head to look at a large black feline lounging on the altar table behind her.

It regarded her with unblinking eyes and then turned its back to lick a long paw. This wasn't the usual arrogance of cats, this was fear, Mrs. Napier could outstare a statue.

"Mr. Crazy was attacked by his Fetch last night and yet somehow fought it off. Mr. Crazy then went home where Sarah Brocklebank and...her friend—," there was a barely perceptible pause, Mrs. Napier felt she should know everyone's name. Yet another thing she would need to discuss with the cats, "...kept watch."

"What does it mean?" asked the one-armed lady.

She had been staring in fascination at Arthur Crazy, desperate to reach out and touch him with her one good hand, to feel something again. The desire had overpowered her sense of caution.

"It means nothing!" snapped the white-haired old lady. "Mr. Crazy here survived the night, which is unusual, but he will not survive another."

She looked down at Arthur, who she realised, was a threat to all the neatness and organisation and order she had brought to the afterlife. She knew he was going to die, she just didn't know how. However, die he must; it would be inconceivable if he didn't. Worse than that. It would be messy.

"So...we just *wait*?" Arthur asked.

"Yes."

"For me to die."

"That is correct."

"But—"

"It is inevitable, dear."

"Umm—"

"I'm sorry."

Mrs. Irene Napier did not seem sorry. She actually seemed relieved. The truth was—and everyone knew it—ghosts and dead people kind of went together. It was a package deal. The fact Arthur's ghost had appeared before his actual death was just a matter of poor timing. It would all be sorted out soon, she was certain of it. In the meantime, they just had to wait. She turned to address the congregation.

"Shall we move onto the next order of business? Doris Clayfield wants to discuss the upkeep of the cobwebs in her crypt. Doris—"

"Excuse me!"

"Yes?" Mrs. Napier turned to Arthur with an impatient smile, tapping her ghostly finger on the lectern.

There was no sound as she did so, but the meaning was not lost. They had moved on. So, then, should he. Young men should be seen and not heard and only allowed out when there were chairs to be stacked, coats to be gathered, or items to be collected from tall shelves. Arthur stood up.

"I don't want to die."

"None of us want to die, dear," said Mrs Napier, "but it's all part of the plan, isn't it?"

She was uncomfortably aware of the way in which the gathered ladies were staring at Arthur, all eyes were on him. She coughed loudly.

"Now—" she started.

"It's not part of my plan. Not tonight anyway."

Arthur had been thinking hard. He had no idea why he'd taken Mrs. Napier at her word. He'd never met her before, he'd had no idea she existed before this night, and yet when she told him he was going to die he hadn't questioned it at all. Some people have such a force of personality they bombard you with it. The words they speak are locked in truth as strong as cement. Part of his brain had been chipping away at the edges and while he had been comforting Sarah Brocklebank she had whispered in his ear.

"Nothing is set in stone."

"Young man, please," said Mrs. Napier.

"No," snapped Arthur. "You're talking about my death as though my life doesn't matter. You just want me to sit here and wait to die. And how long will that take? All night? Into tomorrow? And how is it going to happen? I had a pain in my chest when I woke up." Sarah looked at her feet. "But I feel fine now. There is nothing wrong with me. I'm not going to die."

"Seeing a Fetch is an incontrovertible sign of your impending death," said Mrs. Napier slowly, as though talking to a dim-witted child.

After a pause she added, "My dear," in case the ladies thought her too harsh.

Irene really was losing patience with this young man. There was a lot to get through. Not least of all the appearance of a Shadowman outside her church. How dare they. How dare *he*! Did they not appreciate how important her work was? How *hard* she worked to keep everything ticking along. It had been in shambles before she got here.

"How?" asked Arthur. "How can the Fetch get me? Can it get inside the church? Last night that...thing...attacked me in the street. It must have climbed through the glass near Barley Hall and then followed me into Mad Alice Lane. It didn't look like me then until I turned to face it."

"You faced it," gasped a lady behind him. Arthur turned and nodded to her, noticing for the first time that he had the rapt attention of the room.

"Yes," he said.

"Were you not scared?" asked another.

"Terrified," he admitted.

"But you faced it anyway?"

"I didn't really have a choice," said Arthur.

"You could have run."

"I did," he said, then patted his belly. "I'm really out of shape."

"Enough of this!" Irene Napier snapped.

It had been a long time since she'd had *one of her turns,* but she felt the tension rising inside of her. She pinched the bridge of her nose between two fingers and sighed. Was it possible for a ghost to have a migraine? She did not want to find out, but the man was speaking again. Did he not know his place? This was not neat. It was not tidy. She would have to do something about it before it went any further.

Snapping her fingers, Irene pointed to a highly polished, gold-framed image of the Virgin Mary which rose into the air before Arthur had time to react. Within seconds, the unseen poltergeist held the icon in front of Arthur Crazy and he looked into the eyes of the young woman whose panicked excuse for being pregnant out of wedlock had shaped the entire world. She smiled at him. It was a knowing smile. An inevitable smile. A smile that told of secrets kept and truths revealed. But it wasn't the religious icon that was important, it was the glass she hid behind. Her eyes merged with his as his own features came into focus and they blinked together, Arthur and the Virgin Mary.

And the Fetch.

The face of a blessed virgin changed slowly, dissolving into a blank mask as the eyes, mouth, and nose all bled together before fading into nothingness. Her features vanished as though they had been painted over and replaced by the reflection of Arthur, which moved forward and began to push slowly through the glass. Hands rose and fingers closed around the edge of the frame as the creature pulled itself out into the world.

Arthur was rooted to the spot, absolutely terrified, and Sarah could do nothing this time. The grey ladies screamed and many of them ran, though some stayed where they were in petrified fascination. It all happened so fast. The Fetch dropped head-first to the ground and then rose, taking the shape of Arthur as it did, moulding itself into his likeness, copying his suit, unkempt hair, and scruffy beard. It all happened in moments, and in moments, there were two Arthurs. They faced each other like a strange mime act, the real Arthur unable to speak or move. That his death was imminent was a certainty. This moment would be his last, and what an unusual moment it was.

It is strange where the mind goes in times of mortal peril. Arthur wondered if it would count as murder or suicide if he were to die at the hands of this creature that was him and yet not him. The prospect of another fight brought a whole new meaning to *stop hitting yourself, stop hitting yourself.* He smiled, and so did the creature. There was no malice in the smile, no hatred, no evil. It was Arthur. He tilted his head to the left. The doppelganger followed his movements perfectly. He moved to the right. So did the other. Something snapped in Arthur's fragile mind, and he mumbled,

"Slide to the left. Slide to the right. Crisscross."

He laughed and the action was mirrored perfectly by the creature in front of him. Something had changed. This was very different from last night. The creature that had faced Arthur then had been intent on killing him. He remembered it all now. The chase, the fight, the cat leaping to the rescue. That was the moment Arthur's life should have ended, and in some way, it was, and it did. But he had fought, and the creature had run. He had defeated it, and he knew now with a certainty he didn't understand, that it was no longer a threat. As if to confirm his thoughts the creature bowed slowly and smiled. Then, in perfect unison, the two men slowly raised one hand and touched the tips of their fingers together.

There was a flash of light.

The doppelganger vanished.

The image of the Virgin Mary dropped to the floor and smashed on the tiles where she looked up at him with a crooked smile through broken glass.

Arthur turned to face Irene Napier.

Who backed away.

"You tried to kill me."

"Don't be silly, dear."

"You didn't know *that* would happen."

"Well,"

"You tried to kill me," Arthur repeated, moving closer.

"Now, just..."

"You didn't even give me a chance!"

"You survived, dear. You're a miracle. We need to find out more about you. We should form a committee—"

"You let that creature in here!" shouted one of the grey ladies.

"I did no such thing, I—"

"Yes, you did!" snapped another. "This is supposed to be a place of sanctuary!"

"We have more important things to worry about," snapped Irene, but there was a hint of doubt in her normally steely voice.

She paused and looked around her. The grey ladies were glaring. Even the headless ones seemed to be smouldering with anger. She looked at Arthur.

"I did what I thought was best," she announced with a lift of her chin. "For the greater good."

"You were wrong."

Irene Napier bristled for a moment, but the fight went out of her as she looked into the strange eyes of this man and saw the depth of knowledge there. The realisation of what she was, what she had always been, washed over her and she staggered backwards. All those years telling people what to do, bossing people around, making life difficult for them if they didn't follow her exact directive. In another time and place, Irene Napier could have taken over the world, and in many ways, people would have been happy under her rule. The trains would have certainly run on time. But Irene knew now what she was. She saw it in the eyes of this Crazy man as he stepped towards her. She was a bully. A horrible, self-righteous bully.

"Oh, my Stan," she whimpered, the thought of her poor long-suffering husband rising to her mind.

Everything she had put him through, that lovely, patient man.

She had been by his side when he died and the first thing she said when her spirit saw his was, "Now, Stan. There is a lot of work to do."

It's no wonder he chose to go towards the light. She buried her head in her hands and sobbed with all the painful raw emotion of self-realisation. Arthur stepped forward to put his arm around her, to comfort her and tell her all was forgiven, but when he touched her, a purple light exploded from his hand and engulfed the suddenly frail old lady. Vivid flames crawled over her body without burning and the light intensified. Irene Napier looked into Arthur Crazy's eyes with shock and wonder. She had time to mouth the words *thank you* before the light pulsed one more time and then vanished.

Irene Napier was gone.

No one spoke. No one moved. Arthur Crazy stood on the raised platform at the front of the church and stared at his hand. The congregation of grey ladies stared at his hand. The cat on the altar stared at his hand, and then licked itself.

"What just happened?" Arthur said to no one in particular.

"You happened," came a voice from the back of the church. It was a man's voice, deep and rasping. All heads turned but the back of the room was full of shadows and the speaker remained hidden in the gloom.

"You can feel the power, can't you," the voice said. "You can feel the truth of it. Of what you can do. Of what you can achieve. The possibilities are endless."

"Who are you?" Arthur asked but there was no reply. Sarah ran up to him with Steve close beside her.

"We need to go," she hissed. "Now!"

Arthur looked at her then back to the shadows. Someone was moving back there, just out of reach of the light.

"Who are you?" he repeated.

"We are No one," said the voice.

Suddenly there was a commotion from outside the church, just beyond the stained-glass window behind the altar. A woman shouted and a child screamed, then the tall ghost from the churchyard came through the wall at speed and roared a challenge.

"Shadowman!"

The tall lady swept through Arthur, who would have much preferred her to go around, and floated down the short steps to the central aisle of the church. The black cats followed her as she moved, leaping over the pews, and scurrying along the dark stone tiles. Looking over her shoulder she shouted to Arthur, "Find the queen!"

Then she bore down towards her target.

The man emerged from the shadows and stood still. To Arthur, it was a strange sight. He was just an ordinary man. An ordinary man wearing an incredibly pure shade of black from head to toe, but a man all the same. He was standing at the end of the church staring straight at Arthur, ignoring the ghost of the tall woman and the sea of cats bearing down on him.

"We can show you," the man said to Arthur just as the tall lady reached him.

He thrust out a hand without looking and grabbed her once again by the throat, but this time the cats attacked in a fury.

"Find me," he said before both he and the woman vanished beneath the writhing mass of black bodies.

The grey ladies scattered, screaming and running from the fray, pouring out of the church and into the night.

Sarah grabbed hold of Arthur's hand and dragged him away, running in the opposite direction with Steve close behind. They ran as hard as they could into the night.

It was only much later—after they had left Micklegate, long after they had rested on Ouse Bridge so Arthur could catch his breath, and while they sat in an altogether different churchyard so Arthur could have a shaky drink from a small bottle of scotch hastily bought from Tesco Express—that Arthur realised something very important.

"We ran through the fucking wall!"

CHAPTER 21

"So, to recap," Arthur said, draining the last of the small bottle of scotch and waving it around to make his point. "To recap the events as we know them. You," he pointed the bottle at Sarah, "are dead."

She nodded.

"And you," he pointed the bottle at Steve, "are also dead."

Steve nodded.

"And you," he pointed the bottle at the man who had been watching them for the last ten minutes—well, he assumed it was a man from the clothes and the shape, but as the figure had no head, he couldn't be *entirely* certain. "*You* are definitely dead!" he laughed.

It was all so funny. Wasn't it? It had to be. He had another drink and groaned when he realised the bottle was empty. He dropped it onto the grass where it landed with a soft thunk.

"Forty ounces to freedom," he sang to himself. The headless man nodded at Arthur, which is best not to think too hard about. Arthur continued, "But 'am not dead?"

They all nodded. So far so good.

"But I could have been dead because that...thing."

"Fetch," said Sarah.

"Thas'a one. The Fetch tried to kill me, but I punched it and apparently that's a big deal. And then—and *then*—it chased me tonight as well and we went to church with a lot of lovely old ladies, but not before you..." he tried to focus on Sarah, "...you stopped my heart!"

"Correct."

"You stopped my heart so a Shadowman couldn't find me."

"Yes."

"But he found me anyway."

"Yes."

"But after the Fetch did."

"Correct."

"But the Shadowman and the Fetch are different things."

"That's right."

"The Shadowman looks like something from Peaky Blinders."

"Erm?"

"And the Fetch was friendly? Fetch!" he added with a giggle, as though throwing a ball for a dog.

"Well..."

"But I'm not the Fetch anymore?"

"You never were."

"Then who am I?"

"You're you."

"Who?"

"You're Arthur Crazy."

"You can say that again."

He giggled. Dad would be proud.

"And, and there was a mad old Stalin woman. And I... burned her?" Arthur stared in horror into the middle-distance of his hazy, alcohol-washed memories and tried to make sense of the images.

"No, no! Not at all," said Sarah, quickly. "I think you maybe set her free!"

"What do you mean?"

"She's not a ghost anymore. She moved on."

"Where?"

"No one knows the answer to that question."

"K, then how?"

"Only you and her know the answer to that."

There was a long silence and Arthur looked around the churchyard. He suddenly realised where they were, and he laughed to himself.

"This place is called Holy *Trinty...Trintity...Trinity* Church as well," he said, getting there in the end. "It's the one on Goodram-gate isn't it?"

No one answered.

"It is. It is. We used to climb over the gates and get high in here when we were students. Good times," he muttered to himself. "Good times. Wait. I don't remember climbing the gates. Did we—" but he couldn't finish the sentence.

He looked at his companions. They couldn't meet his gaze. He looked at his own body and poked it, ribs, chest, and arms. It all seemed solid enough. He picked up the bottle and stared at it.

"How did I get this through?"

No one answered.

The silence stretched on. The headless man picked at his nails with a small knife. It was an oddly disconcerting sight that held all their attention for a while.

"I wonder why we keep ending up at Holy...at these places," said Arthur. "Maybe *we're* a..." he concentrated, "...trinity ourselves? Maybe it's important?"

"It was the nearest place to the off-licence," said Steve, coldly. It was the first thing he had said since they fled the church on Micklegate. He was deep in thought and not enjoying the dig.

Arthur looked at the strange sallow man, his face hiding behind neatly combed curtains. Steve looked angry, hurt, and upset. He was shaking. Arthur could always pick up on the emotions of others no matter how drunk he got. As far as he could recollect, Steve had shown no emotion other than painful shyness.

"Are you alright, mate?" he asked.

Steve nodded once but wouldn't meet his gaze.

"Come on, mate. Out with it. What's wrong? I mean, apart from being dead and that."

Steve stood up from the gravestone he had been resting on and walked away. Arthur made to follow him but stood up too fast and staggered. He steadied himself against a statue of a crumbling angel, his hand cupping a familiar shape. He looked, blushed, and moved it.

"Sorry," he mumbled to the angel.

"It's okay," said the stone in a voice like gravel.

In the interests of self-preservation, the part of Arthur's brain that was still functioning on any normal level chose to push that interaction down somewhere really deep, lock it up and throw away the key, then it pointed him back towards Steve.

"What's going on?" he asked the spirit of the office worker.

Steve turned and his face was a picture of fury.

"Why her?!" he snapped.

"Who?"

"That old woman at the church. Why save her?"

"I didn't...I have no idea what happened!"

"You set her spirit free and sent *her* into the afterlife. Why her?!"

"I didn't mean to."

"She was horrible!"

Arthur paused.

"She wasn't. Not at the end," he said, suddenly very serious, the memory of the moment flashing back to him vividly. "I remember that. I remember the...the *feeling* of it. She was sorry. I mean *really* sorry. She had a-a-a...revelation. Sort of thing."

"And that's what allowed you to release her?" asked Sarah.

"I guess so," said Arthur.

"But how?" asked Steve. "Why?"

Arthur peered into the empty bottle of scotch to make absolutely certain there was nothing left.

"I really don't know," he said, softly, and shivered as a cold breeze swept across the back of his arms.

"I do," came a voice.

They all turned.

Standing in the dark, beneath the crumbling wall of the church, stood a boy in grey.

"You!" said Arthur.

"Me," said the boy.

"Where did you go? I was looking for you. Why did you run?"

"You vommed *through* me, dude!" said the boy. "It was gross!"

"Wait," said Steve, "did he just say dude?"

The boy nodded and gave two thumbs up.

"Look at his t-shirt," Arthur mumbled.

Steve stepped closer to the boy, who flinched away slightly but then stopped and pulled the ragged remains of his shirt down to reveal the symbol over his breast.

TMNT.

"Ninja Turtles!" said Steve, in shock.

"Excuse me?" said Sarah.

"Erm, it's a long story. Something from our time. A television show."

"Ahh, I've seen television," said Sarah proudly, looking around at the small group and nodding happily. "The box with the tiny actors."

Arthur chose to ignore that. Explaining television to a two-hundred-year-old ghost would probably push him over the edge. He had a hard enough time explaining video-messaging to his mum.

"You know what's going on?" he asked the boy who nodded and stepped forward.

He was clearly nervous in front of so many people and cast a furtive glance to the darkness beneath the trees in the churchyard, already planning his escape.

Sarah stepped towards him slowly.

"What's your name?" she asked softly.

"Tom," he said in a quiet voice.

"That's a nice name. Where do you live, Tom? Where do you haunt?"

"Stonegate, mainly," he replied. "But I can go all over the city if I really concentrate."

"And how old are you?"

"Do you mean *age* age, or ghost age?"

"Ghost age. How long have you been dead?"

"About ten years, I think. Maybe a bit more."

"Can you remember the year you died?" she asked, kneeling in front of him and reaching out. He flinched away at first but then let this strange lady with the big brown eyes touch his shoulders.

"Nineteen-ninety," he said. "I was eleven. I guess I still am."

"Jesus," said Arthur. "You're older than me." He stared around the odd gathering. They stared back. "I mean, I know you probably all are. What with you being ghosts and everything, but, well, he's just a kid. It's not fair."

"No," said Steve, darkly. "It isn't."

Sarah turned back to the small boy.

"How do you know what's going on, Tom?" she asked. "You're so young. I've been around for hundreds of years but I have no real idea. I know that the Shadowmen are out and that a Fetch tried to kill Arthur here, but I've no idea why, or how Arthur can do the things he can do. Can you help?"

"Do you remember nineteen-ninety?" the boy asked.

"Not really," said Sarah. "It all sort of blends into one after a while. Was that before or after people started staring into little boxes all the time?"

"Before. It was the last time a Fetch came to the city."

"Oh, I remember that, yes!" said Sarah. "That was chaos.

New ghosts and spirits everywhere. Some old, some young, and most with absolutely no idea where they were supposed to be. Wait a minute...were you?"

Tom nodded sadly and Sarah gasped, gathering her to him and holding the small form in her arms.

"Oh, you poor boy, you must have been so scared. What was it doing going after a child?"

The ghosts and Arthur settled on the ground beneath the watchful stare of the stone angel and Tom told them everything he remembered.

He had been on holiday with his parents, staying in the city. They did all the usual tourist attractions and got a particular thrill from one of the famous ghost walks. They decided to spend an extra night in one of the many pubs that claimed to be haunted. Tom was an only child and his parents doted on him, but he was adventurous and spoilt and didn't often do as he was told. The building they were staying in was being renovated and they were under strict instructions not to go up to the top floor, an instruction which Tom, of course, took as a challenge.

When his parents finally fell asleep and he could hear their rhythmic snoring, he had crept out of bed and climbed the stairs to the top of the building. He walked along a carpeted corridor passing closed rooms on either side. The walls were a faint pink with square patches of colour where paintings had been taken down. At the end of the short corridor rose a small set of steps, like a landing, leading to the last and highest room of the building. The Tower Room.

He wasn't surprised to find the door pushed open easily. He knew it wouldn't be locked, he knew, when he looked back on it later, that he was being drawn to the room. What did surprise him when he entered the moonlit space was how utterly boring it was. There was nothing there. No ghosts, no Roman soldiers, no Vikings, no twin girls asking him to come play, no blood seeping from the walls. Nothing of interest to an imaginative young boy who was allowed to watch whatever movie he wanted and read whatever book took his fancy. There wasn't even a silk curtain blowing spookily into the room from an open window offering a faint promise of vampiric activity.

What there was, was a toolbox, some buckets of paint and a lot of white sheets covering the furniture. In the corner of the room, however, there stood two large rectangular shapes a few feet apart covered in thick white painters' drapes. Tom had stepped between the two objects and pulled one of the drapes down. It fell to the floor with a hiss of fabric, and he stood looking at his own reflection. It was a large, ornate mirror with swirling metal filigree encasing the frame. He turned and pulled the drape down from the other. A matching set.

Tom stood in the dark room between the two mirrors and let his eyes adjust. The moon was full and shone brightly through the un-curtained windows. Before long he was looking at a long, curving line of his own reflection, vanishing off into eternity. He had smiled. He remembered that. He remembered it vividly. Smiling at his own reflections as they smiled back at him. Hundreds of them. And then, far down the line, one of the reflections tilted its head from out of the line and grinned.

It wasn't a smile.

It was a grin.

There is a big difference.

Tom had blinked and rubbed his eyes; an action copied by the reflections. He turned to the other mirror and saw all his doppelgangers turning their shoulders to look back at him.

All except one.

One stood up straight and tall.

White teeth visible in the dim light.

Tom turned back to the first mirror and his reflections followed him. He tried to move away, to step out from between the two mirrors, but he was trapped. He couldn't move. His feet were stuck to the floor. He struggled and the reflections struggled with him.

All

Except

One.

One, that leaned out of the line and then leaned back.

He blinked.

One, that leaned out of the line again.

Closer this time.

Tom screamed but no sound left his lips.

The reflections in front of him screamed with him in terrified silence.

All except one.

The one at the front.

Which laughed,

And then attacked.

CHAPTER 22

"Bloody hell!" said Arthur, breaking the silence that had descended on the graveyard after Tom finished his story. "So, you're a Fetch now?"

"No," said Tom. "That's not how it works. I saw my own ghost. *That* was the Fetch. And I died. Now I'm just a ghost like everyone else. Except you," he added, nodding to Arthur.

"About that," said Steve. "Arthur saw his own ghost as well, his Fetch, but he didn't die. So, what gives?"

"I've met a few like me," said Tom. "The presence of a Fetch stirs things up a bit so after I died there were a lot of ghosts around. All sort of out of the loop, away from their usual haunts, that sort of thing. I learned a bit. A Fetch usually takes a person the same night they see it, but sometimes, and this is only a story mind you, I don't know anyone this has happened to... apart from maybe you, dude," he said to Arthur. "Sometimes the vision of a Fetch doesn't mean you're going to die but it *can* mean the exact opposite. That you're going to have a really long life."

"Why does that not sound as positive as it should?" asked Arthur.

"Because things have changed for you now," replied Tom. "You can see dead people."

"Oh, behave!" said Arthur. "You got that from a movie!"

Tom shook his head and Arthur worked out the times, and then, more importantly, the evidence of his own eyes.

"Fuck."

"Yep."

"Is this permanent then?"

"No idea."

"I just figured it was the alcohol," he said, looking down at the empty bottle he still grasped in his hand. "I guess I thought the grog was letting me, I don't know, see things a little differently." The truth was he was hoping that if he maintained a steady level of drunk it might all just go away when he sobered up.

"That is probably what started it," came a voice from behind them and they all looked around. Then they looked down. Then they looked back up again.

"The alcohol allowed you to tap into your pre-existing ability," said the headless man as he strode forward from between two gravestones.

He was tall, well, not as tall as he once was, but still an imposing figure bedecked in rich trappings of velvet and lace. Gold chains and jewels dripped from his wrists and shoulders, and everything about his appearance and bearing spoke of wealth and elegance. Not that anyone paid any attention to minor details such as this when faced with a talking headless man, of course.

The voice was certainly coming from him, there was no doubt about it, and he gesticulated openly with his hands to reinforce his points, but, well, the problem kind of spoke for itself.

Which was the problem.

"Allow me to introduce myself," the man announced, somehow with a flourish. "Lord Percy, Seventh Earl of Northumberland, First Baron Percy, former Warden of the Marches, dead, at your service."

No one said anything.

What could they say?

In any normal situation, Arthur found it difficult talking to a member of the nobility, something he did quite often in his work, but this was no normal situation. And it was made even more difficult as this particular member of the upper classes bowed and openly displayed what remained of his neck, which was not a lot. Arthur swallowed drily and wished, once more, for something else to drink. Sarah Brocklebank had no such reservations. She stood up and greeted the earl with an outstretched hand.

"Sarah Brocklebank. Pleased to meet you."

"My lady," replied the Earl, thrusting his hand out.

Sarah's hand remained outstretched, untouched.

The Earl remained where he was.

It took an embarrassing length of time for the penny to drop.

When it eventually did, Sarah moved a few sheepish steps to the left and placed her hand in the Earl's. She was going for a shake, but he had different ideas. He was a gentleman of the old guard and he wasn't about to let a trifling fact such as his lack of lips get in the way of common decency. A lady is a lady. He lifted her hand to the space above his open neck and the torso bobbed forward slightly. There was the noise of a kiss. Sarah shuddered and stepped away.

"Young man," continued the headless Earl, turning to face no one, "you were targeted by the Fetch, but you survived. You vanquished your foe! And then you saw the creature again, and once more, you survived. You are unique, sir! You are special! One of a kind! The legends say a Fetch has until sunrise to take you and if it doesn't do so in that time then it won't. It can't. Yes, indeed there is a special air about you, Sir. Something *else*."

"How do you know all this?" asked Arthur.

"I read," said the Earl.

There was a polite silence.

Steve coughed, and Sarah punched him. Arthur rallied, gainfully,

"Thank you, your, your, Earlship. Perhaps then, you could tell us about the Shadowman? He came for me as well. What are they...he...*it*? What is the Shadowman?"

"And why did it ask you to find it?" added Steve, suspiciously.

"For that matter, why did the white lady ask you to find the queen. What queen?"

"Alas, I have no answers to such questions, but I perhaps can shed light on the question of the Shadowman," said Lord Percy.

"What is it?" Arthur asked.

"A man—" announced the Lord before pausing dramatically, "of shadows!"

Arthur groaned. He could see the ghosts. He could actually see dead people. Talk to them, communicate with them, touch them.

But why the hell were they all bloody mental?

He sighed and pinched the bridge of his nose. He got the impression the Earl didn't have many opportunities to talk to people. He would have to be patient.

Lord Percy drummed his fingers against the air where his chin should have been then raised a pale white digit and pointed it at Arthur.

He missed.

"They were men like yourself," he said to the stone angel who looked embarrassed. "Fallen beings who can traverse both sides of the veil. They were human once, before the darkness took them. Now they exist only as myth and legend, as stories to frighten small children, they lurk in the dark places of the night and the shadows of the day. They are the creeping feeling of company in solitude, they are the unseen eyes that watch, they are the terrors of our darkest dreams!" he roared this final part with both hands raised high above his neck, and then dropped them dramatically to his side.

Steve clapped politely—the earl seemed to be expecting it—and then he went back to gripping his tie when Sarah glared at him. The ghost of Lord Percy preened, which is quite hard to do without a head, but there was a certain set to the shoulders.

"But what is it?" Arthur asked again.

The shoulders slumped. People just didn't appreciate dramatic flair anymore, the Earl thought.

"The bad guy," said Tom, simply.

"The bad guy," agreed Lord Percy.

"What does he want with me?" asked Arthur.

"What do all bad guys want," said Lord Percy, rallying magnificently and thrusting a hand into the air in an action that was five hundred years and a Jon Bon Jovi perm too early. He made a fist and pulled it tight to his chest. "But power!" he hissed.

Steve clapped again.

"I'm a town planner!" snapped Arthur, getting entirely sick of the whole charade. "I don't have any power!"

"Arthur," said the Earl, facing him and this time getting reasonably close, "right now you are the most powerful man in this city."

"How? This is all bollocks! I got drunk and I'm hallucinating. I'm seeing things. Any second now there will be pink elephants floating along in the sky." He tried not to notice Steve and Tom looking up.

The earl turned to Arthur and this time got it spot on. If there were eyes, they would have pierced his soul. As it was, the words did the job for him.

"Arthur, you have the ability to see the dead, to commune with them, to touch them, and, if I'm not mistaken, you have already freed one lost soul and set her on her merry way to the world beyond this."

"But I don't know how I did that."

"You do. Deep down. It is part of you. It always has been. The true essence of who you are. Take I, for instance, you see me as a Lord, as an Earl, as a fierce protector of the one true faith, but in my heart, I am a thespian! I long only to tread the boards but alas my time never came. That is the truth of who I am. The truth, sir, will set you free!"

"So, you're saying I can free the dead?"

Lord Percy paused.

Steve dropped his tie.

Sarah giggled. Just once.

Tom stared with his mouth open.

The ramifications of that sentence washed over them all. They had skirted around the edges of it in their own private thoughts but to hear it said out loud like that changed everything. The sudden look of hope in all their eyes—well, nearly all their eyes—made Arthur step back.

"No. no," he said, and then, "No, no, no." In case they didn't get it the first two times, he repeated "I can't do that. I can't set you free. I don't know how."

The strange foursome turned their shoulders ever so slightly towards Arthur and what had previously been a not so simple gathering of ghosts he barely knew suddenly seemed a lot more ominous. Now his companions formed a wall—a wall of spirits that needed something. A wall of spirits that burned with an ineffable hunger and desire. A wall of starving ghosts that looked at Arthur like he was food. Suddenly, he knew exactly how the mouse felt when cornered by the cat.

Where were the bloody cats?

They had done a great job of flying in at the last second so far but now that he really needed them, they were nowhere to be seen.

If Arthur had looked up, he would have noticed there were actually three black cats on the rooftops just above him, but they weren't looking down. Not for any particular reason. They just didn't want to.

Arthur stepped back and his head banged against the granite breasts of the angel and she giggled. There was nowhere to go. The ghosts were advancing on him with dangerous intent and the angel, though oddly comforting, was a barrier to any retreat.

I could rush them, he thought. *Push the headless Earl over and run for it; that might work.*

Then the second thoughts in his brain chimed in and reminded him they were ghosts. Just because he had been able to touch the spirits of the dead in the last twenty-four hours didn't alter the fact that they were essentially well-organised mist. The third thought in his brain stepped back, folded its arms, and said it was far too drunk to be of any help.

Arthur went with number two.

He charged.

He ran straight through Earl Percy, then straight through the iron gates of the churchyard, and all the way through three parked cars.

And he didn't stop running until he collapsed below the Minster and vomited up a small bottle of scotch.

Three passing students cheered.

Arthur leaned against the towering monolith and realised what he'd just done. He'd run *through* the gates and *through* the cars. He patted the stone and started to giggle.

The students stopped to watch.

He pushed the stone. It seemed solid enough. He put two hands on it and gave it a shove.

One of the students took out a mobile phone.

Arthur took a step back.

He ran forward.

When the students had stopped laughing, they made sure he was breathing and walked away.

CHAPTER 23

The sound of a horn brought the groggy Arthur back to the real world, or what he had previously assumed was the real world, these days he couldn't be sure what was real and what simply the bottom of a bottle. His head hurt. Not in the normal way he had become used to, behind the eyes and deep in the sinuses, now his *forehead* hurt. He reached a shaking hand to it and winced as he touched raw, bleeding skin and a fairly impressive lump. What the hell had he been thinking?

This is the mantra of drunks everywhere. What the hell was I thinking? What Arthur didn't know now was that he would have plenty of time to dwell on this later as the video of him trying to run through the wall would go viral and bring a lot of attention to the YouTube channel of a local media student. Though none of his subsequent uploads would ever do quite so well as *Man mistakes Minster for Platform 9 and ¾.*

But that was a problem for future Arthur, let him deal with that. Present Arthur had a splitting headache, and he was scared. Deep down scared. In the very core of his being. The whole of the last day had been terrifying, especially now he was certain it had all been real, but at least then he'd had allies. At least he'd had people on his side. Yes, they were dead, but they had been on *his* side and that was bloody important. The image of their hungry eyes flashed in his mind and sent a shiver down his spine, which, up until this point, he'd assumed was a cliché, but he could feel the icy fear in his bones. It was part of him.

They wanted him. They wanted what he could do. And the Earl had been right, he could feel the power within him like it had always been there and was only now making itself known. It was like one of those eye puzzles with the colourful dots where if you squint in just the right way you see an image of a boat or a badger. They were a bugger to get the hang of, but once you got it, you knew how to do it again.

Though just because you could didn't mean you should, right? He'd never been in this situation before.

With great power comes great responsibility and all that.

But then, Spiderman never had to worry about the dead using him as a tour guide.

Arthur groaned and realised he was still lying on the cool grass beneath the towering Minster next to a pile of sick. He pulled himself slowly into a sitting position and leaned his back against the stone wall. He looked up. Thousands of years of history and religion looked down. The giant, gothic cathedral towered over him and propped him up.

Poetic, he thought. *I don't believe in you, but the things I thought I believed in have taken a bit of a hit this last day or so, so if you are kicking around up there, I could do with some help. If you're not too busy.*

The Minster stared down at him impassively.

Fine. I'll do it myself.

The horn sounded again.

So, it was real.

The noise echoed around the open space beneath the Minster's famous Great Eastern window and bounced off the walls of St. William's College, that long, curved, stone and wood-beamed building that was a favourite of photographers and tourists. The echoes made the horn sound as though it was coming from all over the city. From behind the Minster, from St. William's College itself, from the Cross Keys pub, from Goodramgate; the place he had run from.

He glanced all around, but the area was empty. Not a single person in the street. No one walking down The Queen's Path, no one on College Street, no one taking photographs of the Minster, no one on Goodramgate...

Two figures stood at the entrance to the narrow street across the open square. Two black silhouettes picked out from the night shadows by the glow of the pub window. Two adults. A man and a woman. Standing still. Looking. He couldn't tell if they were facing his way or not, but he could hazard a guess.

Then they moved and he didn't need to.

Arthur stood up quickly and lights exploded behind his eyes. The lump on his forehead throbbed so painfully he thought it might explode, he could feel the skin stretching almost to breaking point. Closing his eyes against the pain, he leaned heavily on the coarse sandstone of the Minster as he made his way blindly away from the two figures. He didn't know where he was going; he just knew he had to get away. He pushed himself off the Minster and crossed a narrow street, glancing up at a small square window as he went. It was the last house on the curve of College Street before it turned into Minster Yard. A young wide-eyed girl looked down at him from behind the glass then her eyes darted away and quickly back. She shouted something but he couldn't hear her through the glass. He thought it might be the word 'run'.

Arthur tried but the pain in his head was too much. He couldn't move any faster than he was already going. He staggered into the squat stone house and leaned heavily against the wall beneath the window, pausing for a moment to try to get his eyes to focus before forcing himself on. The horn sounded again. Louder this time. He headed towards it. Why not? There didn't seem to be anything else to head towards and at least it was in the right direction; away.

Arthur bumped his way along the wall and then turned into a strangely lit alley. It was wide, certainly wide enough for a car to travel down, and it stretched off into a brooding mass of stone buildings. The wall to the left was steeped in shadow, towering red bricks visible high above where the streetlight penetrated. To the right was a jumbled row of houses, their doorways shrouded in darkness. None of them had lights on, and the narrow street grew darker as Arthur walked on.

A footpath of large flagstones ran to the left and a river of small cobbles made up the rest of the lane and such light as there was appeared to be emanating from them. Where the walls were dark, the floor practically shone in the moonlight, reflecting the glow of the distant orange streetlamps. Chapter House Street glistened like a river. Arthur half expected his feet to get wet as he stumbled further on, but nothing happened. He walked across the light.

The horn sounded once more, bouncing from the walls and he pushed himself forward, into the noise. Where there were horns, there must be people. He needed people. Ideally, people who needed oxygen. Then he heard the rumble of wheels and the raised voices of men.

Finally! He kept on moving but stopped when he heard the distinctive snort of horses, completely out of place in this urban area. The rumbling grew louder, shouts and yells and barked commands echoed around the walls, so close as to be almost on top of him, deafening, but the alley remained empty. Then the horn sounded again, shattering the still air of the deserted street, and a line of men marched through the far wall in perfect unison, their sandaled feet tramping across the stone in time with one another.

The commander at the front snapped off a smart salute to Arthur by tapping his shining breastplate with an outstretched hand as he roared for the company to keep time before disappearing through the opposite wall. Horses whickered as they were goaded along, steam blasting from flared nostrils as they dragged large wooden carts behind them. Men in armour marched alongside the trundling, spoked wheels as they passed through the alley and one of them raised a long, curved horn to his lips and blew.

The noise bounced back off the walls and joined the tramp and stamp of marching feet. And then, as quickly as they had come, they were gone. The noise of the march and the blast of the horn fading quickly as though vanishing into the distance. One last soldier brought up the rear, impatiently tugging on the reigns of an old packhorse laden with saddle bags. They paused between the two walls for a moment and the soldier grumbled. But the horse wouldn't budge. Instead, it lifted its tail and did what horses do. Only after it was finished did it move. Then they too were gone.

It was while Arthur was staring in wonder at, and trying to make sense of, the steaming pile of transparent, phantom horse shit that he was grabbed from behind by ghostly hands.

"Don't eat me!" Arthur screamed, covering his head with his arms as he was spun around.

Nothing happened.

Nothing continued to happen.

After quite a lengthy time of nothing maintaining its blistering form, Arthur lowered his hands. Sarah's big, beautiful eyes were staring at him. They were filled with laughter in a way only certain attractive people can manage.

"Don't *eat* you," she said softly with a grin curling the edges of her mouth.

She was trying not to smile. She was trying to look serious. She wanted Arthur to know that she was serious. But whatever it was she had been expecting when she grabbed him, it was not for him to scream "don't eat me". That had completely thrown her off course.

Arthur continued to stare at Sarah, completely unsure what to do. A few minutes ago, this beautiful woman had looked at him like she wanted to rip him apart to get to whatever it was she believed was inside. And now, well now she looked like Sarah again. His Sarah.

His Sarah?

Arthur realised he was going to have to give that some serious thought at a later point. He moved his head to look at Steve, who was standing the obligatory few steps away gripping his tie and avidly not making eye-contact.

"Hi, Steve," he said.

"Hi," said Steve without looking up. Same old Steve.

Tom was nowhere to be seen.

"You guys—" Arthur started but Sarah stopped him by stepping forward and hugging him.

"We're really sorry if we scared you," she said in his ear. "We're ghosts, it's kind of what we do. We all sort of...lost control."

"It's okay," said Arthur, trying and completely failing not to notice how her body felt against his. Was that all in his head as well? Was he imagining the way she felt pressed against him or could he, genuinely, physically *feel* her? He could, couldn't he!

If we could touch, we could...no!

He stopped that train of thought before it had time to fully form and pushed her away with a cough. "Sorry. Sorry." he said. "Yeah, I get it. It's totally okay."

"You have no idea how hungry we are!" said Steve with a desperate edge to his voice.

"Steve!" snapped Sarah.

"Not *hungry* hungry," Steve said quickly, lifting his hands in the air, "but it's the best word to describe life as a ghost. We really *really* want...stuff. But we can't have it."

"So, when we realised what you can do, *might* be able to do, we—"

"Can you really do it?" interrupted Steve. "Can you really free us?"

A silence spread through the wide alley and Arthur looked at the longing in their eyes. How difficult it must be. He'd never really given much thought to the afterlife but now he was thrust into the middle of it. Something he previously had no solid thoughts on turned out to be completely, totally, utterly, one hundred percent true. He wished he could go back to secondary school and tell his English teacher. She was great; she loved ghost stories and used to always say that we could never really know the answers to the great questions of life, but poetry came close.

Or maybe he should go tell his RE teacher? That guy was a right twat. He'd belonged to a very small church that met in a remote farmhouse in North Yorkshire, and they'd got it right. They knew the truth. They knew what God wanted. But only them, of course. All the other churches and religions in the world had got it wrong. It took two years and two classes of completely failed GCSE exams before that guy got sacked. But now here Arthur was, in the middle of his own ghost story with a million questions left unanswered but some very important ones as clear as a steaming pile of ethereal horse shit slowly vanishing in the alley.

Ghosts are real.

The afterlife is real.

And, when he reached down deep inside, he knew his power to connect the two was also real.

He looked at Steve.

Then he looked at Sarah.

Then he spoke.

One word.

"Yes."

~

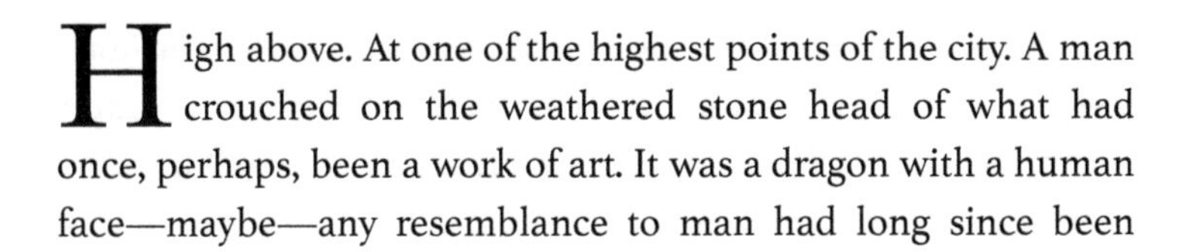

High above. At one of the highest points of the city. A man crouched on the weathered stone head of what had once, perhaps, been a work of art. It was a dragon with a human face—maybe—any resemblance to man had long since been scoured away by the weather. The nose was a stunted nub, one of the eyes was missing and the mouth had been blasted so severely by the wind and rain it was a barely visible thin line. This made it easier for the man in black to issue instructions. He didn't like interruptions.

"Spread the word," he hissed, grinding his heel into the stone and chipping away a small fragment that fell far, far to the ground below.

The creature beneath his feet grimaced and the man smiled.

"I want to know where *it* is, and I want to know now. Make yourself useful gargoyle!"

"Grrrnnesk," said the creature.

"Pardon?"

"NgggaANNann GRRrrnesk."

The man sighed and leaned forward. He gripped the long snout of the stone beast in one hand and with the other he rummaged inside the dark folds of his clothes before producing, from somewhere, a long thin blade that didn't so much appear threatening as exude a sharpness that could cut the light of the moon. It *glistened*.

One lightning quick motion saw the blade swipe across the mouth of the creature, passing through centuries-old stone like a hot knife through ice cream. There was a hiss of steam and the creature gasped in a mixture of agony and relief. The man stood up while the strange thing opened and closed its mouth and tried out a few experimental syllables, smacking its lips together with a sound like a pebble skittering across a cobbled street.

"What did you say?" hissed the man.

"I said," the creature began, rolling its one good eye to glance at the dangerous shadow above it, "I'm a grotesque."

"You can say that again."

"No, I *am* a grotesque. You called me a gargoyle. I'm not a gargoyle. I'm a grotesque. It's a common mistake many people make. They see a figure hanging on the side of a building and they immediately think to themselves, that's a gargoyle that is.

But I mean, they don't look at statues and think, that's a fountain, do they? Do they buggery. That's the difference you see, son. But do you think people care to—"

The man winced at being called son. He hadn't been called son by anyone, certainly not that he could remember. He assumed he'd had a father and mother once, but he doubted even they would have been willing to use the word. He fingered the handle of the dark blade, already regretting allowing the creature to talk and now giving serious consideration to ending that ability permanently. But, for now, he needed it. He tuned back in. The creature was still going.

"Water! That's the issue. Fountains have water. Statues don't. Gargoyles have water. Grotesques don't. It's an easy distinction to make but one most people miss. Back in my early days I—" But the man on his head ground his heel down hard and slammed the mouth shut.

The grotesque gamely tried to mumble a few words but gave up. It blinked.

"Send word," said the man in a voice more dangerous than the blade he held beside the creature's ear. "Tell your people to look out for the man I told you about. I want to know where he is, and I want to know before midnight. Do not fail me," he hissed these last words as a command and released the pressure.

When the grotesque's roving eye finally managed to swivel painfully back up, the man was gone.

"Bugger," it said.

Then it caught sight of an unmistakable collection of twigs that indicated a nearby pigeon nest and opened its mouth in a hideous grin. Years of digestive warfare were about to be repaid.

~

"What if I get it wrong?" said Arthur.

It was a thought that had been scratching beneath the surface of his consciousness since Irene Napier vanished in a ball of purple flame.

"Or, what if I get it right and you don't go where you want to go? What if I just send you...somewhere. We don't know where you go next."

"It could be heaven," said Steve.

"It could be hell," Arthur snapped back. "I don't want to be the person that sends people to hell. I mean, fuck! Yesterday I didn't even believe in a heaven or hell, world of opposites kind of thing and now I can...can..." He sought for a word that seemed suitable—something biblical.

"Condemn?" said Sarah, quietly.

"Yes! Condemn! What if I condemn you to hell?!"

"It's probably still better than this," mumbled Steve.

"Really?" said Arthur in disbelief.

"Try it."

Arthur looked at him and then looked away.

They were sitting on a bench below the Minster facing St William's College, Arthur kept glancing up to see if the girl would reappear in the small window, but she never did. He thought he knew who she was and the realisation that so many people were trapped like Sarah and Steve was beginning to weigh on him. If he started down this road he might never get to stop, which seemed like quite a profound thought for one so tired—so emotionally fraught and still so very drunk.

They'd made TV shows like this, hadn't they? That one with the actress with the big boobs? She spoke to ghosts, and they always had some message to give to the living before they could "pass over." Wendy had loved that show, and Arthur had hated it. Not because he didn't believe in the supernatural—which, at the time, he didn't—but because she never actually told the living person what the ghost really said. She always paraphrased and it got in his tits. "If I do it, I'll tell them exactly what you say," he said in a grumble.

"Pardon?"

"Nothing," he said, a red flush creeping across his cheeks. "Look, we don't really know what happened to Mrs. Napier, do we? For all we know I could have just made her vanish and she'll be back there tomorrow night organising poltergeist poker or bogeyman bingo or something."

"Really?" said Sarah with a look.

"Sorry. But you know what I mean. We just don't know what happened to her."

"But there's hope," said Sarah and she patted his knee. He felt it. He felt it and he wished he hadn't. She seemed so real now—so substantial. That really confused things.

"But what if it's all true?" Arthur said, talking quickly to outrun the other thoughts he did not want to entertain. "What if heaven and hell are real? If you go to heaven, you'll spend eternity bowing and scraping and worshipping and singing and I bet the music is shit! And if you go to hell then you're going to spend eternity getting charred to a crisp or pushing boulders up bloody big hills with crows pecking your eyes out!"

Arthur's knowledge of the afterlife was based entirely on his RE lessons and a slew of movies that did the rounds while everyone freaked out about Y2K, but he was on a roll, so he kept going.

"And what religion are we talking about here? Heaven could be just as bad as hell if we've got it wrong. If it's Islam then there's something about forty virgins and gardens, which sounds alright to begin with, but if you're being rewarded with sex wouldn't you want someone who knew what they were doing? And what happens if you *do* have sex in heaven? Do the virgins get replaced each morning? What happens then? And is it just for the men? What about you, Sarah? Do you get forty virgin men to fool around with or do you join the harem? Is contraception allowed in the afterlife?"

He realised he was steering dangerously close to the territory he desperately wanted to avoid and so he searched the recesses of his education for safer examples.

"What...what if it's Old Testament stuff?" he said. "Then you're pretty much guaranteed a spot in hell anyway. The rules are insane! No pork, no tattoos, no wearing two sets of clothes or something! And you can't get in if you're gay or if you work on a Sunday!"

"Arthur, stop," Sarah said.

He ignored her because her hand was still on his knee.

"Reincarnation!" he shouted, startling a solitary man walking home from one of the bars. The man looked at Arthur talking with such animation on a bench by himself and picked up the pace.

"What if Buddhism or Hinduism got it right and you come back as a badger or a, a horse or a rock or something?"

"Arthur!"

"At least the Vikings have beer!"

"Arthur!"

"What?"

"Stop now." Sarah squeezed his knee. He could really feel it. Really feel her. It was suddenly uncomfortably warm.

"I'm sorry," he said, "it's just too much. I don't know what to do and I don't know how to do it."

He dropped his head and Sarah lifted it gently with a hand under his chin. She turned his face towards her. They were so close. She was so beautiful.

"I don't want to let you down," he said.

What he wanted to say was *I don't want to do it at all*, but he couldn't get those words past his lips when Sarah's were so close to them. He leaned forward. So did Sarah. And then, due to social conventions dictating that all awkward men when finding themselves alone with a couple as a spark ignites must blow the damn thing out, Steve spoke.

"Practice on her then," he said, causing the two to jump and sit back quickly. They had forgotten he was there. They knew it, and Steve knew it, and they knew that he knew.

Nobody looked at anybody else.

"Sorry, mate," coughed Arthur. "What did you say?"

"Why don't you practice on her," said Steve and nodded across the street. He was looking at the last house on College Street, the small brick home nestled at the end of St William's College. From the small, square, upstairs window, the dark-haired little girl was back. She looked down at them and smiled.

Everyone in York knows the story of the girl in the window. She is one of the city's most famous ghosts and Arthur realised that Steve might be onto something. The girl in the window had appeared a few times over the years to lots of different people, and the city ghost walks often gathered beneath he home while the tour guide told shivering tourists a dramatic version of her sad tale.

The house had been boarded up when the plague hit, they said, as was the custom at the time, but those who did it forgot about the little girl! She didn't get sick like her parents. She didn't have the plague like her brothers and sisters. She didn't do anything wrong, but she was locked up just like her family, and, after days and days of vainly beating at the window in the desperate hope of catching the attention of a sympathetic passer-by, the young girl's energy finally gave out.

Eventually, after weeks of loneliness in a boarded-up house with the corpses of her family rotting in the next room, she starved to death. The classic ghost story tells of how the spirit of the little girl appears at the window and tries to get someone to help her, to unlock the door and let her out, cursed to spend eternity crying for help that will never come.

"If anyone deserves to be set free, it's her," said Sarah, reading the silent thoughts of the two men.

"She's bound to go to heaven, isn't she?" said Arthur, giving it serious thought. "I mean if there is one. She's an innocent, just a kid. There's no way I could accidentally send her to hell...is there?" he added.

"I wouldn't say so," said Sarah. "I always feel sorry for the little ones."

"At the very least she'll be free," said Steve.

Arthur stared at the lonely figure in the small window and wondered how long she had been there. How long had she been trapped, looking out at the same view, with no one to keep her company? It was bad enough that her life had ended in such tragedy but to spend eternity reliving the same thing over and over again in the same small room was horrendous. She was just a kid.

Arthur stood up.

Sarah and Steve stood up.

The three of them walked across the grass towards the little girl then crossed the narrow road. Standing in the shadows below the window they looked up. It was much higher than it had seemed from across the street. The little girl looked down at them from a few feet above Arthur's head and stared with wide-eyed amazement. Her face was split across five small panes of glass, and she had to move her head back and forth to see each of her three visitors.

The dark glass and frame distorted her features and so the trio couldn't quite get a good look at her. Two small, pale hands pushed flat against the glass, and she pressed one eye to the central pane. Then she moved back slightly and shouted but they could hear nothing.

"How do I get in?" said Arthur.

"Walk through the wall," said Sarah as though it was the most natural thing in the world.

"I can't—" he started with a laugh, then he paused.

He thought. He swallowed. He touched his forehead. His stomach churned. A shiver rippled through his shoulders as he remembered the sensation. He shook his head to clear it. It felt like déjà vu, like an unwanted memory revisiting and intruding on his thoughts, but he knew that it was real.

"I did, didn't I," he said. It was not a question.

"And you can do it again," said Sarah, placing her hand on his shoulder.

Arthur stared at the wall. Arthur patted the wall. The lump on Arthur's head pulsed sympathetically. It was a very solid wall. The phrase 'solid as a rock' was coined for just such a wall. The stones had had millennia of practice before being dug up and put together with other like-minded stones to form this wall, and they weren't about to give up their general wall-ness now.

"Concentrate," said Sarah.

"On what?" laughed Arthur, throwing his hands up in the air and turning away. "This is bloody ridiculous! I can't walk through a wall. I can't do any of this."

"You can if you just—"

"Don't say if I just believe! Please, don't say it! I know that's what you're heading towards and I don't want any part of it. I don't *believe* any of this! It's all just a bad dream or a bad trip."

"You know it's not," said Sarah, patiently, although she was beginning to feel a little frazzled.

Sure, Arthur was in a tough situation but at least he wasn't dead, which kind of put his situation in a much more favourable light than everyone else she'd spoken to in the last few hundred years.

"You can help that little girl, Arthur. And, when you do, maybe you can help us?" She let out a manic little laugh and then got the giggles. She'd been containing it all so well, but it was a constant struggle.

Arthur looked up at the window. The girl looked down and waved sadly. He looked for a door, thinking in his drunk state that he might just be able to walk in, but there didn't seem to be one. There was just the small window and a larger bay window jutting out from the stonework to the left. On the right, however, a black drainpipe clung to the stones. Drainpipes he could do.

Drainpipes made more sense. Drainpipes were solid and real and that's what normal people would use...when breaking into a house in the middle of the night to make a little girl disappear.

"Are we sure this is a good idea?" he said.

"Oh, for fucksake! Will you climb the fucking pipe already?!" snapped Steve.

Arthur stared at him.

Sarah stared at him.

Then Arthur gripped the pipe and began to climb.

CHAPTER 24

The story of the girl in the window hasn't always been known. For the longest time, there were just mysterious sightings and apparitions, whispers of a spirit, rumours of the deceased, hints of foul play. But then the scared owners of the small house hired a medium to investigate further and the story of the girl in the window was 'uncovered'.

Returning white and shaken from an overnight stay in the room, the medium told them a tale of plague houses and innocent little girls left to starve. They painted quite a picture of loneliness and abandonment before collecting a large fee and never coming back. This tells us two very important things about human nature, that we are, in essence, very positive, but also embarrassingly gullible.

Arthur wedged his foot onto a bracket that secured the pipe to the wall and squeezed his toes between the brickwork and the metal. He pushed down once or twice to test it, there was no give. He leaned out and gripped the window ledge with his left hand, his right clinging tightly to the pipe. He looked up. He looked into the eyes of the girl in the window. She smiled at him and said something he couldn't hear.

"I'm going to help you," he mouthed, then wondered why he did it quietly when surely shouting would be best.

The truth was it was a lie anyway; he had absolutely no idea how he was going to get inside.

"You've got to concentrate," the words of Sarah came back to him.

He groaned.

In the last twenty-four hours, you have spoken to ghosts, touched the spirits of the dead, walked through a metal gate—and Christ! A few cars! And you've tapped into some sort of power that feels like smooth electricity in your veins.

Not sharp or painful. It hadn't hurt when he touched Mrs. Napier. It had flowed like water but crackled with power.

And it was there—deep inside. It had always been there. Somehow, he'd tapped into it and released it through his hands. It had surrounded Mrs. Napier, enveloping her body in purple flame, bright at the edges and darker inside and Arthur knew her spirit had passed on. She had gone...elsewhere. He didn't know where and he didn't want to think about it just in case. Perhaps no one really knew? Mad Alice had mentioned a door, a portal of some description that closed on her, all the other spirits of the dead walking towards it and passing through, but not her. Perhaps Arthur could open doors. Maybe it was as simple as that?

Simple. Sure.

It still didn't explain the walking through walls bit.

He was aware of the eyes on him. Of the girl and of Sarah and of Steve. Of their expectation and hope. Of their hunger. Fortunately, he was entirely unaware of everything else that watched him.

He focused. He closed his eyes to block out the world and he concentrated, trying to remember the feeling he had in the church, the surge of power within him. It was there. He knew it was there. Like something on the edge of his vision that went away when he turned his head. He had to concentrate on *not* looking, on feeling around the edges; it was like trying to hold water.

The effort was draining him, and his head nodded. He was getting tired. He could feel his heart beating faster. He leaned forward and rested his head on the window for a moment. The glass was cold on his skin. The metal pipe crushed his toes against the hard wall. The wood of the window ledge felt rough beneath his fingers and the coarse stone rubbed through his trousers against his knee and his hip. He felt it all. Solid. Real.

Wood, stone, glass, and metal.

He breathed deeply.

And they were gone.

He opened his eyes.

He was inside the room.

Below the window, Sarah and Steve hugged each other in celebration, they didn't notice the palpable change in the atmosphere or the shadows that crept across stone, grass, and wood. They were too happy. The world around them grew smaller as the light fled before the oncoming darkness.

On the tiled rooftops above, a solitary black cat bristled and hissed, turning this way and that, hackles raised, and sharp teeth bared. The problem with cats is they don't just see the things in the shadows, they see the things *made* of shadows. The cat spat and retreated slowly, backing away over the lip of the roof. Then it turned and fled, running as if all the demons of hell were behind it.

High on the side of the Minster, clinging to the corner of the imposing wall beside the Great East Window, a grotesque with long ears and piercing eyes looked down as the living man vanished through the wall of the house below. It saw the shadows descend on the small house, the lights of the city suffocating in an ever-decreasing circle, heading inexorably towards the small brick building. It swore. Then it began to move.

Inside the room, Arthur gasped to catch his breath, his heart raced, and his body prickled with the memory of being briefly inside tons of stone. It was the kind of feeling that could cause a person to never leave the house again, but he had no time to dwell on it. His friends were counting on him. He had a job to do. He was going to free this sweet, innocent little girl and then he was going to free his friends. Starting with Steve. He wanted a bit more time with Sarah first. But one thing at a time.

"Hi," he said, turning to the little girl.

"Hello," she replied. And attacked.

Somewhere deep in the city, in a dark alley between two rows of houses, in amongst the bins, boxes, and tattered rags that make up the detritus of urbanisation, there lay a body. The Shadowman stood over it. He didn't smile. He never smiled. He just did his job. As he wiped the blade – carefully – someone hissed at him. He turned, slowly, and looked into the eyes of a carved Green Man hanging on the back gate of the nearest house. The Green Man spoke.

The Shadowman swore.

It was a curse word not heard in Britain for over three thousand years. The Green Man nodded in appreciation.

The little girl moved with lightning speed and a savagery that would have caused a Viking Berserker to pause and rethink his life choices. Without seeming to pass through the intervening space, she left the ground and was on Arthur, clawing at his face with sharp, dirty nails while her toes dug into his chest like talons. He shouted as she climbed him, flailing with his arms but she was too fast. She darted over his shoulders and struck the sides of his head with clenched fists and open palms, clawing at his ears and yanking his hair.

A flurry of blows battered him before he finally managed to

grab the girl by the tattered rags that passed for clothes. She looked down in surprise as his hand closed about the cloth and that pause was enough for Arthur to yank her hard over his shoulder. He let go as she sailed over his head and her small body smashed against the wall and crashed to the floor in a heap of rags and limbs.

She skittered onto all fours and hissed at him, circling in a low crouch, trying to make sense of this strange creature that had entered her domain. Then she ran up the wall and clambered onto the ceiling, her long dark hair hanging down like shreds of matted cloth.

"What are you?" she snarled.

It was not a voice that belonged to a sweet innocent girl. It was a voice more suited to demons...or traffic wardens who really loved their job.

Arthur backed away and glanced around the room, looking for an escape, still not used to what he could do. He looked with fully human eyes for anything that could help him but there was nothing, not even a door. The room was made entirely of stone. Floors, walls, and ceiling were all the same. The only opening to the outside, the only change of pattern in this strange cube, was the small window through which he had entered.

Every inch of the stone was scratched and scoured with sigils and patterns, and dark shadows crawled across the walls, twisting and turning as though trying to avoid his gaze. Arthur glanced quickly to one corner as the shadows there coalesced and swirled like ink. He blinked and the Shadowman appeared, his face impassive, his peaked cap pulled low. What were once shadows was now a man. A man with a blade in one hand, a book in the other, and a strange expression on his face.

The girl hissed at the Shadowman, but he paid no attention to her. He simply opened the book and ran his finger down the page, then he leaned against the wall as if waiting...as if he had all the time in the world. Which, in some respects, he did. It certainly seemed that way as the girl dropped from the ceiling and the world slowed.

~

See the girl now, between roof and floor, mid-leap, hands reaching, lips curled, teeth bared like a dog. She's older than Arthur first thought, perhaps fifteen, just on the cusp of womanhood but at this moment any and all humanity that may once have existed has vanished. She's more animal than human. Nothing remains except the urge to fight, to hurt, to bite, to kick, to scratch; to devour. Her hair is black. Her eyes are black. Her skin is black. But it is not the black of nature, not the beautiful melanin of African descent. Her skin is filthy, crusting, and flaking like dried oil. She is decay.

~

Arthur's eyes fill with fear as they widen, white surmounting the hazel. But there is something else there as well, something deep in the dark pupils. A spark. He feels the power inside him. He knows where it is, and the fear allows him to grasp it. It is building already, coursing through his veins, rippling through his nerves, part of him, and yet distant all at once.

The girl's hands with their filthy sharp nails reach for Arthur's eyes. Arthur ducks his head and raises an outstretched palm towards the girl. He sees the purple sparks flickering and crackling like static between his fingers. The girl's eyes widen. The Shadowman lowers his book and his blade. Arthur's open hand smacks into the forehead of the girl as they collide.

And the world erupts in purple flame.

The girl screams and falls to the floor on top of Arthur, bringing his awareness suddenly and blindingly into focus. Both of his hands now grip her head, and power surged through him.

But a door is a door, and it goes both ways, and the girl doesn't want to leave. Not yet.

She hangs on, fighting and screaming and Arthur sees her. Sees her for what she truly is. Flashes of a terrified man and woman leap at him, images of two dead children cradled in their arms, the sound of the girl's laughter fills his ears from another time, and he watches as she plunges a wicked blade into the body of a diseased rat. He steps forward with her as she slices at the man and the woman, at her parents, opening filthy wounds in her father's arms as he raises them to protect his wife, to protect the bodies of the girl's dead siblings.

"We're all going to die, anyway!" Arthur screams at them, but it is not his voice. It is the voice of the girl coming from his lips.

He looks down. His hands hold the blood-soaked blade. He feels the warm slick already sticking to his fingers and he feels joy. Her joy. She is taking so much pleasure in their suffering. There is not an ounce of remorse, no sorrow, no regret. Just the wish she had done this sooner. And then the mother rises and swings at them with an axe, the blade turned away from her own child in a pained, final act of love. Arthur feels it as their arms rise to ward off the blow, but they are too slow. And he feels nothing more apart from the descent into the dark.

They wake instantly to the sound of hammering, the passage of time meaningless in this moment. The door has gone, replaced with new bricks, the entire room closed off. He feels the pain as the girl scratches her nails against the stone, screaming and cursing until her fingers run red with blood. And all the while the Shadowman stands in the corner, watching and waiting, following them through time.

Arthur hears the words that are spoken by an unseen person from beyond the walls, a woman's voice, strong and regal. He feels the bonds rippling through the stones, binding them, tying them together with some impenetrable web and he knows that he'll never leave this room...alive or dead. He screams with the girl and pulls his hands away from her, falling back into the real world. He gasps and pants as they fall away from each other, and Arthur knows. He knows he can never set her free. Even if there is a hell, it is too good for her. The girl raises herself to her knees and flashes him a look of such hatred that he feels her nails where they pierced his flesh. The Shadowman steps forward and Arthur's fear overrides any other instinct.

He runs.

One step toward the wall. Two steps and his muscles bunch, ready to jump.

The girl dives for him.

The Shadowman drops the book and opens his mouth to shout.

Arthur leaps.

The girl's hand closes about his ankle as his body vanishes through the wall. Arthur Crazy falls to the street below pulling the girl with him.

~

On the Minster, the grotesques and gargoyle all gather above the Great Eastern Window, peering through the scaffolding at the scene unfolding below.

"Who was on watch?" grumbles one of the oldest stone creatures, a remarkably well-preserved image of a woman with bare breasts.

She rides a beast not unlike a chimpanzee crossed with an imp. No one answers her. No one meets her gaze. They all stare at the small gathering far below. From this height they can see the seething mass of shadows as the creatures on the edge of this reality push and poke their way forward, testing the edges, drawn to the malevolence set free from the stone prison.

Thick, dark mists press up against buildings and trees, growing and spilling over into the street, oozing slowly towards the strange group standing outside the house the creatures have spent centuries watching. They watch now as the smallest of the people, the one that causes even stone to shiver, rises from the ground and screams into the night. The noise reaches them a few moments later, diluted and softened by distance, but there is no mistaking the inherent evil on the wind.

They watch as the girl lowers her hands and turns to the others. They see the way they step back, retreating, moving slowly into the shadow of the Minster. Then they see the girl turn. She looks for a moment at the open city at her back, so much bigger now, so many more souls, and she sees the gathering of the dark things. She laughs and then runs, fleeing with remarkable speed across the grass of College Street to be swallowed by the darkness. The shadows seethe and move like oil, flowing after the small figure of the girl.

A deathly silence descends on the Minster and the bare breasted one turns to look at the newly cleaned glass of the Great Eastern Window. She pats the stone. This tower, with its beautiful window and long history has been her entire life, surviving fire, flood, war, famine, and plague. She is as much a part of the tower as the stone and glass. Nine separate panels, all depicting the beginning and end of the world. She knows them well; she does not wish to catch the live show. The grotesque tugs on the ears of her steed and turns him around, grumbling something that could have been a six-hundred-year-old farewell but sounds remarkably like,

"Bugger this for a lark."

CHAPTER 25

"You idiot!"

The Shadowman radiated fury, the clean black lines of his form quivering with rage. He bore down on the cowering threesome as they huddled against the wall.

"Do you have any idea the effort it took to lock that thing in there? Do you have any idea what you've done?"

"No!" shouted Arthur, finally snapping. "I have no idea at all what I've done, as I keep trying to tell people! I don't have a bloody clue, mate!"

"Mate? *Mate*?" The Shadowman chewed the word around his strange little mouth and tasted it.

He had never come across such a word before. Certainly not in the context in which it was given here. He itched to consult the book, as he always did when something unusual occurred, but that would be an unnecessary waste of resources. They stared at each other in silence. The two ghosts, the man, and the creature made of shadows. They weighed each other up, looked each other up and down, fears and suspicions and curiosity all mixing together. Finally, it was Arthur who broke the silence.

"You know what," he said, "I'm going home. Fuck it!"

"What?"

"You can't."

"Arthur!"

He had no idea who had said what and he didn't care. He was already moving. This was all a fair bit beyond a joke, and he drew the line at spider-legged evil little girl ghosts hanging on the ceiling and Shadowmen with weird faces calling him an idiot.

Now that the terrifying girl was skittering around the city somewhere, he knew only one thing for certain: he wanted to go home. He'd put the TV on, turn on all the lights, lock all the doors, and go to sleep on the couch. When he woke in the morning, he would call in sick and spend the day getting his life sorted out. He'd pay those bills he'd been putting off. He'd clean the house. He'd...shit!

The cat was still in bin liners on his porch! He'd bury the cat. And he'd buy a bloody clock! Maybe he'd even go to the doctor? None of this was normal, none of it natural, there was clearly something wrong with him. He'd rest up for a day. Get everything in order and then see how he felt. Yep, that's what he'd do. All of this was clearly in his head anyway, maybe alcohol poisoning? Could it do this? Either way, none of it was real. Not a single part. Especially not the part that always sent a cold shiver down his spine when Tom the little lost boy appeared in front of him as he did right now. He turned away sharply.

What kind of ghost wore a Ninja Turtles t-shirt and said "dude" anyway? No. This was all clearly psychosomatic. He was having a mental breakdown and he needed to see a therapist. That's what he should do tomorrow, see a therapist! There was one next door to his mum and dad's house back in Richmond. He could go home for a bit. Imagine that. "Hi Doctor, I got really drunk and now I can see dead people and I think I can release them into whatever passes for an afterlife, but I don't want to because one of them is really fit and I think I might have a chance. By the way, did I tell you I can touch ghosts as well? It's far less pervy than it sounds but don't tell Mum and Dad, they think I'm *the least Crazy of all*, which, honestly, is kind of an insult when you think about it."

He picked up the pace, heading back down the side of the Minster, his mind in turmoil. This wasn't the way home, but it was away from the ghosts who trailed behind him. He knew they were there. He could feel their presence. He curled the collar of his jacket up against the chill and thrust his hands deep in his pockets where his fingers touched his wallet. He had money. Why not get the train now? There was one that ran after midnight. Thirty minutes on the train to Darlington, then a taxi, he'd be at his parents' house at some ungodly hour, but they wouldn't mind. He was fairly sure his dad had turned nocturnal since retirement. Nothing is safer, more mundanely normal, more real, than being back at home.

A bacon sandwich for breakfast with his mum. She still cut the crusts off. Perfect.

His mind made up, he passed under the statue of Constantine the Great and tapped him on the toe like he always did. The cat sitting on the emperor's lap hissed at him. Arthur didn't even jump, didn't even flinch. Why wouldn't there be a fucking cat sitting on the Emperor of Rome like he was some sort of Bond villain? Nope, none of this was real. He glanced behind him. The ghosts of Sarah Brocklebank and Suicide Steve weren't real either.

Suicide Steve, he giggled to himself then shook his head. *Poor taste, Arthur. Poor taste.*

He was heading automatically towards the bottom entrance of Stonegate, his usual route through the city, when some memory from the night before surfaced through the sludge and caused him to pause. He looked up. An impossibly large man stood in the narrow gap between two redbrick buildings. A white-faced clock mounted on the wall above him struck midnight because the world loves poetry, and a black cat appeared at his feet.

Then another.

That caused Arthur a few problems. He thought of the triple-lined bin bag on his porch. He thought of the fight with the Fetch. He thought...

No!

He shut his mind to it and marched on. He wasn't going to entertain this farce any longer. He turned and headed towards St. Michael Le Belfrey church, jogging a little to put some distance between himself and the ghosts who weren't real. Especially Sarah. There's no way a ghost could be that attractive. It was clearly all a psychotic episode brought about by the grief he still felt over losing Wendy. But Wendy wasn't dead. Maybe he should call her?

Nope, definitely not.

He stopped.

The ghosts stopped.

He thought about it for a moment and realised that he didn't want to call Wendy. Not even a little bit. He had no desire to speak to her at all.

Well, that's one thing at least.

He smiled and started walking again. So did the ghosts. Then he caught sight of the Shadowman, standing in front of him beneath the large tree that guards the west entrance to the Minster. *How the hell did he get there?* Arthur changed direction once more, stopping dead (for want of a better phrase) in front of Sarah, Steve, the giant man in the beaver fur hat and Tom.

"Leave me alone," he said.

No, he hadn't said it. He'd begged it. The tone of his voice cut through to the ghosts and they all paused. They saw the sorrow and the pain and for just a moment they remembered what it was like to be alive, to be so sure that the life you lead was all there was. Ignorance was a bliss of unimaginable proportions.

"They can't," it was the voice of the Shadowman.

He stepped out from beneath the overhanging branches. Sarah and Steve recoiled as he drew closer but strangely, Tom did not. The boy didn't react at all. Arthur looked at him. The one who came and went. The one who ran away. The first one he saw. The one who perhaps started everything. And he didn't flinch as the man in the black suit approached, drifting like oil over the shadows stretching across the street.

"Their fates are tied with yours," said the Shadowman as he drew closer. Lord Acaster's cats hid behind his boots and hissed.

It was all well and good trying to ignore the ghosts who walked beside you but when they engaged you in conversation it was somewhat harder. Arthur sighed and sat down on a bench. He pulled the packet of cigarettes from his pocket, lit one and shook out the match, flicking it at the Shadowman. He was surprised to see that it bounced off him instead of vanishing through what appeared to be a man-shaped black hole. The Shadowman brushed his jacket (if that's what it was) where the match had hit.

"It has all got so...untidy," the man said.

Arthur tried to watch his mouth as he spoke, but he couldn't quite see it move beneath the shadow of the peaked cap. He certainly couldn't see the eyes. The sharp lines of his cheek-bones and chin stood out as the only colour but even they were grey. It was like talking to a silhouette.

"What are you?" asked Arthur.

"What I am is irrelevant," hissed the man. "It is what I do that matters."

"Well, what do you do then?" snapped Arthur.

The constant riddles, half-truths, and cryptic mysteries were all getting a little too much for him and he was running out of patience. If he was going to do this, if he was going to continue with this charade, he wanted answers. "You're always cranky when you're tired," Wendy used to say.

Oh, fuck off Wendy!

He smiled at that.

He would have been interested to know that this unnerved the Shadowman. No one ever smiled at the Shadowman.

"I keep things tidy," the creature replied but Arthur was having none of it.

"And that's supposed to explain things, is it? What the hell does that mean? Are you a janitor? A groundskeeper? A cleaner?"

"Yes," hissed the Shadowman.

It was Arthur's turn to pause.

"What do you clean?" he asked, slowly, not sure he wanted to know the answer.

"The mistakes. Like you."

Yep. He could have done without knowing that. He looked at Sarah and Steve. They were inching their way closer as they realised the Shadowman wasn't going to strike, though the strange man exuded a permanent sense of danger and threat.

"Why is Arthur a mistake?" Sarah asked. Her voice shook and Arthur smiled at her bravery. If something could scare a ghost, then it must be for good reason.

"Because he shouldn't be here," said Tom.

"Finally, someone is talking sense!" said Arthur, slapping his leg and pointing to his chest. "I shouldn't be here!"

The Shadowman nodded then reached into the folds of his midnight clothes and pulled out the leatherbound black book. It seemed too big to have nestled in whatever passed for a pocket. The cover was worn and old and swirled with dark ridges and strange patterns. Arthur thought he could make out the calligraphic initials AA on the front but then the Shadowman flipped it open and carefully turned the pages. When he found the place he was looking for he tapped his finger and turned the book to show Arthur. All the ghosts craned forward to see.

The pages were full of swirling black text in a language they couldn't read. It was a language no one on earth could read apart from the Shadowman and one forty-two-year-old Reddit user from Wisconsin who went by the username mindthesheeple666 but he had posted too many conspiracy theories about the British Royal family being lizard-people and so no one took him seriously.

As they stared at the pages, the letters shifted and squirmed almost as if they didn't want to be read but even so, it became clear they were looking at a list. And it was a list in which every item had been neatly crossed out with single lines, the letters and words imprisoned behind them. Both pages were the same except for where the Shadowman's pale finger rested. Without being able to read it, Arthur knew exactly what it said. Three words. His name.

"Are you...Death?" he asked breathlessly.

The Shadowman snapped the book closed and tucked it away. It vanished.

"No," he said. "I'm his cleaner."

Arthur looked blank. He turned to the ghosts. "I thought you said he was the bad guy?"

"Well, no one really wants to hang around when they appear."

Tom spoke again, "The Shadowmen take care of all the extras. The ones who slip through the gaps. All the people who don't follow the plan for whatever reason."

"What plan?"

"THE plan."

"There's a plan?"

"Sort of."

"So, God exists then?"

"Which one?"

"Pardon?"

"Which god?"

"*God* god!"

"I've absolutely no idea."

"Then *whose* fucking plan is it?!"

"Language. There is a lady present," Lord Acaster growled, and Arthur just stared open-mouthed at the giant man.

He could feel himself speedily approaching tipping-point

once more. None of this was making any sense and he wasn't sure he wanted it to. He was also kicking himself for being drawn back in, but it wasn't exactly a normal situation. The thought of God had been playing at the back of his mind since all of this began. It was a one plus one equals two—join the dots, sort of thing.

If ghosts were real, then what else was real? Wasn't it all sort of tied together, a package deal? And, standing as he was between two large churches, having a conversation with the spirits of the dead and whatever the hell the Shadowman was, it was kind of hard to ignore. Maybe fate and destiny and predeterminism and all those lofty religious ideals were true? But what did that mean?

Arthur certainly didn't want to have to start going to church. He remembered it from when he was in the Scouts. Once a month to sit on hard seats, pretending to sing the hymns and get all the stand up, sit down bits wrong. That didn't sound like part of anyone's grand plan.

"This is not important," said the Shadowman bluntly.

As a rule, the Shadowmen never talked much. They didn't need to. They certainly never had to explain themselves. This was proving to be a trying evening.

"But *he* is, isn't he," said Sarah, motioning towards Arthur. "Important, I mean."

The Shadowman nodded.

That stopped everyone.

"Why?" Arthur asked.

"You survived the Fetch," said Tom.

"You can talk to the dead," said Steve.

"You can touch me," said Sarah. Arthur gulped and blushed. It had been a difficult night, but he was still a man.

"You are an anomaly," the Shadowman said.

"And you've been sent to...clean me?" asked Arthur, backing away, "to cross me off your list?"

"At first. But you became...even more..." The Shadowman was struggling and left the sentence unfinished.

For as long as he could remember—and that was longer than we could possibly comprehend—he'd followed the rules of the book. Names appeared and names were crossed out. Rules appeared and rules were followed. It was that neat and that simple. He'd never asked questions. There were never any questions to ask. He just did his job and did it well. Last night, Arthur's name had appeared in the book, just another routine task. But then it had vanished. That had never happened before. Then the same name had reappeared on a different page, in a different section. That had certainly never happened before. Then it vanished once again and now it was back and the Shadowman was experiencing something he had never felt.

He was experiencing doubt.

He had hung back at the church when he should have taken the boy the moment he saw him. Instead, he had hesitated. And then he had witnessed what this strange human had done to the old grey firebrand. That was different. That was new.

Fear had opened doors in the one listed in the book as Arthur Benedict Crazy, as it opened doors in many, but something else had wedged them open and entered the room. The man was changed. Arthur Crazy was a different man now to who he was that morning. And different again from last night, and certainly from the day before.

When the name had re-appeared in the book, the Shadowman found it nestled amongst a list of others. Names that had been crossed out centuries ago. Except, now, for one. In the middle of the page, it stood out, a testament to a job incomplete. But the jobs were always sequential. Finish one and another appears. There were never any missed names. Never.

Until now.

The Shadowman had kept looking at the book to see if it changed again, but it never did. And then, when the grotesques informed him of the events at the small stone house, he had felt relief. He knew it was all coming to an end. The man's time was up. He just had to wait for the inevitable and then draw a neat line through the name and everything would be back as it should be. But that hadn't happened. Not only had the man survived, yet again, but the creature in the cage had escaped and was now roaming free about the city. The implications were beyond comprehension.

"It must be set right," said the Shadowman.

"How?" asked Sarah, and Arthur wished she hadn't because he just knew the answer was going to involve him. The Shadowman turned to face him.

Fuck.

"*You* must set it right."

"Go on then," said Arthur, folding his arms across his chest. "How am I supposed to do that? You're the Shadowman. You're the cleaner. Go clean."

"There is nothing I can do," said the Shadowman and when he next spoke it was as if through gritted teeth, though no one could see if he had teeth. "But there is one thing you can do which I cannot."

The admission had clearly been a difficult one for the creature to make. It shook as it spoke, pale fists clenched tight. They all paused for a moment as they wrapped the words he had said around their minds. Steve got there first.

"You have to finish the job. You have to release the girl."

The Shadowman nodded. "You must see the Queen," he said. Then he stepped back into the shadow of the great tree and vanished.

"I guess I won't be having breakfast with my mum then," Arthur said. "And who the hell is the Queen? He can't mean old Liz, surely?"

"I will escort you," Lord Acaster announced. "But clean yourself up first."

CHAPTER 26

"That is indeed a strange story," the Queen said, and Arthur tried not to stare.

She was every bit as regal as he had expected but far more attractive than he was prepared for. His normal propensity to stammer in front of nobility had magnified and rendered him mute. It had been Sarah who did most of the talking, with the occasional interjection from an equally nervous Steve. The giant Lord Acaster, who had brought them into the Queen's presence with a booming and respectful announcement, had remained on one knee with his head bowed and his beaver skin hat clutched to his chest throughout the whole tale. Tom had vanished.

The room was full, crowded on all sides with all manner of people: men, women, and children. There were cats and even a few dogs, and one or two grotesques and gargoyles had managed to make their way inside. Retainers brought large jars for the gargoyles to dribble into. Beside the Queen stood a lady dressed all in white. Sarah Brocklebank recognised her from the church on Micklegate. The lady had smiled and inclined her head to the small gathering as they knelt before the Queen.

They were in a large hall that seemed to have been converted into a library, but the desks, bookshelves, and computers kept fading in and out of view depending on what Arthur focussed on. It made him feel nauseous. It was exactly the sensation you get when you've had too much to drink and your eyes try to swim two sights together into one. This did nothing to help Arthur's already fragile state. He focussed on the Queen.

She was young, in her early twenties perhaps, but she could have been younger. She looked down at Arthur with a gentle, earnest face framed by long, auburn hair. She had a slightly hooked nose and a look in her eye that Arthur recognised and tried not to be captivated by. He failed. There is a certain glint in the eye of some people which speaks of an underlying humour and mischief. These are the type of people who smile with their eyes in such a way that they can capture the attention of anyone. You would follow them anywhere, knowing full well it might only lead you into trouble. Sarah had the exact same look and Arthur was sure the two women recognised it in each other. He already felt like they were conspiring.

"We are confused by your tale," said the Queen and Arthur bowed his head away from her as she flashed a smile at him.

She wore a rich green dress and held two red roses in her lap which she plucked at with her thumb and finger, bending and breaking the thorns and dropping them by the side of the raised ornate chair on which she sat.

"It appears to follow no normal narrative pattern. You are thrust into a new world and find you have a foe, then you vanquish said foe. This is where your story should end. Perhaps you even get the girl?" she added with a look to Sarah who somehow blushed and looked away.

The queen laughed, it was rich and deep and infectious. Everyone in the room laughed with her but she shushed them into silence, a look of annoyance creasing her face.

"Leave us!" she announced and there was a strange susurration as the ghostly courtiers vanished through the walls without argument.

The queen rose and made her way down the steps towards the bowed group.

"Sycophants," she said under her breath.

Then, entirely unexpected, she sat down on the bottom step of the raised dais, stretched her long legs out in front of her and sighed. Lord Acaster panicked and rose in a half bow, dropping his hat as he searched frantically for a chair.

"Calm yourself, my Lord," the Queen said with a raised hand. "We are quite comfortable, we assure you. One would think a ghostly throne would be less hard to sit on," she added more to herself.

"Now, Arthur," she continued. "It appears you are in quite a bind. Where your story should have ended was either with your untimely death at the hands of this creature called the Fetch—we had quite some fun with one of them a few years ago did we not, Lord Acaster."

"Your Majesty," he nodded.

"Oh, Jonathan, do sit up!" she scolded him. "If you bow any deeper your head will go through the floor. How many times must we tell you?"

"At least once more, your Majesty," rumbled Lord Acaster. "As always."

"Oh, you charming man," purred the Queen. Lord Acaster bowed so low his giant forehead dipped through the floor, but Arthur could still see the smile creasing through his beard.

"Now, where were we?" continued the Queen. "Oh yes, your untimely death. As this did not transpire it seems as though you should have been free to live a long and happy life, yet you somehow managed to become embroiled in this realm of ours once more. How was that?"

"I don't know," said Arthur. Lord Acaster growled, and he hastily added, "Your Majesty."

"You don't know?"

"I was drunk, your Majesty."

"Ah," she said, picking at one of the petals of her red roses. "We are well acquainted with the effects of drink."

She appeared distracted for a moment, turning the rose petal over and over in her fingers then she shook her head and continued.

"And then you meet a new foe, who turns out to be nothing of the sort. This...Shadowman. We have heard of them of course, though one never expects to see one, let alone converse with such a creature."

"What are they, your Majesty?" asked Arthur. "I never really got a straight answer."

"They are the book and the blade of death," said the queen. "They clean up all the little mistakes." She sensed that this was not enough for the young man at her feet, and she leaned forward. "Death comes for us all, but *that is not dead which can eternal lie, and with strange aeons, even death may die*," she whispered.

The words floated into the room and rested heavily on them all. Arthur was certain he had heard them before, but he had absolutely no idea from where and they did nothing to help his understanding of the Shadowman. Thankfully, the Queen was not done. She sat back and sniffed the roses.

"When we die," she said, violently ripping the head off one rose, "we either pass over," she tossed the rose head over her shoulder, "or we remain in this realm." She held up the last remaining rose, the headless stem beside it. "No one knows why some pass and others linger. One thinks there may be something yet that binds us to the Earth, some tragedy, some task unfulfilled perhaps, a deeper connection in the minds of those left behind than one can fully comprehend."

"Power in a name," whispered Arthur. The Queen looked at him sharply.

"Indeed," she said. "And yet you have the power to break all of these rules and set the spirits free."

"I think so."

Another growl.

"Your Majesty."

"And yet you chose to set free the most vile, most repulsive creature this city has ever seen." Her voice had changed, now brittle and sharp. "Why?" she demanded.

Arthur couldn't meet her gaze.

"I didn't know," he stammered. "I thought she was just an innocent kid. I wanted to set these two free, but I didn't want to get it wrong."

"Well, you certainly did not get it right," snapped the Queen. "Now that foul beast is running through this beautiful city. That mistake must be rectified!"

"I will fix it, your Majesty," said Arthur, completely entranced. "I don't know how, but I will fix it. If I release her from this world and send her over then she can't cause any more harm."

"That seems almost too good for her," mused the Queen, turning the headless stem over and over in her fingers. "She should be punished for her crimes, not rewarded."

"I don't know what else to do," said Arthur sullenly, looking at the wooden floor. *I should have got on the bloody train.*

"Worry not," said the Queen, her voice returning to normal, a smile playing on her lips and twinkling in her eye. "We trust that you will think of something. If you need to release her, then do so, far better that than to allow her to run rampant in the world."

"I could release *you*, your Majesty," Arthur said, suddenly. "I mean, I've only really done it once, but I think I know what to do."

The Queen smiled at him sadly.

"No," she said, "I died a Queen, but I would much rather have died..." she paused then, her eyes misting as she looked far away.

She shook her head to clear whatever thoughts tormented her and turned back to Arthur.

"No, thank you," she said, again composed and assuming her royal role. "We are a Queen. There are those here who need us. Our duty does not end with death."

Beside Arthur, Lord Acaster sniffed and ran a hand across his eyes. They all stared at him. He ignored them and maintained his focus on the floor.

"Now go," commanded the Queen, rising to her feet with all the majesty brought about by centuries of practice, and—she would say—breeding.

She stared down at them like a goddess.

"Go with our blessing and rid this fair city of that foul creature. You have our promise that you will not be held nor hindered in your endeavour. The city is yours, Arthur Crazy." She giggled slightly then, which kind of ruined the moment and she climbed back up the steps to the throne.

The Queen reached down beside the ornate chair and turned to face them once more. In her hands, she held a sword. She stepped purposefully back down the steps and stood in front of Arthur. She held the sword out towards him, concentrating hard on her grip.

"Take your sword and go forth, Knight of the Realm!"

Arthur stared at her, his mouth hanging open.

What the fuck did she just say?

The Queen raised a perfect eyebrow and looked at him from over the proffered blade, a single bead of sweat made its incomprehensible way down her face, the merest hint of the immense strain she was under holding the very real weapon.

Arthur didn't move.

The silence stretched on—dumbfoundedness versus regal eyebrows.

Lord Acaster coughed, "Take the damn sword, boy!"

Arthur reached out with trembling hands and clasped hold of the dark red scabbard.

He lifted it reverentially from the Queen's grasp.

He stared at the ornate swirling patterns cast in shining metal filigree across the hilt and pommel.

He marvelled at its feel in his hands.

Solid, heavy, real.

Then he dropped it.

The sword clattered and clanged onto the floor with an almighty racket and Lord Acaster sighed heavily.

Arthur snatched up the sword and stood awkwardly with it clasped in both hands.

The Queen looked at Sarah Brocklebank with a raised eyebrow and a question in her eyes. Sarah just smiled and bowed.

Arthur continued to stare from the Queen to the sword and back to the Queen. Every story he had ever read, every movie he had ever seen, every dream he had ever had as a boy (and many as a man) had brought him to this moment. He couldn't believe he had been going to get on a train. This was the greatest night of his life!

In the end, they had to drag Arthur away, his eyes aglow with patriotic fervour, his mind aflame with tales of daring do.

Sir Arthur Benedict Crazy. Knight of the Realm!

The lads would never believe this!

Of course they bloody wouldn't!

Outside King's Manor, in the cooling night air, besides the fountains of York Art Gallery, Arthur pulled the sword from the scabbard with the most satisfying silken hiss and raised it high above his head. The moonlight winked off the shining blade in a way that touched Arthur's soul and reached back through time to tell his childhood self that life, though strange, would turn out to be fucking awesome! The ghosts watched as he roared into the night,

"Cry God for...the Queen, England, and Saint George!"

Five minutes later, Sir Arthur Benedict Crazy sat in the back of a police car and gave his name and address. He did not use the title 'sir'. He did not mention the Queen. He did not mention any of his actions that night, nothing since leaving the pub on Micklegate anyway. The officer looked at his watch, then looked at the address Arthur had given him, and then looked at his watch again.

"It's taking you a long time to get home," he said. "Get lost, did we?"

"I got distracted," mumbled Arthur.

He did not know what was worse, being arrested for drunk and disorderly conduct while wielding an offensive weapon or the fact that the ghost of Lord Acaster had not stopped laughing since the blue lights flashed. There he was now, standing beside the car with tears streaming down his face. *Ghosts shouldn't be able to cry. It doesn't make any sense.*

"Right you are, Mr Crazy." the cop said with a smirk.

Clearly, he was thoroughly enjoying this strange break in normal proceedings. Once he realised Arthur wasn't a threat, and once he'd been handed evidence that the surname was real (and stopped laughing) he knew this was one to tell the lads in the canteen. He was already mentally preparing the conversation in his mind. If he played his cards right, he might just win this month's 'funniest nick'. The kitty was up to nearly sixty quid!

Just then his radio crackled, and he answered it. Arthur only caught one side of the conversation.

"Go ahead, over. Can you repeat that? Over. What?!" There was a long pause then, "You are saying *cats*, aren't you? Over...Decaffeinated? Shit. Look, are you taking the piss? Headless?! Christ almighty! On my way! Over and out!"

The officer jumped out of the car and yanked open the back door. "Get out!" he snapped to Arthur. Arthur tumbled out of the car.

"Leave the bloody sword!" the policeman shouted.

Arthur reluctantly dropped it onto the back seat.

"Look," continued the officer, as he ran back round to the driver's door, "you're getting off light. Just go home and...don't be a dick!" He jumped in the car and sped away, blue lights flashing and sirens blaring.

Lord Acaster was still laughing.

Arthur thrust his hands in his pockets and walked away, the three ghosts followed behind him. There was silence, though he was certain there were glances and smiles flitting back and forth between them.

Arthur stopped in front of a fast-food van and bought a kebab, completely unaware of the figure in black watching him from the roof of The Theatre Royal. He was starving. He also needed the toilet. He wondered why toilet breaks and food never seemed to crop up in adventure stories. Surely even heroes needed to have a pee.

You're not a bloody hero. You're just trapped in a really, really strange situation you can't get out of.

As he nipped behind a tree to answer the call of nature, he couldn't help but feel a little disappointed. The feeling of elation he'd had on holding the sword had quickly fallen away to a consuming melancholy at losing it. He didn't realise how much he could miss something he'd only had for such a short time. The sword seemed right. It felt right. It felt...he hated the word... like destiny. He gave himself a shake, zipped up his pants, and stepped out from behind the tree.

"Right then," he said. "Let's get this over with."

"What?" said Sarah.

"Setting you guys free," said Arthur.

He'd given it some thought. He liked these guys. One of them he *really* liked. He didn't want any of them to get hurt. He said he would free them, and if he could, he would. Plus, it would be good to have a bit of practice before coming face to face with the little girl again. He shuddered at the memory.

"What are you talking about?" Sarah asked.

"I'm setting you free," he said. "You're not coming with me. You might get hurt."

"I'm dead!"

"Yeah, well, you know what I mean. Come on, you all asked to be set free so let's get it over with. It'll give me practice and then I can take care of that...*thing*. Lord Acaster," Arthur turned to the giant, "you're a brave man. You go first. Show them how it is done."

The giant shook his head.

"I will not abandon my Queen. While she remains, I remain."

"Last night you were talking about the king," said Steve, who only ever seemed to pipe up with controversial titbits like this.

"The crown is the crown," rumbled Lord Acaster. "I remain."

Arthur sighed, "Steve?"

Steve shook his head and backed away, gripping his red tie tightly. Arthur closed his eyes and breathed slowly. He didn't want to do this, but he turned to Sarah.

"Show them how it's done, please."

Sarah looked at him with her big, beautiful brown eyes and shook her head slowly.

"Why not?" pleaded Arthur.

"You didn't wash your hands," she said with a smile, nodding to the tree. Arthur smiled at her and she laughed, though it didn't reach her eyes. Arthur shivered suddenly.

"I'll do it," came a voice.

They all turned.

Tom was back.

CHAPTER 27

The small group sat on a ruined stone wall beneath overhanging trees in the gardens to the north of the Minster. They had crossed through iron gates to get here but Arthur hadn't noticed, his mind had been elsewhere. It's all well and good being the hero of your own story but when that hero has to bring an end to a person's existence it comes with a great deal of soul searching. He'd even walked through an old oak tree, but everyone had been too polite to mention it. He'd scared the shit out of a sleeping squirrel though.

The Minster towered above them all now as they sat in their strange huddle. The living and the dead. The city planner, the soldier, the daughter, the office worker, and the orphan. As groups go it was an unusual one, and no one had talked for quite some time. They were being watched from high and low, from near and far, from flesh and from stone and from spirit.

But you knew that, didn't you?

"It's okay," Tom said, eventually. "I want this."

"Are you sure?" Arthur asked, wringing his hands together.

"I'm sure. I hate...this."

There was such sorrow in the young boy's eyes that Arthur had to look away.

"Where do you go?" Sarah asked. "When you...vanish?"

Tom looked at her.

"Arthur will tell you," he said simply.

Then, turning to Arthur he winked. "Come on...dude."

Arthur grinned and Tom smiled back at him. Wordlessly, Arthur reached up and held his hands on either side of the boy's head, not quite touching him yet summoning the power. The boy turned to Lord Acaster, then Steve, then Sarah and he smiled.

"See you on the other side," he said. He looked at Arthur. They both spoke at the same time.

"Cowabunga!"

Arthur closed his hands over the boy's head and purple flame rippled instantly from beneath his fingers. Arthur had full control. He knew exactly how to tap into the power and where to direct it. It was like he had always known.

It didn't make it any easier.

He saw the young Tom creep through the silent corridors of the hotel.

He saw him enter the room and stand before the mirrors.

He saw the Fetch drag the poor boy screaming through the glass and he went with him.

Then he saw his parents. Distraught. Scared. Agonised.

He felt their pain. The pain of their loss. He saw them turn on each other as they scoured the city as days turned into weeks and weeks turned into months. He saw them blame each other. Saw them fall apart.

He followed the ghost of Tom as the boy visited each one of his parents in turn, night after night. In separate houses now, though both in York. Neither able to let go. To move on.

He watched as they walked the city each evening, talking to their lost son, unaware that he was right there beside them listening and answering.

He felt the passage of years. The parents growing older but Tom remaining the same, forever. The pressure to hold the flame became almost too much as the sorrow overwhelmed him but Arthur clung on. He cried out as Tom knelt by his mother's side on a floor strewn with empty bottles. He felt the boy's heart sore and then break into pieces as the spirit of his mother caught a glimpse of her boy only to be torn away from him by a familiar black-clad shape dragging her towards a blue-rimmed door.

He saw the father's body swing.

And the Shadowman collect.

He saw Tom alone at the foot of the stairs.

At the foot of the stairs leading to Micklegate Bar.

Saw him run from a drunk man in a blue suit.

The purple flames roared with white intensity and Arthur looked into the eyes of the young boy for the final time. They were full of a hope that broke his heart. And then they were gone.

Tears streamed down Arthur's face as he collapsed to the floor beneath the Minster. Sarah knelt beside him and placed a hand on his shoulder. No one spoke. None of the creatures moved. Not even the cats.

It took a long time for Arthur to sit up and even longer for him to compose himself. He was exhausted. Bone-weary, as his mother would say. He didn't want to go on, he just wanted to sleep. It was the chirping of a bird that did it, the sound so alien in this long dark night. The promise of a new day. Of new beginnings. He sat against the cold stone and listened. It was a sound he had always loved.

From his childhood bedroom and the trees outside to his university halls of residence then the flat in the city, there had always been birds chirping in the morning. This night had seemed endless. Full of pain and wonder. But now it was coming to a close and he had one last job to do. Here, at the end, he was running out of time. Arthur groaned and stretched then rubbed his face with his hands. There was no doubt in his mind anymore, no indecision; he was going to do what needed to be done. This was his story, and he was going to finish it. He wasn't going to walk away, and neither was he going to hide at the bottom of a bottle. Arthur Benedict Crazy was going to fix things.

Sir Arthur Benedict Crazy, he grinned. *Knight of the Realm.*

He looked up at Lord Acaster.

"How do we find the girl?" he asked.

"We follow the screams," the soldier replied.

CHAPTER 28

The girl had not been idle. There were indeed screams, and plenty of them. She knew they would come for her as soon as they realised she was gone. They probably already knew. And so, she made haste. It had, after all, been a very long time since she'd had anyone to play with. Only twice before this night had anyone come close enough to contact her. The first had been two brothers many years ago. The younger boy had watched in horror as his older brother cut the throat of a priest outside her window. She had delighted in the sight but hid her glee from the boy when she saw his pain.

She beckoned him to her with a sad, sympathetic smile and he came. The fool. He climbed the wall and she whispered to him through the glass. She told him that a good boy should not have done such a thing, that a good boy should hide away. There was an attic room in the building next to hers, she whispered. There was a closet there. It was the perfect spot. Run now, young man. Run. Hide. Before they catch you! As the boy fled, the older brother had turned to see where he had gone.

Catching his eye also, she whispered in his ear when he too climbed the wall. She told him that his brother had run to tell the authorities. That they would blame it all on the influence of the older sibling. That he was doomed. The only way to stop this was to get there first, but fret not young man, for she had convinced his brother to rest for the night in the room above. If he went to the authorities now, he would be saved their wrath.

It was almost too easy. The older boy fled in panic and soon the authorities arrived at the house, where they searched the attic room and dragged the younger boy from the closet. They executed him the next day and the girl laughed with glee as the older sibling, full of remorse, locked himself away in the very same closet and slowly succumbed to madness. His wailing kept her company for centuries. Which was good because those who held her had made sure her window was soundproof after that.

The second occasion had been when a new family moved into the house. The room became a study with a door in the wall she could not access, but the man who wrote at the desk by the window could feel her presence, or rather, he could feel *something,* and so they had paid good money for someone to tell them if the stories about the house were true. Was there a spirit who inhabited their new home? The woman who arrived bedecked in chains and amulets was nothing more than a charlatan without a single trace of the gift—no sight, no vision, nor even any style. But she charged a fortune and so the girl decided to do a good deed. She gave the lady visions. Real visions of plague and horror, of poor, lonely little girls being made to suffer so unjustly. She could feel the atmosphere of fear shift as the world slowly bought the new story. They even prayed for her! Fat lot of good that would do.

But all that was in the past and now she was out. She'd had centuries to plan and wasted no time when she tumbled to the world outside her cage. She didn't even pause to rip the heart out of the one who had freed her, or the strange companions he kept. She ran into the city, marvelling at how it had grown, at the strange sights and things she could not possibly understand. She felt a single moment of panic when her destination was blocked by new buildings; structures that already looked old and worn but she need not have worried. She heard the laughter, and she heard the cries coming through the bricks as she passed down an alley. They were still there.

The children.

~

Arthur, Steve, and Sarah walked with Lord Acaster to the entrance of Stonegate where the giant soldier whistled once. Almost immediately two black cats detached from the shadows and trotted to his feet with their tails high in the air. They purred and butted his boots, curling the tips of their tails around his legs as he bent to scratch them between the ears.

"How is that possible?" Arthur asked. "Your cat...last night... it died saving me."

"And now would be a good time to say thank you," said Lord Acaster with a look.

Well, it wouldn't be the strangest thing that's happened tonight, and the brave animal certainly deserved it. Arthur crouched to his knees and whistled softly. The cats, as expected, ignored him completely.

"You'll be telling me it's because they have nine lives next," said Arthur as he tried to coax the animals towards him with a click of his fingers.

"Six now," said Lord Acaster.

Arthur looked up to see if he was joking, though he needn't have bothered, there was no humour in that voice. He gave up the clicking and whistling and spoke instead.

"Thank you for coming to my rescue last night. You saved my life, and I can't thank you enough. I owe you a debt."

One of the cats stopped circling Lord Acaster and took a step towards Arthur. It seemed to incline its head slightly, just for a moment, and then it sat down, cocked a back leg, and proceeded to give itself a thorough clean.

Arthur wrinkled his nose and stood up.

"Apology accepted?" he asked Lord Acaster.

The giant nodded.

"So, what now?"

"Now we listen," said the giant.

"To what?"

"To the cats."

Arthur grinned and looked at the others, but their faces were deadly serious, staring solemnly into the night.

When am I going to stop questioning all of this? he asked himself. *If you stop questioning it, you really will go mad.*

Too late.

Arthur put his head in his hands and groaned.

"Are you okay?" Sarah asked.

"Uh-huh. Just arguing with myself."

The clock above them ticked loudly as silence descended on the small group. The city was beginning to wake up though there was still an hour or so before dawn. The occasional car or truck rumbled quietly through the streets and more and more birds could be heard singing from the rooftops and trees. A lone cyclist came out of the dark following a single pinprick of light and then sped away on silent wheels.

It was peaceful, calm, and yet full of life.

They stood together in companionable silence.

Then Steve said, "That column is upside down."

"Pardon?" said Arthur.

"That Roman column over there," Steve said, pointing to the tall stone structure a few feet away that stood opposite the statue of Constantine. It was delicately lit from beneath and glowed like an inverse lighthouse just before the entrance to Minster Gate, the short street leading to Stonegate where they all stood, "it's upside down."

"Sure it is."

"It is, you know, they found it on its side, and someone messed it up when they stood it up there."

They all looked at the column. It seemed perfectly normal.

Arthur and Sarah both tilted their heads to make the world tip. It looked exactly the same. They gave up.

They fell back into silence.

And then they noticed the cat sitting on the top of the column (or the bottom, if Steve was to be believed). Perhaps it had always been there, perhaps not. They watched as it stretched languidly, clearly in no rush, and then walked sedately down the side of the vertical column before daintily stepping onto the pavement to join the rest of the world at an appropriate angle.

At least it didn't smile.

The cat trotted over to the small group, completely ignoring the two young ghosts and Arthur, and climbed into the outstretched hand of Lord Acaster. The officer inclined his head to the animal and appeared to be listening. Then he whispered some words and gently lowered it to the ground. The newcomer gave a desultory look to Lord Acaster's two cats, proving that the animals are even dicks to each other, and sauntered away.

Lord Acaster stood up straight.

"To Bedern," he said with a dark look in his eyes. "She is at the Ragged School."

CHAPTER 29

Ragged Schools popped up all over Britain in the nineteenth century to help those poor unfortunate waifs and strays who found themselves destitute and alone on the streets. Charities, churches, and institutes banded together to provide food, shelter, and accommodation for young orphans from even the most degenerated of areas. Slums and workhouses were often overflowing with bedraggled and starving children. It was the Christian thing to do to see that they were well cared for.

And so, in York, the Parish Beadle volunteered to run a Ragged School in one of the most run-down areas of Bedern, just off Goodramgate. Suffer ye not the little children, smiled one Mr. Pimm obsequiously in front of the City council, entirely misquoting his scriptures, which, given due consideration, may have been their first clue. Of course, Mr. Pimm worked hard out of the goodness of his heart and his strong sense of Christian duty. The small stipend he received for each body in his care (an unfortunate turn of phrase as it would turn out) was more than enough to feed, clothe, and educate the poor wretches. He would keep nothing for himself. Serving the Almighty was reward enough.

No one questioned Mr. Pimm. Why would they? He clearly took great care of the children in his charge. None left his Ragged School after they entered it and there were very few reports of casualties, which clearly meant he was doing a dashed fine job of meeting their needs and wants. Healthy children educated in the proper Christian manner raised to contribute to society, and, more importantly, off the streets and out of sight, hey. Top work, that man!

In the winter he couldn't bury the bodies, the ground was too hard. And he couldn't declare the dead because the money would stop. Thankfully, it was cold enough to store the little wretches in one of the large cupboards on the top floor. They'd be okay there until Spring.

Mr. Pimm accounted for everything as he counted his money.

Everything, that is, except the noises.

The pathetic screams of the little beasts never went away. He was certain it was the children on the floor upstairs trying to torment him and he lashed them into silence. What more did they want? They had a blanket each and were fed a decent soup last week! Be silent you foul beasts and be grateful!

But they were never silent.

They cried and moaned throughout the long winter nights. No matter how many beatings he gave them, they just wouldn't learn. Mr. Pimm couldn't sleep, he couldn't concentrate on his counting, he shivered in front of his fire no matter how much coal he added. And his hands! Oh, how his hands ached. He rubbed them together and blew on them to add to the warmth, but it was so fleeting, the cold seeped back immediately and it seemed as if the very fire itself was made of ice.

And the screams never stopped.

His hands curled and spasmed as if grasping the round, rough handle of his pick and shovel, memories of shallow graves ached his nerves and still they screamed, night after night until

Mr. Pimm prayed for the first light of dawn to creep through the soot-filled sky outside.

But on this night the dawn never came.

Mr. Pimm's aching hands gripped the handle so tightly the blood drained from his skin. He rose from his chair and ascended the stairs in a daze.

Why would they not stop screaming?

Monsters!

He lashed about him in a blind rage, cutting through thin blankets and thin bodies, it was not the handle of a shovel he held in his hand but that of a large knife. He caught sight of it, slick with blood as the sun finally rose and crept fearfully into the dark room, afraid of what it might see.

The bodies lay about his feet. They had finally stopped screaming.

He looked up.

He saw the cupboard standing like a tomb at the end of the long workhouse room.

The heavy oak door slowly opened and a man in black stepped into the room. The Shadowman took the bowed form of Mr. Pimm who never once lifted his head. He left the children.

And their screams filled the Ragged School once more.

Arthur paused before the black arch that led from Goodramgate into the warren of streets behind. The sign on the wall said *Bedern* but it seemed to Arthur as though the alley sat like a portal to a different world. Heavy mists lay thick in the red brick tunnel, blocking all sight of what lay beyond. A single streetlight managed to penetrate the gloom some distance away but by the time the orange glow reached Arthur, it had been reduced to a size no bigger than that of a match, offering neither warmth nor comfort.

Even Lord Acaster's cats paused on the threshold, hissing and spitting into the swirling mists, crouching low with hackles high. Arthur looked around; the night sky was changing. It was no longer black but touched with watercolour grey. He did not have much time. There were no mists out here, the air was fresh and young and clean. A hint of baking bread wafted through the city. Home and comfort. One last temptation.

Arthur gulped and stepped forward, crossing the threshold and allowing the mists to take him.

He could see nothing. Not even the hands he waved at arm's length to feel his way through the dark void. He aimed for the soft pinprick of light; it was the only thing to aim for. Arthur blinked and blinked, trying to clear his vision, but his lack of sight had nothing to do with his eyes. The mists were so thick he could almost taste them as they settled on his skin and caressed his flesh with cold matter. His dad would have called it a 'pea-souper' but there was nothing natural about this mist. He'd been in thick fog before, up on the Moors and across the Dales.

There were pubs his family loved to travel to, The Lion Inn on Blakey Ridge and Tan Hill, the highest pub in the United Kingdom. They had been forced to stay at both when the fog rolled in and the roads became too dangerous. Well, his dad said "forced," but the decisions were made swiftly as more beers were bought and warm fires stoked.

Images of Arthur's parents and their smiling faces danced through the mists before him. He couldn't tell if they were real or in his mind's eye, but they were there, happy and smiling. His parents were always smiling. Simply happy and content to be with each other and so very proud of their only child. He didn't call them enough. He should. Happy memories of home bombarded Arthur, assaulting his mind and his heart, causing him to doubt his path and to hesitate.

He paused and felt the power that flowed in his veins move of its own accord, stirring and crackling through his body. He struggled to contain it, but the effort left him breathless, and he clutched his chest as he gasped against a cold, damp wall. Before, he struggled to summon the power, but now it seemed to be moving by itself, dancing to some unknown rhythm. The effects had begun already, heightening the emotions, raising memories and feelings both latent and active, though this time they were all his own: his father holding him after a nightmare, his mother bandaging scraped knees, holidays, warm meals, and laughter—happiness, warmth, safety, and love.

So much more powerful when they may never be experienced again.

Turn back, Arthur. Turn back and go home. There is no need for you to be here.

He concentrated and clenched his fists, feeling the prickle and spark of power in his nerves as it crackled along his skin. He sought to control it. To take the purple flame and direct it away from himself. To shut out the voices. His body shuddered violently with the effort...and they vanished. So too did the warmth and life and memory of love. It leached out of his heart and Arthur staggered against the wall as the dark mists caressed him with cold fingers like vapour, gibbering and whining across the earth. Icy tendrils of despair wrapped around his heart and he panicked, gazing wildly about the empty mists.

"Hello?" he cried.

No sounds came back.

Not even his own echo.

He was utterly alone. Desperately so.

He felt the emptiness like a leaden weight in his chest. The agony and loss of Tom's parents came back in a flash, mingling with his own heartache when Wendy stepped onto that train. Images of his grandfather trussed to a bed with wires weaving in and out of his frail body mixed with those of the little girl's parents as they cowered before her. He felt the pain and loneliness of Mad Alice, and of Steve. Poor Steve, alone in the basement, looping his tie over a cold metal pipe with shaking hands and tears in his eyes, his body swinging, alone for four days. Arthur cried out in despair and sagged to his knees, his head in his hands. What was he thinking? He couldn't possibly do this.

Yes. Turn back, Arthur. This is too much. Too much for one person to bear. Too much sadness and despair. Turn back. You'll only make it worse.

I can't do it, he raged in his own mind, his hands gripping the side of his head as if to shut out the voices.

No. You can't. You'll lose everything. You'll die alone.

"Alone," he gasped, his breath pushing the mists away from his mouth in a swirl.

A gentle hand settled softly on his shoulder then and squeezed. A voice spoke quietly in his ear.

"No one is ever completely alone."

Arthur looked up and the mists cleared slightly to reveal the sad blue eyes of Steve. "I don't want to go anymore," the man said with a smile, "I have friends now. *You* did that. You can do this." Steve helped Arthur to his feet and Sarah appeared at his side. Lord Acaster stepped out of the swirling mists to join them and his two cats ran ahead, still unsettled, still wary, still poised and ready. Arthur looked at each of them in turn and felt their strength and their determination. The power crackled through his body like electricity. *I'm going to have to think of a better name than power,* he thought. *It makes me sound like Ryu from Street Fighter.* He wondered briefly if he might actually be able to make fireballs appear from his hands and then dismissed the idea.

But why not?

You are strong enough.

He looked at his hands and felt the power surge within him. Purple sparks crackled across his fingers and, as he concentrated, they began to coalesce and swirl together in his palms. He put his hands closer together and felt the ball of energy build between them, sparking and crackling. He grinned in delight at the sensation, all other thoughts abandoned, imagine what he could do!

Yes. Imagine.

People would marvel at him. He would be a sensation. His face on the cover of every magazine. Television shows.

The adoration. They would worship you.

He could bend the world to suit his needs. He would never have to work. He would be rich. Go anywhere. Do anything. Be anyone.

There are no limits to what you can do.

I can walk through walls.

You can. And you can burn them down.

"I..." Arthur paused and turned to his companions.

They were staring at him with fearful eyes. Lord Acaster had stepped in front of the other two and placed his large arms protectively across them, like a father looking after his children. They had seen the look in Arthur's eyes, the single-minded concentration and unmasked glee as he built and caressed lightning in his hands. They saw what he could do, what he might become, and they feared him. Arthur saw it in their eyes and looked at his hands. The pulsing fire in his palms spluttered and died.

A child laughed, somewhere close, long and mocking. It echoed for a moment then was gone. The small group looked at one another fearfully then another laugh sounded, coming from a different direction, cheerful this time, a musical lift to it that spoke of happiness and joy. Soon the whole alley was ringing with the sounds of laughter. Children at play. Full of life and innocence and fun. The kind of full-bellied, high-pitched laughter that only comes with the sheer wonder of being a child.

Then the laughs turned into screams.

From joy to terror all in one breath and soon the early morning was full of horror; stark and visceral, nightmares come real. The two black cats burst back out of the mists and sprang up the body of Lord Acaster, cowering on his shoulders beneath the large beaver fur hat.

"I tried love!" an angry voice spat. It filled the world around them and seemed to come from all directions.

"But you care not for love! I tried loneliness!" it hissed. A girl's voice but wrapped in an ageless, timeless evil.

Arthur walked forward slowly, hesitantly, aiming for where he thought the voice came.

"But you find solace in the company of the dead!"

Arthur spun in the mist, but the voice was everywhere.

"I have shown you power!" it screamed. "But you are too weak to wield it!"

A shadow passed over Arthur's head as he ducked through an opening and into a large, cavernous room. It was old and filthy; the wood of the floor, walls, and ceilings crumbling with age and rot. Broken barrels and boxes lay scattered across the cracked floorboards and bundles of rags filled every available gap and space. At the far end, in a dark reflection of the Queen's Hall, the girl from the window sat on an ancient chair in front of a large wooden cupboard.

"You leave me with nothing now but fear!" she screamed, and the room erupted.

Children of all ages burst from the shadows, the dark rags lifting to reveal emaciated grey bodies and desperate, hungry eyes. They crawled over the barrels and broken wood on all fours, cursing and hissing. They were filthy, their skin covered in bruises and scars and dirt and mud and blood. More of the creatures dropped from the dark places in the rafters, and the cupboard behind the girl burst open to release yet more of the terrifying and tragic figures. They surged toward Arthur, and he would have been instantly overwhelmed if not for his companions.

The three ghosts and two cats charged forward and grappled with the demon children, grabbing and throwing their small bodies away from Arthur. But they kept coming. No sooner had they hit the floor than they turned and came screaming back. One small boy, perhaps no older than four, hit the wall hard after Lord Acaster flung him away but he simply laughed as he landed, then raced up the rotting wood on all fours before clambering with long limbs across the ceiling and dropping once more onto the giant soldier's head. Lord Acaster roared as sharp nails gouged at his eyes and cheeks, the wounds very much real.

Sarah and Steve were faring no better, both were already swamped and covered in cuts and gashes. A girl so slick with grime and filth as to be barely recognisable as human swung from Sarah's hair, pulling the woman to the ground. Steve tried to help her to her feet but was tackled by three boys who grabbed the red tie and pulled it tight around his neck. They dragged him backwards across the floor as the creatures tugged and pulled at him. Arthur wondered how they could possibly get hurt but the wounds were so savage and their howls of pain so real he did not doubt it. His friends were being ripped apart.

For him.

"You think pain hurts when you're alive!" hissed the girl. "You should try it when you're dead!"

She snapped her fingers in the direction of Lord Acaster, and suddenly two boys, their mouths sewn shut and their eyes dark pits in sallow faces, stepped towards him with jet black blades gripped in filthy hands. Arthur didn't even have time to shout before both daggers were plunged deep into the back of the towering giant and he arched backwards in a great spasm, screaming his agony to the uncaring and unhearing world.

"No!" screamed Arthur and finally he moved.

He punched and kicked and shoved as hard as he could, lashing out blindly as he moved, striding forward over the bodies of Lord Acaster's two cats who lay still and limp on the dirty floor. He battered the two boys away and tried to support the big man as he sagged to his knees, panting and gasping, blood dripping from his mouth as he struggled to take a breath. Lord Acaster reached a crimson hand to Arthur's chest and pushed him away.

"Finish it," he gasped, and his body tumbled to the floor.

Arthur rose from the dirt, death, and decay, and locked eyes with the girl on her makeshift dark throne. The purple light coursed through him, and time slowed. She sat up and regarded him curiously. He realised then that she didn't care about the little children, she didn't care about his friends, she didn't even really care about him, she just wanted to know what he was so she could destroy him, and if possible, take his power. She smiled as he thought this, and he knew also that somehow, she understood his mind. She raised her hand, and the creatures slowed their attack. The maelstrom stuttered and drifted into slow motion around them and Arthur looked around, taking it all in.

He saw Steve hanging from the rafters by his red tie, his face struggling as he gasped, his eyes full of fear. He saw Lord Acaster lying on the floor, reaching out towards the bodies of his cats, no longer fending off the blows that still battered him from all sides. And he saw Sarah Brocklebank, her head forced painfully sideways by grasping filthy hands. They were going to break her neck.

"Balance," the girl on the throne hissed. "It all hangs on the blade of a knife. What is written is written. Until we cross it out," she added, her eyes darting quickly to the side of the room.

Arthur glanced in that direction but could see nothing in the shadows, though he knew now this didn't mean they were empty. He turned back to her.

"What do you want?" he asked, though he already knew the answer.

"You."

"I'm here."

"We shall see."

The girl rose slowly from the throne and stretched like a cat, her fingers interlocked as she reached towards the ceiling, she closed her eyes for a moment and then glared at him, the room around them froze completely; a tableau of pain and torment, the agony etched onto the faces of the dead.

"I'm glad we have this chance to talk," she said. "When I snap my fingers again the world will continue to spin and you will have, oh, seconds, before your friends die."

"They're already dead."

"Do you seriously think that's the worst thing that can happen to a person?" she scoffed.

Even though Arthur was talking to a girl who looked to be in her early teens, it became clear she was far older than he could possibly comprehend. Human life was but the blink of an eye to her. Fragments and shards of her true nature were splintering around his mind, he knew he didn't have the whole picture, that something was hidden from him, hidden even from the vision his power had shown him in the small stone room. Every time he thought he was getting closer to the truth it seemed there was another layer beneath the one he dug up. Always something hiding in the shadows.

"You will have to choose," she said. "Love, loneliness, power, or fear? One of these things will guide your hand. I can sense it, you know," she said, with a look to her left as she took another step forward.

"I can sense the power in you, I can smell it! I can taste it! I can feel you building it, trying to control it, wondering what you might do, what you can do. It feels good, doesn't it?" She picked her way through the frozen bodies, stepping carefully and quietly, doing nothing to disturb the world around them.

She moved like a wild cat, hunting its prey, patient and dangerous, entirely confident in her own prowess.

"But you're a child!" she spat. "A child with a new toy and absolutely no idea what to do with it. You don't even know what you have, do you!"

Arthur ignored her. He knew it would be the one thing he could do that would infuriate her the most and perhaps buy him some time while he thought, and so he looked away. He looked at his friends.

To his left, Arthur saw the pain in Sarah's beautiful, dark brown eyes, saw the way her neck was twisted almost to breaking point and he realised that she would not be here if it weren't for him. He hadn't asked for this, but, as his grandfather had whispered on his deathbed with a smile that transported Arthur back to long country walks when he seemed as indestructible as Lord Acaster—*we do our best with the hand we are given*.

The memory of Sarah's hand on his leg came to Arthur and he thought of the connection they shared, the stolen looks and glances, but more than that, the knowledge that passed between them through Arthur's power. They were bound to each other in some strange, inexplicable way, her fate and his tied together.

The dark girl said something he didn't hear, but he tore his eyes away from Sarah and glanced up at Steve. He saw the fear there, the loneliness on the edge of death, the regret and the fear and the awful, terrible hope. Steve did not want to die. All he ever wanted was friendship and companionship and, at long last, he had found them.

Arthur looked at the giant form of Lord Acaster, bowed, broken, and beaten. All his strength, all his might, all his nobility counting for nought in the face of death, but the great man's eyes were locked on Arthur's and his last words still rung in his mind. Arthur couldn't hold that gaze and so he looked away. He looked into the shadows and knew what he had to do.

Arthur Benedict Crazy lifted his eyes to the evil child and grinned savagely, the fire in his body intensified with the rage he felt at being forced into this situation.

The girl stopped, suddenly uncertain.

She looked into Arthur eyes and her own widened.

Was it fear?

She clicked her fingers.

The world spun back into motion.

Arthur clasped his hands together in a loud clap, felt the energy build instantly between them, felt it course through his body and ripple in purple flashes from every fibre of his being. His eyes widened as the girl stumbled back but it was too late for her, too late for them all. He thrust his hands out with a scream and roared one word,

"Hadouken!"

Arthur felt it all. All the pain, all the misery, all the love, all the hope, fear, anger, and loneliness. He felt the stories of every soul in that room as the purple light burst from him and smashed into each being. It erupted from his outstretched hands like lightning and rippled instantly outwards, enveloping everything in its path.

The girl screamed in rage and raised her own hands, but she was instantly silenced as the fire washed over her, devouring her, the flames shimmering and swirling until they exploded into whiteness. She vanished in the blaze and Arthur thought she was gone. He relaxed his hold and opened his eyes, daring to hope. But the girl was still there, crouched and defiant, hissing and spitting beneath a stygian cloud that seethed above and around her. She raised her hands and fought back, lifting the purple fire with dark mist, her lips curled back in a snarl over sharp teeth.

Anything that had been human was ripped away as she pushed against the light. Arthur struggled against her, reeling for a moment as tenebrous clouds rolled beneath the purple flame in an oncoming storm. They pressed their wills against each other and found themselves locked in a stalemate. The girl gasped, "To take me...you'll have to take them all!"

Arthur screwed his eyes shut and focused all his remaining energy, everything he had, everything that he was, on the power. Tears streamed down his face and he felt his heart beat with agonising sorrow in his chest. He opened his eyes, and through gritted teeth said,

"They know."

Then he screamed.

The whole room turned white, and Arthur felt it all. He felt everyone.

The girl.

Sarah.

Steve.

Lord Acaster.

The orphans.

And the man standing in the shadows who gasped in sudden terror.

"Not me," he said.

And the book and the blade fell to the floor and vanished into shadow.

CHAPTER 30

Arthur woke in a room that smelled of antiseptic and cabbage. Everything was white. Even the people talking beside his bed were dressed in white. They were laughing about his name. He closed his eyes before they could notice he was awake, and he listened. Just another drunk passed out in an alley. What a loser. Funny name though. He'll be alright when he wakes up. Was there anyone with him? No. Does he have any family or friends in the city? None. He lives alone. Sad really. He's too young to be on his own.

A single tear rolled down Arthur's cheek and soaked into the crisp white pillowcase.

Si gathered a handful of empty glasses and placed them at the end of the bar as his last few customers put on their coats and loaded their pockets with wallets, phones, cigarettes, and lighters. He held the door open as they left, chattering and laughing and talking about where they would go next. He brought the advertising board inside and turned the key in the lock. As he flicked the sign over, he glanced across to Micklegate

Bar and saw the solitary figure standing on top of the city wall. He sighed and walked inside.

A short time later, Si climbed the steps and stood beside Arthur at the top of the wall.

"You know you're not supposed to be up here," he said with a grin. The young man didn't reply.

"Here," Si said, offering a small glass of scotch.

Arthur took it with a nod and a sad smile and continued to stare into whatever world he was lost in. Si raised his own glass and they touched them together. Arthur noticed then that the barman held a third glass in his other hand.

"Who's that for?" he asked.

The barman lifted it in salute then slowly poured the contents onto the wall.

"Absent friends," he said.

The two men stood in silence as the scotch glistened in the moonlight, watching as it slowly soaked into the centuries-old stone and vanished forever.

"You know," said Si, looking into his own glass. "When I lost my dad, I didn't know if I would be able to keep going. It hurt. Like physically hurt, you know."

Arthur nodded.

"Grief is a bitch," said the barman. "And don't let people tell you it gets easier with time. It doesn't. It's just...life grows around it. It never stops hurting but we owe it to the dead to keep on living."

The two men drank in silence by the light of a full moon.

They were watched.

~

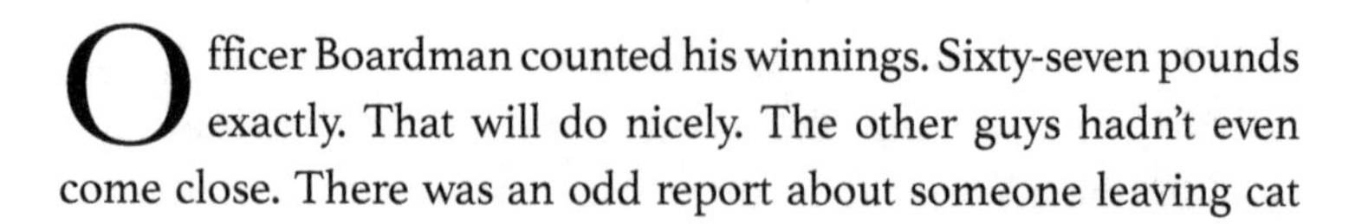

Officer Boardman counted his winnings. Sixty-seven pounds exactly. That will do nicely. The other guys hadn't even come close. There was an odd report about someone leaving cat food outside the door of the Ye Olde Starre Inne every night but other than that it was business as usual, except for his arrest last week, the one ended prematurely by a prank call. Officer Boardman closed his locker and picked up his bag. A few quid in his pocket and two days off. A good end to the week, but there was something he wanted to see before he left for home. He tapped the passcode into the pad beside the door and walked into the secure room.

It was full of bags and neatly labelled boxes, rows and rows of them, but he knew exactly where he was going. They had filed it under weapons though it didn't fit on the shelf, so in the end, they placed it with the baseball bats and cricket bats in the sporting section. All the lads had had a go. Sergeant Sheehan even had a crack at knighting one or two of the community coppers, though Officer Hepworth got a little bit carried away and they were all told to leave it alone by the Chief Inspector. But Officer Boardman wanted one last look before he went home.

He reached the cage and opened it.

He stared for a moment.

Then he opened the next cage, though he knew full well it wouldn't be there. He checked the paperwork. He checked the cage again. There was nothing there. Just a space where something should have been. Something long and sharp that was too big to fit with the other knives. Officer Boardman ran back into the station.

Arthur Crazy walked down Low Petergate with a large bag slung over his shoulder munching on a bag of chips. They'd put too much vinegar on, and he wasn't enjoying them. It was stinging his eyes. He'd been into work that morning and taken extended leave. They hadn't complained, he hadn't taken a day off since the day he started. Plus, his supervisor thought if

Arthur took a few weeks off it would give everyone else chance to catch up.

She gave him her personal number, just in case he needed anything. Anything at all. Arthur had smiled and left quickly, but not before going down to the basement for a few last-minute searches. Now he had one last thing to do before he caught the train home. Something important.

Arthur leaned against a wall and watched as groups of tourists clustered outside an art shop and took photograph after photograph. It wasn't the stunning paintings in the window they were taking pictures of, though, it was the small sign hanging above the alley next door. It was the alley that Arthur was interested in.

He finished his chips and put the vinegar-soaked paper in a bin, crossing the road as an opening in the tide of people appeared. He ducked under the low entrance to Lund's Court (formerly Mad Alice Lane) and walked slowly down the narrow passage. About halfway, he stopped and lit a cigarette, checking to see if anyone was in earshot as he did so. A kitchenhand appeared from a doorway and dumped a black bag in a wheelie bin, then disappeared again. Arthur had the alley to himself.

He looked around.

"I can't see you anymore," he said to the emptiness. "I can't see anyone. But I did some digging."

He took another drag of his cigarette and blew it out slowly, half expecting—even hoping— that the smoke might settle over the form of the old lady. Instead, it billowed against the bricks and circled in on itself, forming a cloud.

"Your name is Ann Barber," he said. "And I'll remember you."

On the way to the train station, Arthur paused to touch the foot of Emperor Constantine, looking up at the general whose world was forever changed in this city and who in turn, forever changed the world. The man gazed benevolently out from his seat below the Minster and Arthur couldn't help but stretch on his tiptoes to take a look at his lap. There wasn't a cat in sight. He grinned and crossed the street to the tall stone column at the entrance to Minster Gate. He read the plaque affixed to the base and smiled.

"Good on you, Steve," he said.

And then he went home.

Arthur rode off into the sunset on the 19:45 York to Darlington express with connecting X26 bus to Richmond.

He went back to where the Crazy people live.

ABOUT THE AUTHOR

A.B. Finlayson makes things up and occasionally writes them down. He's been a fighter, a poet, and a preacher. He went to school and then became the teacher (only some of these things are true). He's a Yorkshireman living in the sun and can usually be found hugging the air-conditioning when he's not playing bass guitar (poorly). He has an awesome wife, two amazing kids, two cats who apparently own his house and tolerate his presence, a loyal dog with the world's saddest face, and his wife's bloody bird (which he pretends to hate). His real name is Alexander but only his mum calls him that...when he's in trouble. He doesn't like writing about himself in the third person and frequently makes mistakes when trying. In the immortal words of Paul Simon, you can call me Al.

WWW.ABFINLAYSON.COM

facebook.com/abfinlaysonauthor
twitter.com/ABFinlayson1
instagram.com/a.b.finlayson

Ingram Content Group UK Ltd.
Milton Keynes UK
UKHW011703130323
418485UK00004B/353